the pursuit of happiness

the pursuit of happiness
tara altebrando

POCKET BOOKS MTV BOOKS

New York London Toronto Sydney

POCKET BOOKS, a division of Simon & Schuster, Inc.
1230 Avenue of the Americas, New York, NY 10020

ISBN-13: 978-1-4165-1328-5
ISBN-10:   1-4165-1328-0

This MTV Books/Pocket Books trade paperback edition March 2006

10 9 8 7 6 5 4 3 2 1

Manufactured in the United States of America

For information regarding special discounts for bulk purchases,
please contact Simon & Schuster Special Sales at 1-800-456-6798
or business@simonandschuster.com

For my mother

acknowledgments

I'd like to thank the founding fathers and also these good people:

My editor, Lauren McKenna, and agent, David Dunton—two unabashed saps who apparently cry as easily as I do. The wonderful crew at Pocket Books and MTV Books, notably Louise Burke, Liate Stehlik, Jacob Hoye, and Megan McKeever.

Also: Adrienne Wieland and the fine folks at Richmondtown, past and present. Especially: My family—and Nick, for sharing the pursuit.

chapter 1

The day my mother dies is a Thursday in mid-June and Loretta's scolding me for leaving my cell phone on the kitchen table. If it were my own family's twenty-first-century kitchen table, there wouldn't be a problem. But the kitchen table where my stuff is right now happens to be in a restored colonial-era farmhouse. Anachronisms are a big, bad no-no at Morrisville Historic Village and employees like me are expected to know better than to leave such modernisms lying around.

It's a day like any other at work. Mary and I complain about our itchy Early American clothing and the ninety-degree weather; if colonial women actually wore as many layers as we do, we joke, they must have stank to the high heavens. Loretta bakes corn bread to show off the authentic brick oven and swats visitors' hands when they reach out for a taste. "Not enough for our guests," she sings. "I'm sure you understand." It'd be breaking character to say "health code" or "lawsuit"; she winks deliberately instead.

Mary and I feed the ducks in the pond out back and give tours of the house, pretending not to know anything about modern-day life. ("George Bush? Who's he? The cobbler up the road?") We explain the origins of the phrase "sleep tight" to packs of camp kids and detail the long-ago tragedies of the families that once called the farmhouse home. James, the lanky blond who works in the carpenter's shop, wanders over for a chat. He leans over the half-cut front door, his sloping shoulders silhouetted against blazing daylight, as I sit in a rocker in the darkened front hall drinking warm Coke from a clay mug. He says, "If Will tells me 'measure twice, cut once,' one more time I'm not responsible for my actions." He just graduated from a different high school, in the next town over, and is going to Princeton come fall. He surfs and always has a book in his pocket and that's about all I know about him at the moment. It will be another few weeks before he'll start carving me things out of wood—a duck, a name plate, a Ferris wheel—and a couple more before he'll say "wow" after we kiss.

Loretta hollers from the kitchen; she has a chore for me to do. I spill soapy water on my burlap skirt while emptying the metal bucket off the back porch. "If you don't rush so much, you won't get it on yourself," she instructs, and I say, "Thanks, Mom" without thinking. Immediately, I feel guilty. It's like I've already begun to replace her.

Mrs. Rudolph, the village head honcho, comes to the kitchen door a full hour before my shift ends and catches my eye. "Someone's here to take you home, Betsy." She has a perpetual redness to her nose, an unfortunate fact considering her name.

I slip into the nursery and unpeel my work clothes, hanging them over the side of the wooden crib before shoving them in my backpack in place of the shorts, T-shirt, and Sketchers I've put on. When I return to the kitchen, Mrs. Rudolph is still waiting for me and my stomach clenches. Escorts are never good. I know that it's happened, that she's gone. Thank God I went to see her last night.

Mary ditches colonial-speak and says, "Call me?"

The fact that no one chides her modern usage means trouble for sure.

Mrs. Rudolph and I walk through the village in silence, crossing the busy street that carelessly cuts through it, and I realize it's unpleasantly hot—Early American clothes or not. I'm mad that Mrs. Rudolph knows something I don't—rather, that she's actually been told—but I don't ask her what she knows. I don't even ask my Aunt Patty and Uncle Jim, who've been sent to bring me home; they're an aunt and uncle I rarely see so their mere presence confirms the level of crisis. I sit in their oversize backseat, my thighs sticking to the tan leather, and wait for Patty to start smoking. She's fidgeting—I know she wants one—but she doesn't give in. I could tell her it's okay, that I know the difference between breast cancer and lung cancer—that I could probably use a smoke myself—but I decide to let her sweat.

It feels like revenge. I just don't know what for.

I get out of the car in front of my house, and my aunt and uncle hang back. I grew up inside this house—a three-story white Victorian, with a big wraparound porch—and it has never, ever looked so menacing. I almost don't want to go inside but I do. When my eyes adjust, I see the grandparents I have left—my dad's parents—loitering in the kitchen. My father's at the top of the stairs and beckons me with his eyes.

We sit on my bed and he tells me what I already know. Together we cry and await my brother's arrival. Ben's younger than I am—fourteen years old—and he's been summoned from basketball camp. He joins us in my room a while later and the three of us cry and cry.

I call Brandon, who I've been dating for six months; he's my first bona fide boyfriend. In minutes he's at the front door, his car parked poorly on the street—a solid two feet from the curb. He wouldn't have his license if he parked like that during his road test.

"I'm going out," I shout to the house.

Brandon hugs me limply on the front porch. His eyes are perpetually sad to begin with, just by design; now they look something else, too. Sad and maybe a little bit scared. Like this is more than he bargained for. He doesn't say anything and I say, "Let's get out of here."

In the car, he says, "Where to?" and I say, "The wall." It's a concrete wall at the end of a wooded street that dead-ends at the beach. We go there to watch the waves and to fool around—sometimes just to talk. We've been going there less and less lately. I'm not sure why.

I step out of the car at the wall and am immediately grateful for the shore breeze. It's cooler by the water than anywhere else I've been all day. We hop our butts up onto the scratchy concrete and spin around so our legs dangle down over the sand. I wonder why I'm not crying and figure I'm now officially in shock. Brandon says, "I'm so sorry," and I just nod and stare at the water. We supposedly knew she was going to die but I guess you never believe it until it happens . . . and maybe not even then.

I want Brandon to say something more. Something insightful and comforting, something that will crush the feelings I'm having about his complete inadequacy as a boyfriend. I don't know what I expect from him, but I know that it's more than this. He takes my hand, which is a start, but when I look up at him, he's got nothing for me. "Why don't you *say* something?" I ask.

"I—" He sighs. "God. I don't . . . I don't know what to say."

I know that I should say something reassuring. Like "that's okay," or "just being here is enough." But it's not okay. It's not enough. I'm already wondering whether I'll ever see him the same way again, whether I'll ever feel my stomach flip at the sight of him—or anyone—and that makes me mad. She's gone and now everything's going to be different.

I pick a swell of ocean in the distance and try to track its progress to shore. When it finally crests and crashes on the beach, I turn to Brandon and say, "I should get home. My dad and Ben'll be worried."

We go home a different way, past the junior high I went to. Even though I'm only going into my senior year of high school I suddenly feel ancient, like junior high was a lifetime ago. Like I've aged twenty years in the space of an hour.

Brandon pulls up in front of the house. "Call you later?"

"Yeah," I say. "Sure." But I'm not sure I care whether he does.

Then, a blur of memories: Picking out a casket. Streams of people hugging me, squeezing my hand. Someone—a grandparent? an aunt?—saying it's for the best, she's at peace, my father can move on now, me storming out of the room. Deciding what dress to bury my mother in, feeling guilty for loving its deep pink-brown silk so much that I want to keep it, and shopping for something to wear to the funeral myself.

My Aunt Kay, the mother of two boys, takes me to the mall. She's already stepping up to the challenge my mother, her sister, apparently presented her—of looking after me in whatever mysterious feminine ways my father can't. And amidst the racks of tank tops and capris in The Gap, I run into Missy Vetter from school.

"Is that your mom?" she asks when she sees the blonde woman hovering near me. I hiss, "My mother's dead" before disappearing into a fitting room alone. I've got a long, blue floral skirt and a white cotton shirt with three-quarter sleeves hooked over my finger on plastic hangers. My mother, I was sure, would have insisted I was too young to wear black, even on her account.

My phone beeps a text message at me. "How R U?" Mary wants to know. And I want so desperately right then to be able to text back "gr8," to have my life be normal again.

People crawl out of the woodwork for these things, turns out. Cousins I never knew my father had pop up in every corner. Girls I barely know from school turn up at the wake, like it's the social event of the summer. Brandon is there, too, of course. I bring him up to the casket with me at one point—kneel in front of my mother's dead body with an arm slung around his shoulders. I think I'm giving him an opportunity to redeem himself, to say something insightful or meaningful, but he doesn't. He mostly seems to avoid looking at my mother, and who can blame him? I keep stealing glimpses at her myself, trying to figure out why she looks so different, but I can only conclude that the difference is that she's dead. I watch Brandon later, as Lauren Janey—barely an acquaintance from school—flips her hair in his vicinity. I think, Flirting at a wake. Nice.

I nearly die myself when I see Danny Mose's car pull into the cemetery. I'm standing with my family, sweating through the new clothes that I'll never wear again and, I imagine, getting sunburn. I think the priest has already started saying whatever it is he's saying when I see the car—a red sportscar—pull up. Danny gets out, with Meaghan Armstrong trailing behind him, and they hurry over to join the congregation. I think, Better late than never. I haven't seen either of them since the end of the school year a few weeks ago but there have been rumors they're kind of sort of dating. I guess they are. I barely know Meaghan, though, and I think it's weird that he brought her here. Like it's a date or something. Not that I know Danny well, either, but I've always wanted to. He's unbearably hot. I decide to pretend he came here because he's secretly in love with me, not because his mother worked with my mother and probably told him he had to. In school, Danny Mose never gives me the time of day.

The casket gets lowered. The crowd disperses. Then it's back to the house where there are lasagnas and baked hams to be pushed around on the plate; the salad dressing's oily, a cancer poisoning everything around it. When I'm finally able to escape the concerned looks of relatives and neighbors and retreat to my room, I lie down on my bed and see my work clothes—my brown burlap skirt, white cotton shift, and brown striped top—hanging on the back of the door. To my complete astonishment, I can't wait to go back to Morrisville, to put on layer upon layer of farm-girl gear. I've hated my dopey job from the get-go but right now it seems like the only place where I can escape. I think back to the first time I met James; I was feeding the ducks down at the pond and he walked over and said, "You new to these parts?" I smiled and said, "Yes," and then he said, "I'm James," and I said, "Betsy."

"You here all summer?" he asked.

I said, "Yup."

"Cool." He squinted and looked up at the sky; I'd just felt a drop of rain and I guess he had, too. "You ever say more than one word at a time?" he said.

I smiled, not even looking at him, just watching one duck launch itself back off the shore. I said, "Nope."

He looked at me with a sort of disbelief and for a second I liked the idea of it; that I could reinvent myself with him as this weird girl who never said more than one word at a time, a girl who couldn't say "my mother" or "breast cancer" or "I have a boyfriend." I liked the idea that he was a clean slate. But then I felt compelled to say, "Just kidding."

"Aha!" His eyebrows shot up. "That was two!" And then it started to rain and we each went off—me toward the farmhouse, him toward the carpenter's shop. "I'll see you around," he said. And I said, "See ya."

I wonder if the ducks have missed me.

chapter 2

My father pretty much orchestrated my job interview at Morrisville Historic Village. Not only is he a history professor and history buff—my full name's Betsy Ross Irving, for chrissakes, and my brother Benjamin's middle name is Franklin—but also he's on the board at Morrisville. I didn't want to go on the interview at all as I'd hoped to get a job checking badges on the beach all summer. The beach—where Danny Mose is a lifeguard—is only a few blocks from my house, whereas Morrisville is a long-ass bike ride away, closer to the strip of shops and restaurants we call "downtown." My aunt owns a café there—and there's a really cool record store—but it's hardly a bustling metropolis. This is, after all, New Jersey.

I might have even liked working for the catering company where my friend Sandra works when she's not on some exotic trip with her parents but I didn't really have much choice in the matter. My father gave me just one opportunity to get out of the interview. He liked devising tests for me and I failed this one miserably.

"Fine," he said, when I stormed up to my parents' room on the top floor and moaned to my mother for the umpteenth time about how wearing colonial clothes would ruin my chances of ever being popular. "Name the original thirteen colonies and you're off the hook."

He lowered his newspaper, took off his glasses, and crossed his arms.

"Mom!" I moaned.

But she just shrugged. "I think you'll look cute," she said from the bed. She was weak from the last round of chemo and didn't come downstairs much anymore. Her blond hair had grown back a steel-wool gray. "And I know you'll like the money," she added.

"I don't believe this," I said. I plopped down on their window seat; it's never been quite as comfortable and cushy as the one in my room and I've never been sure why.

"How do you expect to get into college if you can't name the thirteen colonies?" my father said from his rocker. With his salt-and-pepper hair and beard and glasses, he always looks like he's playing the role of history professor to the letter.

"I'm pretty sure they don't ask you that on the SAT," I said. I looked out the window: the pool out back wasn't yet uncovered and I felt a wave of anticipation for summer.

"Humor me," he said. "Just give it a whirl. And don't forget, your popularity is on the line."

"Massachusetts." I began a count using my thumb. "New Jersey, New York, North Carolina, South Carolina, Connecticut, Georgia, Virginia." Then I started to run out of steam and

I wasn't even sure of them up to that point. I cringed and starting naming other states more slowly. "Rhode Island . . . Delaware . . . New Hampshire . . . Vermont . . . and . . ."

Only one more to go . . .

"Pennsylvania?"

"Ooooh, so close." My father shook his head and lifted his paper up in front of him. "Better get your interview clothes ready."

"Fine." I stormed out of their room and went down their hall to mine, where I promptly slammed the door shut. I turned in the general direction of my dad—who yelled out "Not Vermont! Maryland!"—and raised my middle finger. I said, "Yeah, well, colonize this!"

To be perfectly honest, Morrisville sort of freaked me out. My parents had taken Ben and me there for various exhibits and festivals over the years and the grounds never ceased to spook me. The whole village had been assembled around the ruins of Buckman House, a brick mansion that a wealthy merchant built for his young wife in the early 1800s. She died tragically young—of some old disease like cholera or consumption—before the house was finished and she is believed to have guided her husband through the construction's completion and the planning of the estate's elaborate gardens and garden maze *from beyond the grave.* But her devastated husband never recovered from the blow and the estate eventually fell into total disrepair. It was abandoned for close to a century, then it was taken over by the local historical society in the 1970s. Other historic houses from random parts of New Jersey were moved to the grounds and Morrisville was born.

So the focus of the village is this massive crumbling brick

structure that has been stabilized but only partially restored. Morrisville offers special private candlelit dinners on the grounds during the summer, and they bill it as a haunted dinner. Though I can't for the life of me imagine why anyone would want some dead chick hanging around on their date, it's one of Morrisville's most popular tickets. Like I said. Creepy. The fact that I once got lost in the maze—a mile's worth of pathways and dead ends created by high hedges—and screamed bloody murder until my mother found me probably didn't endear me to the place, either.

As if the idea of Morrisville itself weren't bad enough, I soon discovered that Liza Henske, only the weirdest freak of a girl from school, worked at Morrisville, too. Apparently she'd been working there for years, stuffing her spiky black-and-bleached-blond hair up under a white bonnet, covering her tattoos with colonial garb, and taking out her piercings before every shift. We barely acknowledged each other when we passed on the grounds and I was hoping it'd stay that way. I was a relative goody-two-shoes who built sets for school plays, played midfield on the JV soccer team, got mostly good grades. Liza, on the other hand, practically lived in detention and was widely believed to have had an abortion during a long break she took sophomore year. We were complete social opposites, and when the new school year started, I didn't want to have to actually talk to her in the hallways.

The only redeeming factor was the fact that Mary, my best friend forever, was so excited about my job interview and the chance to play dress-up that she insisted she go on one, too. We both got hired, then suffered together through a training program that reviewed some basic American history, taught us details of colonial home and farm life, and provided scripts we'd have to participate in. We were also expected to improvise when appropriate but, two weeks in, I still hadn't discovered my improv skills. Thankfully, though, Mary had a knack for it and she and I were assigned to the same house, a farmhouse built in 1816, where we were supposed to be the teenage (duh) daughters of a young widow, played with a bit too much enthusiasm by Loretta.

My mother had insisted that it'd be fun if I would just give it a chance. But this was a woman who talked to strangers constantly: in the supermarket, on line for popcorn at the movies—even, more than once, stopped at a red light. I'd clearly not inherited this trait. In fact, if someone had asked me before Morrisville what my notion of hell was, it would most likely have had something to do with rats nipping at my feet. Barely a month into my summer, I was sure my personal hell would be an eternity spent giving strangers tours of Satan's crib while wearing horns and a tail.

I had a feeling it was going to be a very long summer.

chapter 3

the day before I'm supposed to go back to work at Morrisville, two weeks after my mom dies, tragedy strikes again. Mary calls to say her parents weren't as keen as she was on the idea of her working at Morrisville—or working at all.

"They've enrolled me in an SAT prep class," she tells me. "And my mom thinks I should practice more for cheerleader trials. They say work will distract me. I already had to call Mrs. Rudolph and tell her I quit."

This shouldn't be a surprise to me. Mary's parents are the most hardcore parents I've ever known and they've been trying to get Mary into an Ivy League college since kindergarten. Mary and I have known each other since before we were even born—our parents were friends—and her parents have always pushed her to get straight As but also to be well-rounded. More recently—after years in school bands and taking dance classes—Mary's energy has been focused on the school newspaper and on writing in general; she won third prize in *Seventeen* magazine's fiction contest last year. Her parents were, of course, thrilled but I secretly think they decided that the writing award and the job at Morrisville would make her look too bookish on her college applications. They would've preferred it if she'd made the varsity cheerleading squad, something Mary has yet to do despite many tryouts.

"I'm so sorry," Mary says. "I'll come and visit, I promise."

"But it's not the same." I feel like crying.

"I know. It's not my fault. I could kill my mother."

"Don't say stuff like that," I snap.

"I'm sorry," she says. "I didn't mean it." And now she's crying and I'm crying. "I don't know how you're holding it together," she says. "I always wished your mom was my mom."

Mary actually has the same body type and mannerisms as my mother did so we all always joked that Mary was her daughter and I wasn't.

Mary wails, "She was so cool."

I sigh and say, "I know." Because I know it's true that my mother was cool even if I never wanted to admit it before. I somehow wish I had, that'd I'd told her I thought so. That we hadn't spent most of the last year fighting about clothes and curfews and boys.

When I walk into the farmhouse, Liza Henske, who usually works at the parsonage/schoolhouse up the road, is in the front hall sweeping. She looks up, then back down again, and she says, "I'm not any happier about it than you are." She resumes sweeping and I go into the kitchen, where Loretta is preparing cornbread mix in a big wooden bowl. She's already fired up the brick oven so the kitchen's hotter than Hades. You have to burn an actual fire inside the oven to heat it. Then you yank out the wood—it falls onto the stone hearth and then you sweep it into the fireplace—and the oven retains the heat for hours. It's actually kinda cool when you think about it. Sometimes the broom even catches fire.

"What is she doing here?" I say.

"With Mary gone, we thought we could use an extra hand around here," Loretta says.

"I could've managed."

"Aw, honey." She puts her spoon down and twists her hands in her apron. She's about forty-five years old and looks like she actually could've lived in colonial times, like she might have preferred it. I don't think she's gotten a haircut in ten years and I doubt she even wears makeup when she can. (Did I mention how we can't wear makeup????) "We weren't sure when you'd be coming back and, well . . ."

"Well, what?"

"What kind of shape you'd be in. I'm so sorry about your mother." She's coming around the kitchen table to hug me, so I head for the stairs and say, "I better go change."

She backs off and looks offended but I don't especially care. I'm through letting people hug me just because it makes them feel better.

When I return to the kitchen all dressed and demodernized and ready to get back to colonial living, I fear she'll want to pick up where she left off so I shove my twenty-first-century belongings in the closet and say, "I'm gonna feed the ducks before any tours arrive."

James finds me by the pond, which you can see from the carpenter's shop. He pushes a strand of his dirty blond hair out of his eyes and says, "Hi."

"Hi," I echo. I toss some feed out for a group of ducks that have come to welcome me back. I'm surprised by how excited I am to see them—and him.

"I wanted to call you." He brushes a foot over the grass, looking down like he's nervous. "But I guess I was a little afraid to."

I say, "Things were kind of crazy."

Plus, I want to remind him, it's not like we're *really* friends, or like he's ever called me before. I don't know why people think they should treat me any differently now. I'm getting sick of it already.

"Well, I'm still sorry I didn't call," he says. "I should've. I mean, I wanted to."

My face gets hot. "Well, thanks."

"I guess I didn't know what I would have said." He's got something in his hand and he slides it into his pocket. "Because even now I don't want to ask you how you are or tell you how sorry I was to hear what happened or any of those stupid things people say." Hearing this guy I barely know talk like this to me feels weird and I just stare at him, having a hard time believing there are words coming out of his mouth, directed at me. "I guess I just want you to know that I've been thinking about you. That you're really all I've been thinking about. And that I'm glad you're back."

I nod and realize I'm crying.

"Oh," he says. "I didn't mean to—"

"No." I wipe my nose, thinking that it would've been nice if my own boyfriend had been able to say the same, thinking James looks a lot cuter right now than he's ever looked before. Then I feel guilty for thinking that when we're talking about my dead mother. "It's okay." I take a couple of sharp breaths. "I better go."

"I made you something," he says. "While you were gone." He reaches into his pocket and says, "Close your eyes and hold out your hands."

I do as I'm told and feel a smooth object being placed on my palms.

"Okay," he says. "Open."

I open my eyes and study the object. "It's a duck," I say. "A wooden duck."

We both let out a quick laugh.

"What'd you expect," he says. "A real one?"

"I didn't mean—"

"No, it's okay." He smiles and runs a hand through his hair. "I know it's stupid. It's just you're always feeding the ducks and I . . . I don't know. It was dumb."

"It's not dumb." I slide the duck into my apron pocket. I want to tell him it's the nicest thing that anyone's ever done for me. "Thanks."

It's a busier day for Morrisville than any I've worked before—or maybe it just feels that way since I've been doing mostly nothing for two weeks; my father and I sorted through some of my mother's stuff to give away but other than that we mostly moped around the house avoiding each other.

Liza and I take turns picking up tour groups as they arrive on the doorstep and we barely have a break all day. We pass in the halls but since we've usually each got a tour going at the same time we can easily avoid actually talking to each other. I hear snippets of her spiel as the day wears on. Her tour members are always laughing and asking her questions, and she answers them confidently in what sounds like authentic colonial-speak. Colonial Liza is a far cry from the modern Liza I've seen around school, where she hangs out with pale guys with black hair and black boots who are rumored to be in punk bands or own motorcycles. I'm sure I've never seen her in a skirt off the Morrisville grounds.

The general store gets robbed three times a day every day and it's our job to rush out into the streets in a tizzy. We fret and ask visitors if they saw any suspicious characters fleeing the scene and they mostly laugh at us knowingly. I find it hard to muster the requisite level of shock and excitement three times a day but Mrs. Rudolph swears the guests love it—"This is really living history!" she says. Liza does such a good job of playing a ditsy, alarmist farm girl that I think maybe I should practice at home in front of the mirror so I don't suck so bad by comparison.

At day's end we both collapse into chairs by the kitchen table. "Nice work today, girls," Loretta says. "Nice team work," she adds. It's all I can do not to roll my eyes.

Liza says, "If you'll forgive my saying it, I'm not familiar with this phrase, 'team work'? Is that modern?"

"Point taken," Loretta says.

I get up and get my stuff out of the closet. I say, "I'll see you tomorrow."

"Okay," Loretta says. "Have a good night."

I hope to. I've got a date with Brandon—our first since it

happened. He's picking me up in the parking lot but on my way up Main Street I hear Liza call after me, "Hey!" I stop and turn and she stops where she is, maybe ten feet away.

"I heard about your mother," she says. She looks ghostly white in broad daylight and I'm tempted to tell her she should get out more, go easy on the sunblock once in a while.

"Yeah?" I say.

"Yeah," she says.

I'm not really looking to be touchy-feely with Liza Henske and wish she'd left well enough alone. Ignoring each other suited me just fine.

"That really sucks," she says.

I nod and almost want to laugh. No one's said as much but it does suck. It sucks big time.

"Yup," I say. "It sure does."

I slide into the passenger seat and say "hey," then lean over to give Brandon a kiss. It lands on his cheek, though that's not what I intended. I'm not sure whether he turned away at the last second or whether I imagined it.

"Where are we going?" I ask. I'm hoping he's planned something extra special since we haven't been *out* out in weeks. Something romantic. Like maybe dinner at Nadia's, one of the nicer restaurants downtown.

"Well, it turns out everybody's going bowling," he says. "I thought it'd be fun. We're supposed to meet them at Bowl-a-Rama in half an hour if you're up for it."

My face burns. I can feel my heart pounding against my ribs. I see James coming up to the parking lot—still in Early American clothes but suspenders dangling down by his legs—

and he sees me and we meet eyes and he waves and I just tilt my chin up to say "hey" as the car glides past. I have the worst feeling of wishing he hadn't seen me here with Brandon.

Brandon says, "So are you up for it?"

I'm speechless. Stunned into silence by his apparent inability to do anything right anymore. He's got something stuck between his teeth and I think how he can't even brush his teeth right. When my phone beeps at me and it's a text message that Mary sent hours ago about bowling, I realize I'm also just caught off guard, out of the loop. Colonial farm girls can't get caught text messaging and I'm always playing catch-up at the end of the day.

"Is that okay?" He pulls up to a red light.

I'm wondering why he's not squeezing my hand or rubbing my knee or anything, like he used to. "Yeah," I say. "Fine. But can we swing by Burger King first?"

"They have food at the Bowl-a-Rama."

I'd forgotten that, but I say, "I know." I want to get one thing I want today, even if it's just a BK chicken sandwich.

"Everybody" turns out to be Mary and her boyfriend, Trevor, and our friend Libby and her sister, Natalie. It also includes Lauren Janey, She Who Flirts at Wakes, and I don't really understand why she's there. "Everybody" has never included her before. We've occasionally hung out with Natalie, who's close to Lauren, during the summer months but she's never before brought Lauren along. I can't say I like it.

We've got two lanes next to each other and somehow Brandon and I wind up playing on different lanes. He doesn't seem to care that we're separated and I wonder how it is that we ever started going out at all, how he ever got up the courage or level of interest to ask me out on a date in the first place. I remember how easy I made it for him once I'd heard he maybe sort of liked me, how I kept throwing myself into his path so he'd have no choice to say something . . . eventually. He'd finally done it when we were breaking down the set of our school's production of *Pippin*. We'd gone to a movie the following weekend and then just kept going to movies, and footballs games, and then we were a couple before we maybe even knew what hit us. No fireworks, no drama, and that suited me fine. There was already plenty of drama at home after my mother's diagnosis.

I decide to focus on my game. I'm a good bowler so a couple of strikes or splits might distract me from the looks on everyone's faces. They seem to say "Shouldn't you be at home?" and "You're ruining our good time just by being here." But I need to be out and around people I know and not home, undistracted—even if it makes them all uncomfortable. Ben's neediness is more than I can handle. I'm not his mother. I don't want to be. My father can't seem to find a way to talk about what's happened and his newfound affection for forced cheeriness is wearing on me. He's supposed to be writing a book this summer—in the academic world there's this idea called "publishing or perishing," which I guess means he has to get a book out or risks losing his job—but he spends most of his time staring blankly at his computer screen or watching the History Channel. I'm hoping that'll change soon. Like maybe now that I'm going back to work, he'll do the same.

I get strikes on my first three gos—everyone claps reservedly—and I become so focused on the game that I lose track of Brandon for a while. "Where's Brandon?" I ask Mary, finally.

"He went to get food," she says. Once again I feel the anger rising up. He didn't even ask me if I wanted anything. I already had a chicken sandwich, sure, but I might've liked a Coke.

"Everything okay?" Mary asks. She and Trevor have been all lovey-dovey all night; I can't say it doesn't irk me.

"Yeah," I say. "Fine." Because that's what I'm saying to everybody these days.

I start off in the direction of the snack bar across wall-to-wall carpet dotted with gray circles of old flattened gum. I smell grease, smoke, popcorn, and beer as I approach the entry to the kitchen area and stop when I see Brandon and Lauren Janey standing on the cafeteria-style line talking. Guys are so dumb, I think. He doesn't even realize she's flirting.

I turn and go back to the lanes just as it's my turn again. I don't pay attention to what I'm doing and throw a terrible gutter ball. Just then Brandon and Lauren rejoin the group. "Nice one," she says, wryly.

I don't turn around but wait for my ball to pop up out of the return machine. I hold my hand over the cooling fan and wish it could blow air into my skull so I wouldn't be so hot-headed. When I take my second shot I knock all the pins down.

"Too bad it's only a spare," Lauren says.

I look up at the scoreboard overhead and say, "Yeah." I decide to let the scores speak for themselves. The closest person behind me, Brandon, is trailing by a full twenty-three points. Lauren's got a whopping forty-eight in the sixth frame. I'm discovering the virtues of small victories, I guess. I'm putting on a show for Lauren and my friends because I don't want to make a scene. I save that for later, for the car.

"You practically ignored me all night," I snap. We're driving by my old school again on the way home and Brandon suddenly pulls over and turns off the engine. It's the most decisive thing he's done in weeks, possibly ever.

"We need to talk," he says.

"We didn't talk all night. Why talk now?"

He huffs and grips the steering wheel and suddenly it dawns on me. The flippy hair. The French fries. He's not as dumb as he looks.

"You've got to be fucking kidding me," I say.

"What?" He's defensive.

"Lauren Janey?"

"I tried to tell you."

"You did?" I nearly laugh. "When exactly did you try to tell me?"

"I don't know. But I wanted to. Everyone said I shouldn't."

"Everyone? Who's everyone?"

"We didn't want to hurt you."

"We?" I nearly scream. "Now you two are a 'we'?"

More silence. Shocker.

"Have you hooked up with her?"

"Betsy. Please."

"You hooked up with her?"

His guilty silence is answer enough.

I think of Brandon's hands, his mouth—on her breasts. I think of the basement of his house, the backseat of his car—the places where we've come close to having sex but haven't—and I try to picture *her* there instead of me. I feel like maybe I'm going to throw up.

I say, "Take me home." Then I'm astounded by the fact that he does. That he takes me home and lets me get out of the car without so much as another word. That he lets me go that easily. That I wasted six months of my life with someone so cowardly. I think of Lauren and her big breasts and, awful as it sounds, I think, Good, that's more room for cancer. When I think of all the times Mary and I used to chant, "We must, we must, we must increase our busts," arms pumping, I'm embarrassed for us. We had no idea. We had no fear.

At my house, I get upstairs and into my room without drawing the attention of my father, who is glued to the History Channel as usual. My brother appears in my doorway just as I'm about to shut myself in. He says, "Can you help me with this questionnaire I have to do for camp?"

"Ask Dad," I snap. I close the door on him.

I just can't seem to be anything but mad. I know Ben's done nothing wrong, nothing but have to slog through this misery with me, but I'm pissed off at him for placing demands on me, for looking at me like I know how to do things better than he does, when I don't really know much of anything.

Suddenly, I'm mad at my mother for not preparing me better, for not teaching me a million things I imagine will now seem more essential to survival on this planet than ever before, things I've yet to even conceive of ever needing to do. I'm mad at her for getting sick in the first place. For not insisting the doctors do chemo the first time around, for falling for their promises of having "gotten it all" with surgery. For relapsing. For not fighting harder. For not protecting me from a whole catalogue of awful images I can't seem to shake when I crawl into bed at night. Clumps of hair falling out when she finally succumbed to chemo. The scar, and the bandage, and the void where her breast used to be. The sound of her voice, screaming from the master bedroom that she needed help getting to the bathroom, or a glass of water. I'm mad at her for leaving. For not defying the odds. For becoming a statistic. For turning me into a charity case. For screwing everything up for all of us.

A couple of months ago, when my mother told me Brandon seemed like a bit of a dud, I wanted to strangle her, but now—now that he's dumped me—I want to hear her say it again. To hear her say, "He's too short for you. And he talks like he's got marbles in his mouth."

My father knocks on my door. I say, "Come in."

"Everything okay?" He pokes his head in and looks at me over the top of his glasses.

"Brandon and I broke up," I say. I think of the things I let him do and regret it all. I'm so grateful I never went all the way with him and already imagine that Lauren Janey has. Maybe that's all he ever wanted from me to begin with.

My father shakes his head. "Yeah, well, he had a wimpy handshake."

I smile weakly, but it doesn't feel the same coming from him. "Did you help Ben with his camp thing?"

"Of course," he says. "I'm packing him a lunch for tomorrow. You want me to make you one, too?"

"No," I say. "I'm good."

He turns and goes and I reach for my phone; I mistakenly call Mary's home number, not her cell.

Her mother picks up.

"Hi, Mrs. Giacomo. I'm sorry I'm calling this late."

"Oh, Betsy," she says. "I've made a lasagna I want to drop by. Is there a good time?"

"Oh, we've already got too much food. But thanks anyway."

I know I'm being rude but I'm tired of hand-me-downs, of everyone acting like my father's some imbecile who has never cooked a meal in his life. He's a better cook than my mother was and, besides, we've already tossed about three frozen casseroles that we knew we'd never eat.

"Oh, well, of course." Mrs. Giacomo says. "If there's anything you need, honey. Anything at all."

"Is Mary home?" I ask.

"Yeah, she just came in a few minutes ago. Hope you girls had fun tonight. I'll get her now."

Mary picks up on another line and I hear her shout, "You can hang up!"

"Hey." We wait for the click. "Sorry about that."

"It's okay."

"I tried to tell her that her lasagna sucks," Mary says. "She thinks she's Italian just 'cause she's married to my dad. I keep reminding her that her maiden name's McGinty."

"Brandon just broke up with me," I blurt.

"Oh, Bets. I'm sorry."

There's something wrong with the way she says it, though.

"He's been seeing Lauren Janey behind my back," I explain.

"I'm so sorry," Mary says again.

I feel my ears start to burn. "Now see, this is really interesting to me," I say. " 'Cause you don't sound surprised." I'm looking at a picture of me and Brandon and Mary and Trevor at Six Flags together, arms around one another's shoulders on the line for Batman.

Mary takes a deep breath. "Nobody knew what to do. We just didn't think anyone else should be the one to tell you. And it's so soon. He was supposed to wait at least a little while longer."

"This is unbelievable." My head spins and throbs. "What were you thinking? Why didn't you tell me?"

"I was afraid to, I guess. You've been through so much. I thought you'd get mad."

"Well, I'm mad now," I say.

"But—"

"I'm gonna go," I say.

"I'm so sorry," she says.

I hang up and start to de-Brandonize my room. I take down the picture of Six Flags. I hesitate before ripping it into shreds but then go ahead and rip away. I do the same thing to a couple of other pictures: at a birthday party at his house, in the cafeteria at school, one of him in his track clothes on the bleachers at school. I take off the silver necklace he gave me—a swirly B on a chain—and toss it into the trashcan.

Satisfied, at least for the time being, I change into my pajamas—a shorts-and-tank set that my mother ordered for me online when she could no longer manage our trips to the mall. The tank says HEAVENLY across the chest but I don't feel that way at all. I wonder for a second whether my mother's gone to heaven, whether it really exists. I curl up on my room's window seat. It's one of my favorite places in the whole world—you can see a slice of ocean—and tonight it feels especially magical. A warm breeze blows through the open window and there's a full moon casting silver light over the trees in the yard, making the water in our pool shimmer like liquid silver. I'm more tired than I realized—drained to the core. I should climb into my bed, but I don't. Instead I try to look toward the skies for signs of heaven, for a clue about what happens to us when we die.

I let myself cry like a baby, but immediately I feel foolish, like a drama queen, so I stop. I get up and get my backpack and hang up my work clothes so that some wrinkles will fall out. I pull the wooden duck out of my apron pocket and feel its smooth lines with my fingers. I put it on my night table before crawling into bed, and I find myself fantasizing about my own wake. I run through a list of my friends and newly sworn enemies and imagine how they'd feel if I were dead tomorrow, if they never got the chance to say they were sorry. I picture Brandon finally showing the kind of emotion he's never shown with me before. I imagine Mary wailing, "I should've told her!" and starting a catfight with Lauren Janey. And I see James walking into the room, stepping up quietly to the casket. While everyone else is wondering who he is, he's whispering to my corpse, "I think maybe I could've loved you. Now we'll never know."

I wake in the same spot seven hours later when my alarm blasts a new Strokes song at 8:00 A.M. The sun is shining right in the windows and I feel feverish, my skin hot to touch. I head for the shower, making it as cold as I can bear.

chapter 4

Mary has text-messaged me three times by the time I've biked to work the next morning, but I turn off my phone and put it in the kitchen closet without responding. I feel like I've been made a fool of and I'm just not ready to forgive and forget. I still can't believe it. Brandon. And Lauren Janey. Behind my back. And people knew!

I take a broom out to the front hallway and find Liza dusting the parlor with a feather duster with a wooden handle. I say, "Hey."

"Good day," Liza says back. I make a face when she looks away. It's not like there's anyone around to hear us talking out of character. Secretly I'm both embarrassed for Liza for taking her job so seriously—and for me, for not. I've never really found anything to really sink my teeth into, anything that really excites me enough to give it my all, so I sort of coast through a million things and nothing. Between my father's obsession with history and my mother's career as a professional photographer—she made most of her money selling "stock" images on the Web, for other people to use on book covers or in magazines—I've always felt like an adopted child of sorts. Someone born of less passionate people. My mother used to always ask me, "But what are you *passionate* about?" I'd always think real hard, then draw a blank and say, "I don't know." Ben would dribble by and say, breathlessly, that he was *passionate* about basketball. She always thought I was being evasive but it was and still is, pathetically enough, the truth.

I quickly finish up the sweeping, then go back to the kitchen, where Loretta's preparing ingredients for chicken soup. "Feel like chopping carrots?" she asks.

"Sure," I say. I take a seat at the kitchen table and get to work. I still can't believe that this is my summer job. That I'm sitting in a colonial farmhouse making chicken soup that'll cook in a wrought-iron pot that hangs over an open fire. In the middle of summer. I mean, come on. Why would anyone *do* that? Sometimes the whole thing's so trippy I can't quite get over it. I feed ducks and eat chicken soup and get paid for it.

"Mrs. Rudolph's looking for people to sign up to work the end-of-summer benefactors' banquet," Loretta says. "You should do it. It's fun."

I just look up at her skeptically.

"You'll get paid," she adds. "We serve up a big dinner for about fifty people and teach them how to play old games and puzzles and such."

"Sounds like a blast." I move onto a celery stalk.

"Well, you might be surprised." She turns and busies herself with tightening a knot on her apron. "Liza and James have already signed up."

I look up but she's still looking away. Liza I couldn't care less about, but James . . . well, maybe it *would* be fun. "I'll think about it," I say.

Loretta turns and examines my celery with a knowing smile. "Smaller pieces, if you can."

The morning seems endless. We're short on tours today—the grounds seem deserted—and even Loretta's at a loss as to how to while away the hours. The first general store robbery of the day is cancelled, since there aren't enough visitors to make it worth the charade. In our house, we've already dusted and swept the whole place—no small task—and made more soup and cornbread than the three of us can possibly stomach.

"Why don't you two go play dominoes in the parlor?" Loretta suggests, after we've all been sitting around the kitchen table in silence for too long.

"What a glorious idea," Liza says.

I'm wondering how it's possible that one person could be so completely one way in school and entirely another here at work. Troublemaker Liza, who gets sent to the principal's office for cracking wise in class, is a colonial kiss-ass.

"Go on, Betsy," Loretta says, when Liza has walked off in the direction of the parlor. "It won't kill you."

In the parlor, Liza quickly refreshes my knowledge of the rules and we play quietly for a while.

"There's something I think you should know," she says eventually. "It may be none of my business, but if it were me I'd want to know."

I say, "What is it?" but I'm pretty sure I already know. That everybody knew but me.

"I've seen you around with Brandon Fields, and he picks you up here and stuff, so I take it he's your boyfriend or something."

I just put down another tile, two dots against two dots, and wait.

"Well, it could be nothing, but I saw him out last week, at the movie theater." She pauses for a second, looks me in the eye. "With Lauren Janey."

Eyes quickly diverted from mine, she puts down another tile. I quickly make another play.

"I just thought you should know," she says.

I'm so grateful I want to cry. My own best friend kept me in the dark and a practical stranger comes to me with the news instead. "He broke up with me last night," I say.

Liza shakes her head and snaps, "What an asshole" more loudly than is necessary.

"Girls!" Loretta yells from the other room. "Language!"

Liza raises a middle finger toward the kitchen and I laugh. She laughs, too, and her face seems transformed. Maybe she's not the bitch she seems like in school.

"Thanks for telling me," I say, when we've quieted down.

"I wish I had told you sooner." Liza starts packing up the game after she wins. "Then you could've at least broken up with him."

"I know," I say. "I feel like a fool."

"Well, you know what they say." She looks at me like I'm actually supposed to know which particular thing they say she's referring to.

She says, "Living well is the best revenge."

I smile weakly and go to get my wallet and a clay mug so I can buy a Coke at the café. We have to slip into the kitchen to pour since we can't be seen with cans. I think about asking Liza to come with me but I don't.

The afternoon takes a turn toward deathly hot and people stay away from un-air-conditioned Morrisville accordingly. Loretta can't seem to stand the boredom on Liza's and my face another second. "Why don't you girls go out back for some air?"

We make our way down to the pond and lay down on the grass. "We're probably lying in duck shit," Liza says.

I spread out like I'm making a snow angel. "I'm too hot to care."

We lie there in silence for a while, too hot to talk.

"Hello ladies," James says, all cheesylike. I squint up at him and Liza says, "Whassup, Jimbo?"

"Nothing much." He squats down. "You guys are probably lying in duck shit," he says.

Liza says, "We're too hot to care."

"Oh, fuck it," he says. He lies down next to me. "You think colonial people were ever this bored?"

"Nah," Liza says. "They were probably too busy raising chickens for real and tilling the fields or whatever you do to fields. We're only faking it."

"I don't know," I say. "I kinda like it." I don't really realize it's the truth until I say it, that maybe I've been thinking I'm *bored* when I'm really *relaxed*.

"You *like* being bored?" Liza says.

"No, not that," I say. "I mean that I find it relaxing. Being here."

"Yeah," James says. "But what if you had to use an outhouse and stuff. What if you couldn't flush?"

"Or use tampons?" Liza says. "Or drink Coke?"

"Yeah yeah yeah," I say. "But don't you think things were easier before e-mail and the SATs? We have to worry about getting into college and then paying for it, not to mention Al Qaeda and AIDS and a million other things that colonial people didn't have to worry about."

"Yeah, you're right," Liza says. "That's hell compared to worrying about the plague and getting pregnant and dying during childbirth—without a freakin' epidural—and war with England and consumption and—"

"Fine, fine." I breathe heavily. "I'm just *saying*. Sometimes having nothing to do—or not being able to do it because we're not allowed to have our phones on us or whatever—it's kind of fun."

"Don't take this the wrong way." Liza perches up on an arm, starts playing with a blade of grass, and smiles deviously. "But based on what I've seen of you at school I never would have guessed that you were such a freak."

I pretend to be shocked, then say, "I'm not the one who got all excited about playing dominoes."

"You're still a freak," James says, half laughing.

"Oh." I raise my eyebrows; there's something about being around people who barely know me that makes it easier to *be* me. "This from someone who carves ducks out of wood!"

Liza sits up. "You made a *duck*?"

"It was hard!" James protests.

"I'm just saying." I sit up. "You guys have been working here for, what, two, three summers? And you signed up for the end-of-season dinners? You can't exactly hate it, the whole colonial scene."

"The colonial scene?" Liza laughs.

James says, "Is that a popular alternative to the Goth scene?"

"Ohmigod, we should totally open up a club." Liza's excited by the topic—her eyes alive, crackling. "What could we call it?"

James says, "The Colony."

"Too obvious," Liza says.

I decide to lie back down and join in the joke, even though it's sort of on me. I think really hard of something witty or funny to say, wanting to impress them.

"I got it!" James says. "Jamestown!"

"No fair. You don't get to have your name as part of it," Liza says.

"How about Salem?" I say.

"Ooooh," James says. "That's good."

"It has nice witchy overtones," Liza declares. "But it's still too obvious. This is going to be the first colonial club of its kind, remember? We want to set the right tone. Something meaningful, yet mysterious. So it doesn't draw any old crowd, only the hardcore colonials."

The conversation has taken several turns for the absurd but I like it. And I'm feeling inspired. "Wait." I sit up and hold my hands up, palms out, to silence them. "I've got it."

Liza and James both sit up eagerly.

I say, "Thirteen," and it takes a moment for the genius of it to dawn on them.

"Thirteen," James repeats reverentially.

"It's perfect!" Liza concludes. It's silly to get so excited about such a ridiculous idea but we're all in it together. She says, "It'll be called Thirteen and then we'll have all these cool specialty drinks, like a Salem Witch Trial."

"And a Jamestown Massacre," James says.

"What about a Boston Tea Party?" I try. "Like a Long Island iced tea, but different." I've only had one Long Island iced tea in my life—with Brandon—and I hated it.

"We'll be rich in no time," James says.

"Yup." Liza sighs. "Any day now."

We indulge our reverie in silence and I realize how weird it is to be here, making plans—imaginary or not—with two people my mother never met. I wonder whether she would've liked Liza in spite of her raccoon-style hair, whether she would have thought that James's lanky body and mussed-up blond hair were cute.

"Anyway." James goes to get up. The mood has passed. "I should get back."

"See ya," I say, wishing he wouldn't go, wishing we three could hang out into the night, wishing I never had to go home.

"Wouldn't want to be ya," says Liza.

Liza and I pop back into the house to wrap things up and bid Loretta good day, then we change and head up Main Street together.

"So listen," Liza says, "I know we've had this too-cool-for-school vibe going between us but we're stuck together all summer and, well . . . there's a party at Midland Beach tomorrow night. If you wanted to maybe hang out and stuff."

She actually looks nervous, her eyes darting around uncomfortably and I figure she's nervous that I might actually say yes. She was probably put up to it by her parents, who told her to take pity on the girl with the dead mother and loser boyfriend. If there's one thing I don't want these days, it's pity.

"Thanks," I say. "But I can't." My father waves from the car; he's come to pick me up, thank God, and save me biking in this heat.

"No big deal." She can't possibly be disappointed but for a second it feels that way. "Just thought I'd ask."

"Thanks." I head off toward my dad, who is readying the bike rack on top of the car. "I'll see you tomorrow."

"Nope. Not me." She walks off toward her car with a quick wave. "I've got the day off."

And now I'm the one who's disappointed.

"I forgot something," I say to my dad as I toss my bag into the car. Then I run back into the main building where I find the sign-up list for the end-of-summer banquet. There's a pen dangling from the bulletin board. Under James Manning—I never knew his last name before—and Liza Henske, I add my own.

I watch a movie with Ben and my dad that night and we're all too uncomfortable to laugh, even though it's a comedy. There are a couple of things I find funny, but it mostly seems dumb and I wonder if I've lost my sense of humor. My mother was the jokester of the house, always doing a silly hoedown sort of dance move to lighten the mood of a room, always pouting— bottom lip turned out—or just poking us. Ben stifles a giggle at one point but beyond that I'm not sure anyone has laughed in this house since she died.

I try to remember what her laugh sounds like, and I can't. It has already begun: the forgetting. I wonder how much will be gone before it's done.

Upstairs, I turn on my computer and Google "grieving" and

come across countless sites explaining the so-called five stages of grief. Number one is denial/isolation and I figure I've pretty much got that one covered, even if some of my isolation wasn't by choice. My friends screwed me over and helped me along with that one quite nicely. The very fact that I'm turning to Google for help in my time of need should confirm how isolated I am. I'm more than certain that I've got anger absolutely in the bag. So check, and check. That leaves bargaining, depression, and acceptance, which doesn't exactly sound like a barrel of laughs.

I print out a page that lists the stages and then post it on my wall so I can measure where I've been and where I'm going. I look at it and think, Yes, definitely going to be a long summer.

chapter 5

the village is packed on Saturday, as is the rest of town. Since we're by the beach, we get a lot of daytrippers and vacationers during the peak of summer; there are a handful of really big B&Bs within a few blocks of my house and their NO VACANCY signs are out.

Since it's Fourth of July weekend there's all sorts of Early American fun planned at Morrisville. I'm churning butter on the front porch all day—it all goes to the restaurant at Buckman House, which boasts about the fresh butter on the menu at every opportunity. With Liza off—apparently for some family thing—one of Mrs. Rudolph's village pals has been called in to take over tours of the house. I'm relieved I don't have to help out on that front at all.

Outside the town hall—a big white building with columns—Mr. Larman is standing at a podium swathed in red, white, and blue, reciting the Declaration of Independence at the top of his lungs. "We hold these truths to be self-evident," he declares, "that all men are created equal, that they are endowed by their creator with certain unalienable rights, that among these are life, liberty, and the pursuit of happiness." I almost choke up, hearing it read aloud with such passion, and then feel foolish. I can't help but wonder, though, where death fits it. It seems to me that that's the most unalienable right of all.

A new exhibit, "Profiles in History," has opened up in the main gallery space and I stroll through it on my lunch break. The walls are covered with small frames featuring individual silhouettes—people's profiles cut out of black paper and pasted on white paper. There must be a hundred of them and all I can think is how many people lived in colonial times and before and after and how many dead people there are out there.

I sense James standing behind me before he says, "Good day."

I turn and say, "Good day yourself." I scan the room for my father and Ben, who are coming by to see the exhibit and to spend the afternoon kicking around Morrisville. At day's end they will driving me home.

"Good day *yourself*?" James smiles. "A lot of attitude for a lowly farm wench, don't you think?"

"Maybe." I smile. "You'd have lots of attitude, too, if you'd been churning butter all morning."

"Oh, and I suppose chopping wood is a walk in the park."

We turn and look up at the wall of framed profiles. There are tiny scenes, too. Small silhouettes—of a group of people gathered by a piano, a string quartet, a woman trailed by a couple of kids, one of whom is pulling a wagon.

"Look at the nose on that guy." James nods his head toward one image. An old lady overhears him and shoots us a look.

"Jeez," James whispers to me, after the lady has moved away. "Nobody told me colonial people never had any fun."

I see my father and Ben enter the gallery and tell James, "I've gotta go." I can't handle the idea of introductions, the idea of saying "my dad" and "my brother" and not being able to say "my mother."

"Oh." He looks to where I've been looking but of course he doesn't know what my father or brother look like. "Okay. Catch you later."

I make my way over to my father just as Mrs. Rudolph grabs him. The site of her freckled hand on my father's arm irks me to no end. "God, Mark, I'm so sorry." She sees me then, just as I meet Ben's sad eyes.

"Oh, good day, Betsy," she says.

"Hi." I use the word defiantly. "Hi, Dad."

"Well, I'll leave you be, then," she says. "But if there's anything, anything at all, and I mean—"

"Okay," I say. "Got it."

"Betsy," my father says. "Apologize right now."

"I'm sorry," I say to Mrs. Rudolph, looking at her nose and thinking of the most famous reindeer of all.

"I know you didn't mean it, Betsy," she says. When she walks off my father says, "You better watch it."

"These are kinda neat," Ben says, looking up at the wall of black cutouts. My father and I have no choice but to look, too, and I realize that they actually are kind of cool. It's sort of hard to believe how distinct they are from one another, how a simple cutout of someone's profile in black paper can capture so much, be so expressive. Some folks are wearing caps, others have ribbons in their hair. Some look stern, severe, while others appear light, elegant. The handful of scenes are my favorites, though. I see one, a group of aristocratic types at a dinner party, and smile. I don't know why.

"We had ours done years ago," my father says, surprising both Ben and me. "The four of us. In Disney somewhere."

I suddenly have the vaguest recollection of this, a flash of memory of a cart set up on cobblestone streets in the shadow of the castle. "Do we still have them?" Ben asks before I have a chance to. "Where are they?"

"I haven't the foggiest," my father says and it sounds like much more than the answer to Ben's simple question. We all know that if my mother were here she'd know exactly where they are. That this is just one of a catalogue of things that my father has no clue about. I want to yell at him, "Snap out of it," or "Get a grip." If not for his own sake, then for ours.

"You look dumb," Ben says, looking me up and down. I always change at work so he's never seen me in my colonial getup.

"Yeah, well," I mess up his hair. "At least *I* can blame it on the clothes."

"Betsy," my father says sharply.

"What? It's a joke."

He shakes his head and I tell them I have to get back to work.

I take over tour duty when Mrs. Rudolph's pal calls it quits because her feet hurt. The afternoon passes in a blur of tours and I hate every second of it.

When things wind down and I head into the kitchen, Loretta tells me to have a seat. "I hate to have to say this," she says, "but I was listening to Mrs. Rudolph's friend doing the tours, and your tours, well, they're a bit on the dull side. Maybe you can review the script, find things that you get excited about, and sort of spruce it up a bit."

There it is again. Find something you're excited about.

"Are you giving me homework?" I ask.

"Sort of. I'd also like you to run this over to Buckman House." She picks a basket off the table; there's something wrapped in a cloth in it. "There's a private dinner tonight and they need this."

"What is it?" I ask, as she hands me a basket.

"Fresh butter," Loretta says. She adds, "Some of the stuff you churned this morning!" Like that's going to make this errand real special for me.

I grab the butter and head out the front door and as I start off toward Buckman House, I feel eyes burning into the back of my head. I turn and see James standing out front of the carpenter's shop, ax in hand, piece of wood on a block. He waves, then dramatically wipes his brow. "Hard work!" he yells.

I hold my basket up. "Not as hard as churning butter!"

He shakes his head, takes up his ax, and hefts it overhead. He's only a year older than me but it's such a manly act that I find something terrifying about it. The idea that he might be flirting with me makes my stomach clench. And I'm pretty sure he's flirting.

Buckman House looms ahead of me, a jagged tower of brick that stretches high, a topless cathedral. I try to imagine when there was an actual mansion, try to picture Buckman House in all its glory but it's a sad and spooky place to me now. I see a member of the Morrisville waitstaff and follow him through a few rooms of the ruined mansion. I hand off the basket of butter without much fanfare or conversation—oddly, costumed and noncostumed employees don't interact much at all—and try to rush out of the labyrinth of crumbling rooms. I happen upon the small chamber where a table has been set for two. There's white linen and wineglasses and shiny silver on the table, and lush vines growing up toward the open sky. There's something beautiful and melancholic about it all.

Without knowing how, I find myself in the Buckman House gardens. Instantly, my heart calms and I decide at once to find a bench and sit. I watch as a village security guard locks down the gates to the garden maze. According to the literature we were given in training, garden labyrinths were considered to be an essential part of well-designed European gardens in the sixteenth and seventeenth centuries. Julia and John Buckman had one in England before coming to young America and then decided to duplicate it here. Of course today's maze isn't the one they planted, but it has the same trapezoidal shape, the same pattern of pathways and dead ends. Remembering how I got lost in there once, I think maybe I'd like to walk in there and stay lost forever.

"Whatcha doing?" James says, scaring the shit out of me.

I jolt and turn, pulling something in my neck. "Ohmigod," I say. "You scared me half to death. What are you doing here?" I rub my neck.

"Looking for you, why? Expecting somebody else? Maybe ole Julia Buckman?" He waves his hand in my face and makes a ghostly *wooooohooo*ing sound.

"I don't believe in any of that." The second I say it I'm not sure it's true. Maybe I do believe. Maybe that's why the Buckman estate gives me the heebie-jeebies.

"I don't know," James said. "A lot of bad shit went down in this place."

"A lot of bad shit went down everywhere. I mean, the whole world's really one big cemetery when you think about it."

"Jeez." James takes a seat beside me on the bench.

"I'm serious. All those people today, looking at all those profiles. They're profiles of dead people."

He just nods and looks into the distance. "When you're right, you're right."

I realize my father's probably waiting for me with Ben in the parking lot. "Do you know what time it is?" I ask.

"As a matter of fact, I do." He pulls a timepiece out of his pocket and looks at me all cocky. His eyes are brown like dark chocolate. Everything Brandon's eyes weren't. For a second, I remember the reality of my life, the reality of the fact that Brandon is probably sleeping with Lauren Janey. I wonder who'll be the next person to touch me like that, wonder whether it'll be James.

"Nice touch," I say.

"Thanks."

"Where'd you get it?"

"It was my father's, and his father's before him."

"*Was* your father's." I'm confused.

James nods, still looking off into the distance. "Before he died."

I feel like I've been slapped and I just stare ahead, at a row of purple flowers, because it's too much to even look at him. "How did it happen?' I say next.

"He got hit by a car. He was walking on the side of the road."

"Ohmigod. I'm so sorry."

"I know."

"How long ago?"

"Two years in a couple of weeks."

"Why didn't you tell me?"

He exhales loudly. "Because I didn't want you to think that I was implying that I know what you're going through."

"But you do."

He shakes his head. "Only sort of." He looks at the timepiece and says, "Moms are different."

I feel like he must have seen it in my eyes these past few weeks, must've seen that I know this to be true. "I feel like I'm already forgetting," I say. "Like I'm going to forget everything."

"I know what you mean. I feel like I should've paid more attention or something." He reaches out and plucks a flower off a plant beside the bench and props it up in his front shirt pocket. "Maybe we can help each other remember."

"How?"

"I don't know." He's staring intently at one spot and I follow his gaze to an ugly black beetle crawling on a peach rose. "Telling stories about the things we don't want to forget?"

"I'm not sure I even know what those things are." The beetle disappears between some petals. "Whether I have any stories."

There's only one I can think of that seems interesting enough to tell. But it's too bizarre, too sad. I haven't told anybody it and I'm not sure I ever will. It's not a happy story, none of the ones I remember are.

"I'm sure you do." He looks away from the rosebush and slides the timepiece back into his pants pocket. "It's five after six. By the by." He nudges me with an elbow.

"My father and brother are waiting," I say. It feels weird not to say "family" or "parents." "I should go."

"Right," he says. "I'll walk with you."

We walk in silence past the parsonage and the general store and it feels nice just to be next to him, this person I barely know. Maybe that's why it feels so good. He barely knows me and I've been feeling like I barely know myself. Strange as it sounds, I feel like maybe he knows this person I'm becoming before I've even discovered her myself. I desperately want to be the person he thinks I am.

"Was there something you wanted?" I say, when we get to the parking lot.

"Uh, what do you mean?"

"You came to find me in the garden."

He half smiles. "I did, didn't I?"

"Yup. You did."

"I'm sure I had a reason," he says. "I just can't seem to think of it right now."

"Okay." I start to back away. "I've gotta get going."

"Oh!" He smacks his head. "I remembered!"

"Yes?"

"You working tomorrow?"

"Nope."

"Monday?"

"Yup. Why?"

"I could give you a ride home. I mean, if you want."

"I bike to work," I explain reluctantly. "So if you don't have a bike rack, there's no use, really."

"Hmmn." He strokes an imaginary beard, deep in thought. "I have a bunch of bungees for surfboards. I'm sure we can figure something out."

chapter 6

the house smells like home, like mom's chicken cacciatore, when the three of us walk through the door. For a minute I think that it was all a horrible dream and that I'm finally awake. She's alive! She's cooked us dinner! We can all go back to being normal now. My father can stop watching TV every night and get back to the business of actually being a professor. Ben can become a kid again and climb all over my mother the way he used to. I can go back to being a normal teenager whose biggest concern is whether I'll have a pimple tomorrow. I can stop worrying about how if anything happens to my father now, Ben and I will be orphans. I can stop looking at the printout I put in my night table drawer, the one that shows you how to do self-examinations of your breasts, how to look for cancer, how to find out whether I'm going to die, too. I can stop getting nauseous every time I try to do it.

I want to say, "Smells great, Dad," but I can't. Who knew

that basil and garlic and oregano and whatever else goes into chicken cacciatore could smell so sad?

My father goes to the Crock-Pot and stirs it and the aroma spreads even more. "Okay," he says cheerily. "We need a salad made, Betsy, and the table set, Ben. I need to make a quick call and then we'll sit down."

I head for the stairs. "I've got to run my stuff up to my room."

Upstairs, I check my phone for messages and do a quick check of my e-mail. No voice mail or texts, a lot of spam, and an e-mail from my friend Sandra. At last. A lifeline! She's been in Italy with her family for a few weeks but now she's back. She's a friend of Mary's and mine and her e-mail tells me she's going to be in the same driver's ed class as me. We start classes a week from Monday.

When I get back downstairs Ben has fired up a video game and I plop down on the couch. He's some kind of military dude, walking around an abandoned warehouse and shooting bad guys.

"Ben," I say. "Set the table."

"*You* set the table if you want it set so bad." He opens fire.

"Uh, some of us work all day." I can hear my father wrapping up his phone call. I hope maybe he's doing some actual research for his book, maybe setting up an interview or appointment and making an effort to get back into the swing of it.

Ben says, "Not my problem."

"Ben." My voice is sterner this time. "Go set the table."

"I don't see you making the salad." Another bad guy gets detonated.

"I will," I say. "As soon as you set the table."

I hear noise in the kitchen and know that we're gonna be in trouble in a minute. But when my dad doesn't call us again, I figure we're off the hook. I hear the fridge snapping open, a clean slice of iceberg being cut, silverware being pulled from the drawer.

"You're such a spoiled brat." I shake my head, not that Ben can see me.

He mutters, "Takes one to know one," and opens fire on a group of guys.

When many, many minutes pass and my father still hasn't called us to dinner, I finally get up and peek into the kitchen. He's sitting at the table eating his dinner, having made himself a salad and set the table for one. Ben comes up behind me and neither of us can think of anything to say. My father takes a last bite—his plate is already near empty, his salad gone—and then takes a big gulp of water. He pats his stomach, gets up, and starts loading the dishwasher like we're not even there. He takes a rag and wipes off his placemat, then puts it away, on top of the fridge. Looking around as if impressed with his work, he says, "Apparently it's every man for himself around here now," then goes upstairs.

I look at Ben and he's baffled and scared.

"Come on." I go for the fridge. I make us salads as Ben sets the table and then we eat in silence and clean up without speaking a word. As I add our plates and bowls to the dishwasher, I wonder what dinner is like over at Mary's house, where I imagine they're all laughing, and talking about their days, and deciding which board game to play after dessert—maybe Sorry! after strawberry shortcake. I wonder whether

Brandon's mom has invited Lauren Janey to dinner yet, the way she used to invite me. I wonder whether they sneak down to the basement and turn the TV on and get hot and bothered on the nubby brown sofa. I wonder if she says yes when I said no. Then I wonder whether James and his mother ever laugh over dinner together, whether she ever makes chicken cacciatore, whether he has a hole in his heart like I do, whether he's thinking about me at all. I try to think about whether there's some funny dinnertime story about my mom that I remember. I draw a blank.

"What should we do?" Ben says, once we've finished cleaning up.

"Come 'ere," I say, and Ben follows me down the hall to the foyer.

"Dad?" I call up the stairs. Ben looks at me expectantly. A little louder, I say, "We're gonna go fly a kite."

"A *kite*?" Ben whispers, like it's the dumbest thing ever, and I tell him to shush.

"You wanna come?" I call up the stairs.

"No." My father sounds strangely far away. "Don't be long."

"A *kite*?" Ben is unable to contain his contempt for the idea and I remember that he used to get upset when playground bullies would tell him to make like Ben Franklin and go fly a kite.

"Come on," I say. "It's better than sitting around here."

Up at the beach, Ben forgets he's a cool fourteen and warms to the idea of kite flying. After walking the kite away from him and helping him get it in the air, I just sit down and watch from a distance as he yanks the string spool up and down and left and right, trying to get the kite—a big black bat with wide yellow eyes—to do flips and dives. This part of the beach is just a short walk from our house but I hardly ever come up here anymore. I got in the habit of going to the wall with Brandon . . . and, like any good makeout spot, it's nowhere near where anyone would ever think to look for us. This beach is more calming, more familiar on account of the hours I've spent here over the years: flipping through fashion magazines with my mother, or doing cartwheels when I was younger, or just sitting and daydreaming about having a boyfriend before I ever did. I wonder how I'm going to survive the summer, and thank God for driver's ed. I'll have a goal. Something to aspire to. And at the end of it, I'll be free.

I see a couple walking along the shoreline in the distance and it makes me a little sad about Brandon, and then I take a closer look and see that it *is* Brandon. He's holding hands with Lauren Janey. I can't believe he has the nerve to come here—to my turf—and then I see why he has. He and Lauren walk up toward two people sitting on a blanket on a ridge formed by the tides. It's Mary and Trevor, and this is Mary's turf, too. The four of them look all cozy and happy, laughing and talking, and I feel like maybe I'm gonna explode. They'll find pieces of me all over the shore: a nose here, a flip-flop there.

"Ben," I yell over the wind. I realize they might have heard me and turn and see Mary look my way. Then she looks away. "Start rolling it in," I say. "It's getting late."

Ben looks over at me, then follows my gaze back toward my former friends. "Hey," Ben says. "There's Brandon." He shouts down the beach, "Brandon!"

"Ben!" I storm over to him and start pulling the kite string in. It hurts my hands, which are already sore from churning butter, but I don't care. We need to get away from here and fast.

"What are you *doing*?" Ben whines.

I hear Brandon say, "Hey."

I stop what I'm doing as Ben tries to catch up, winding up the loose string dangling from the kite in my hands. I turn around and my ex is right there, looking to me like an alien. I can't believe I ever kissed him. Ever touched his hair. I can't bear to think of the other places I touched him, the places he touched me.

"Hey, Ben," Brandon says. He's in desperate need of a haircut. "Good night for kite flying?"

"I guess," Ben says. He looks at me for guidance, sensing something's wrong. I guess nobody told Ben that Brandon and I split.

"Why don't you come hang out?" Brandon says to me. He gestures down the beach and I look over and Mary waves stiffly, like a tired beauty queen on a float in the final leg of a parade. "Lauren says she doesn't mind."

"Who's Lauren?" Ben says, all naïve.

"Start walking." I hand him the kite parts. "I'll catch up in a minute."

"Who's Lauren?" Ben repeats.

"Ben!" He gets the point and starts toward the boardwalk. I look at Brandon, speechless.

"You look good," he says.

"Brandon!" Lauren calls from down the beach and I just shake my head, regretting suggesting flying a kite, regretting not going to the party with Liza tonight. I imagine her hanging out with all sorts of cool people, people who have yet to stab me in the back. I imagine her laughing and the two of us talking about something I've never talked about with Mary or Brandon, like what kind of tattoo I'd get if I were to get one. "Maybe a bat," she'd say. Or an I ❤ mom.

Brandon says, "You coming?"

I shake my head again. "You really don't have a clue, do you?" I turn and walk away.

I catch up with Ben and tell him Brandon and I broke up and he just shrugs, which is about what I expected. At home, we peek into my father's room. He's asleep in front of the TV and I feel certain he'll perish and not publish. You can't write a book when you watch that much TV; it's just not possible. Over the years, I've seen my father in his highly productive periods, juggling a full load of classes and writing some article for a journal or magazine. This is about as far from that as you could get. I wish there were someone he had to answer to about his behavior but no one's likely to notice it but me.

In my own room, I feel for the light and then see something on my bed. Going closer, I see it's a framed silhouette like the ones we saw at Morrisville. Only it's me. Probably around eight or nine years old. I've got a high ponytail and a pert little nose that flips up at the end. The frame is oval and gold, with a ring so you can hang it. I take a picture off my wall—of me, in the back row, with the cast of yet another school play for which I helped build the set—and replace it with my silhouette. My father must have found them in the attic.

"Hey," Ben says from the doorway. "Look what I got."

He shows me his own silhouette, in the same style of frame.

I can almost remember him looking like that, like a little boy. It strikes me for the first time that Ben's going to be a *guy* soon—that he pretty much already is. When he stopped being a *boy*, I'll never know, and I wonder whether my mother noticed it, maybe noted the date. Or maybe it only happened when she died. Maybe that tipped him over the edge. "Pretty cool, right?" he says, still a little bit of a kid at heart. I envy him that.

"Yup," I say. "Pretty cool."

"But I don't look like this anymore." He stands in front of the mirror above my dresser and struggles to see his profile before realizing it's impossible.

"I bet we can make you a new one," I say.

"No way. How?"

"I don't know." I pull the silhouette closer, to study it better. "I'll figure it out."

Ben and I mostly stay off my father's radar on Sunday. I sit by the pool trying to get into the new Harry Potter but, instead, alternately daydream about James—maybe sneaking a kiss in the pantry of the farmhouse or visiting the wall together when he gives me a ride home from work—and replay last night's encounter with Brandon. I'm still kicking myself for not going to the party with Liza and am determined to make her my friend.

Ben goes out and plays kickball with kids from the block. My father spends the day in his office—occasionally popping out for a glass of water. As dinnertime approaches, I take a quick swim, then shower, and try, unsuccessfully, to cut Ben's silhouette out of construction paper. I search through a photo album for a picture that shows him in profile and then try again.

Later, Ben pokes his head into my room and I slide the paper and scissors into my desk drawer. "Do you know where Dad went?" he asks.

"He went out?"

"Yup."

"That's weird."

Ben and I play basketball lazily in the driveway until our father comes home with a pizza. We follow him inside and he slides a slice onto a paper plate. "I'm going to work through dinner."

"Are you working on the book?" I ask, hopeful.

"No. Just dealing with some financial paperwork. Getting organized."

He goes to get a can of Coke out of the fridge and Ben and I look at each other and shrug and then take our pizza into the den and turn on the TV. I think that my mother is probably turning in her grave. Watching TV during dinner. It's all gone to hell.

I lull myself to sleep the same way I did last night—with elaborate revenge fantasies. I replay that scene at the beach, over and over, imagining that James is with me but that Brandon doesn't know it. So Brandon comes over to ask me to join them and right then James turns up—with ice cream for me and Ben. That's where he was, getting us ice cream. James, looking all manly and cool compared to Brandon, who's still got food in his teeth, says, "Who's your friend?" James kisses me with lips sweet and cold from vanilla and it's like a dream.

chapter 7

I wake up too early for work on Monday and can't fall back asleep I'm so filled with nervous energy. I want to see Liza again so I can get her to invite me out again and, more importantly, James is going to be driving me home at the end of the day. I pack a tight-fitting tank top to change into after work, strap on my backpack, and set out on the bike.

The day proves to be an extraordinary disappointment. Liza is pulled away for training on a loom all morning—she volunteered!—and hours upon hours pass with no sign of James; the general store gets robbed twice and he doesn't participate once. Finally, when Liza comes back to the house, I go over to the carpenter's shop to say hi. No big deal.

Will says, "Well, good day, miss" when I step into the shop. My eyes need a few seconds to adjust and see that Will's got company: tourists. They're clustered by him, surrounded by wood walls, like a log cabin, and tons of dangling metal tools and scraps of wood. There's a light coating of sawdust on the floor and even the air seems slightly thick.

"Good day." I have to stay in character so I form my next sentence slowly. "I was wondering, perchance, if your apprentice is in today?"

"Kind of you to ask." Will bangs a nail into a piece of wood; it looks like he's building a wheelbarrow. "I'm afraid his wife has taken ill."

"I see." Of course, I don't see at all. "Well, good day then." I curtsy and turn to leave.

Back at the house, Liza has just started a tour. "And here is my sister now," she says, when she sees me. "And did you find Mr. Manning well, then?" she says to me. To the tour she says, "Mr. Manning is apprentice to the town carpenter. It's expected he'll have a shop of his own before long."

She looks at me expectantly and the people on her tour do, too. "Apparently his wife has taken ill," I say.

"'Tis a pity, that," Liza says.

"Indeed it is," I add, then she finally goes on her way.

At lunchtime I revisit "Profiles in History," this time reading a display about how silhouettes were made. I'm trying to distract myself from obsessing over James's whereabouts, over the sinking sensation that there's someone else in his life. To make a silhouette, people would sit in such a way as to cast a shadow on a piece of paper, where an outline would be drawn and then cut. A leaflet at the information desk shows teachers and camp counselors how to take a more modern approach. Take a kid's picture, have them graph it, then transfer the image to graph paper, then cut it, then use that as a sort of pattern to cut black paper. To me, this all sounds needlessly complicated. I resolve to try again freehand—like I remember them doing at Disney—but with smaller scissors. Ben's profile wasn't perfect but it was getting closer.

Liza comes back to the farmhouse to help close up at the end of the day and we head up Main Street together. "You want a ride?" she asks me.

"I wish," I say, "but I've got my bike."

"I've got a hatchback," she says. "And some twine. I'm sure we can figure something out."

"That'd be awesome," I say and I mean it. I'd have preferred the ride from James, obviously, but this'll be great, too, for different reasons. I still can't seem to get my mind off wondering where the hell he is, why he didn't come to work.

My bike mostly fits into the hatch of Liz's car but we have to tie the back down. She does this seemingly expertly so I just stand and watch as she concocts a knot that I can't imagine she'll ever be able to untie on the other end.

When we're finally ready to climb in, she looks at me and cocks her head sort of birdlike and says, "Do you have to go home right away?"

"I could probably call." I'm intrigued. "What'd you have in mind?"

"Nothing specific."

I just sense she doesn't want to go home. "You could come over and hang out," I say. "I mean, if you want. We have a pool. I probably have a bathing suit you could wear if you don't think that's gross. I mean, it's clean. But—"

"Why don't I swing by my house and grab mine real quick?" She suddenly sounds excited.

"Okay," I say. "Cool."

*   *   *

Liza's house is cute and old—almost old enough to be moved to Morrisville by the looks of it—with a front garden over-flowing with wildflowers. "Come in for a minute," she says. "I don't think anybody's home and it's cooler than waiting out here."

Her car doesn't have A/C and it's torturously hot out. For a second I worry about my bike being stolen but it's a cute street and, again, that knot was a work of genius.

"Anybody home?" Liza yells when she opens the door. Her call meets silence. "I'll be right down," she says, heading up the stairs.

The house is airy and cool. Sheer white curtains billow ever so slightly in the breeze from an open window and they draw my eye to a far corner of the living room, to a shelf full of tro-phies and plaques and framed pictures. I move closer to see what they're all about and it turns out they're cheerleading awards. I figure Liza must have a sister—someone who's her so-cial opposite—but then I look more closely and realize the tro-phies are Liza's. I know in a flash right then that Liza never had an abortion, that nothing I've heard about her is true because the truth would have included this.

"I always forget that stuff is still there," she says.

I turn to see her coming down the final step. "You must've been good."

"Yeah, I guess." She comes closer—she's got a swimsuit in one hand—and picks up a photo and examines it. "To be hon-est, it was mostly my parents' thing. They were kind of psycho about it all and I was too young to know how miserable I really was. I finally cracked under the pressure—I mean, I used to practice with a coach like fourteen hours a week—and I flipped out on them and I never competed again."

"Wow."

"Yeah, it's pretty freaky. It's like it was another lifetime. Like I was a different person. It's such a boring story, really. Parents trying to live out their own dreams through their kid. They wanted a cheerleader and they got me."

"Well, it seems like you were pretty good at it."

"Yeah." She does this funny skipping thing across the room then jumps up—both legs tucked—and poses with her hip thrown out and arms snapped back over her head like a gymnast would, then stands normal again.

I start laughing and she does, too, and finally I say, "I never would've pegged you as a cheerleader. Maybe you should try out for the varsity squad this year."

Liza lets out a snort. "Could you imagine how that would upset the delicate balance of bullshit at school?"

I smile and pick up a picture to look at it more closely. "Meadow Montgomery and her mother would probably put a hit out on you."

"Like, ohmigod," she says, all cheerleadery. "You're totally right."

"Do you miss it at all?" I put the picture back. The sight of Liza with long hair and pigtails is almost too much to take.

"I miss being good at something, yeah."

"You're good at lots of stuff." I follow her as she heads for the door. "I've never won a trophy in my life." I think for a second how sad that is for me.

"Well, don't beat yourself up about it." Liza opens the front door and a wall of heat steps right in. "I think that might be the sign of a healthy individual." She smiles and puts on her sunglasses.

When we step out onto the deck at my house, my father says, "Well, hello hello." He puts his newspaper down and climbs off his lounge chair. "Who do we have here?"

I'm mortified. "Dad, this is Liza. Liza, my dad." The whole thing is replete with hand gestures.

Liza steps forward, extends her hand, and says, "A pleasure to meet you, Mr. Irving. I'm very sorry about your wife."

My father seems stunned and I guess I am, too, but for different reasons. He's astounded by the fact that a teenager could be so eloquent and polite and I'm astounded that she could be so bold as to just come out and say it. The combined effect of our responses is awkwardness all around. My father looks like he might break down and I'd follow right behind him for sure.

He clears his throat and says, "Well, thank you." He bends down and fumbles to collect his sunglasses off a side table. "The pool's still getting sun," he says. "You girls should get in there if that's what you have in mind." He heads for the sliding doors. "Nice to meet you, Liza. Make yourself at home."

Once we're alone, Liza goes to the edge of the deck and looks out at the yard. "Nice pool," she says.

"You want to change?" I ask.

She says, "Sure."

I lead Liza upstairs and show her the bathroom, then slip into my room to change. I do it real quick, like it's a race. I guess I'm sort of afraid she'll walk in and catch me in the act? And of course, I hate my bathing suit all of a sudden. It's too girlie and bright. Something about being around Liza makes me long to be more sophisticated and edgy. I wonder how you get to be that way, whether Liza's mother is more sophisticated than mine was. Whether there are stores of things I'll just never be because of who raised me, like daredevilish or prone to violence or a cat lover or a good joke teller.

When I'm done changing, I open the door to my room and sit on my bed, trying to seem all calm and nonchalant until Liza opens the bathroom door. She's holding her clothes in front of her chest and looking as nervous as I am. "You can leave your stuff in here," I say, then I go into the hall and open the linen closet door and grab two beach towels. "Here," I say, and hand one to Liza, who takes it from me faster than I can let go. She quickly wraps it around her body under her arms and then follows me down the stairs. Just then I hear the thwack of running feet and see Ben coming up the front walkway. He bursts through the door like the force of nature he is and I feel my heart sink. I was kind of hoping it'd be just us girls. Liza's already had to meet my dad and now Ben's probably going to want to come swimming with us—or worse, play Marco Polo. This whole thing is starting to feel like a really bad idea.

Ben says, "You're going swimming?"

"Yeah," I say, "but it's an adult swim."

"Says who?" He looks at Liza. "Who are you?"

"Well, it's nice to meet you, too," she says.

"Seriously," he says. "Who are you?"

"I'm Liza. Who are you?"

"I'm Ben." He surveys her more closely. "How'd you get your hair like that?"

"Like what? On top of my head?"

I'm leading the charge for the backyard and Liza and Ben

are following. I can practically feel Ben rolling his eyes but he isn't dissuaded. "How'd you get the two colors so mixed up like that?"

I've gotten so used to Liza's black-on-blond mix that I don't even really notice it anymore.

"I was born this way," she says.

"I'm not stupid," Ben says.

"All right, Ben," I say. "That's enough."

"But I want to know how they do it."

I steal a line from my mother and say, "Yeah, well, it's nice to want."

We step out onto the deck and suddenly I'm nervous about having to drop my towel. A week ago Liza and I had barely spoken a word and now we're having a swimming party for two. Or three if you count Ben, whose presence doesn't seem to bug Liza nearly as much as it bugs me.

"Ben. Go inside."

"He's okay," Liza says to me.

"So," he says to her. "How?"

"I do it myself. I put this cap on and pull a couple of hairs at a time through holes I poke in the cap," she says. "Then I dye what's outside the cap and when I take it off, voilà!'

"Cool. Could you do mine?" he asks.

"Ben," I cut in. "You're not old enough."

"Says who? You?"

"Go ask Dad," I say. This, at least, sends him inside, calling out a singsong, "Da-ad."

The sun has just dipped behind a big tree but it's still hot and muggy out. I walk down to the step entry of the pool, push two floats away, drop my towel on the cement walk, and descend into cool blue as quickly as I can without going into shock. I'm in up to my shoulders before I turn around and see that Liza's walking toward the deep end. Her suit is simple and black, like something from another era, maybe the thirties, and I regret that my mother never allowed me a black suit, always said I was too young. On Liza, it makes her tattoo—a shooting star—look extra dark. I get my first good glimpse of her body. It's compact, muscular—I see the cheerleader now—and she has remarkably small breasts, even smaller than mine. "How deep is it?" she says.

"Only eight feet at the deepest, and it slopes up so it's not really safe for—"

She dives in and I watch as she shimmies under water, arms down by her side, then resurfaces almost at the opposite end of the pool. She comes up and takes a huge breath. "Man, that feels good." She wipes water from closed eyes. "I'd go in every day if I were you."

I used to but I don't anymore and I'm not sure why. I guess it was just more fun when I was younger and interested in holding my breath for as long as I could or racing Ben or trying to do half-submerged cartwheels. The way Liza says it makes me feel guilty, though, like I'm some privileged brat and I wonder what her deal is. Her house is old and small but it hardly seems like they're poor. "Do you have any brothers or sisters?" I ask, as a way of maybe collecting clues.

"Nope, not a one."

Right then Ben shouts out the window. "Dad says he'll think about it if I save up enough money! So there!"

"Good for you!" I shout. I say to Liza, "God, he just bugs the shit out of me."

"They're better when they're not your own."

"Maybe," I say. I push a float toward Liza and climb up on my own.

"My mother has a history of depression." She gets up on hers and it makes a squeaking sound. "They thought they'd better not take too many gambles. I'm already more than they can handle. And they're always worried I'm going to curl up in a ball and flip out like she does every couple of years. Especially after the cheerleader meltdown."

I don't know what to say to this, so I don't say anything.

"Anyway!" Liza says a bit too cheerily. "Enough about me! An old habit from therapy, talking too much about myself. What's the deal with you and Jimbo the carpenter?"

I play with the water around me, pushing my hands forward then back, diverting her glance as I do. "What do you mean?"

"Don't be coy, Irving."

"I'm not!"

"I think he likes you," she says. Then she flips over and stays underwater longer than anyone should. It's got to be like a whole minute or two and I'm actually starting to get worried and cold. I say, "Come on, it's not funny," as if she can hear me and then she shoots up out of the water, heaving.

"Don't do that," I say. "You scared me."

My father calls out the window, "Betsy, does Liza want to stay for dinner? We're having spaghetti and meatballs."

I look at her, as curious as to what she'll say as my dad sounds. She calls up to the kitchen window where my dad's torso appears in a gray shadow created by the angle of the sun on the screen. "Thanks, Mr. Irving, but I've got to get going."

She stands up in the shallow end, water to her waist, then strides out of the pool. She dries off quick like a bunny, then pulls on her shorts and says, "Thanks for having me over. I'll see you tomorrow."

"Let me show you out." I scramble to get out of the pool.

"I'm okay," she says. "I'll find the way. But be careful with James. There's a lot of stuff you don't know yet." She disappears through the sliding doors and I can hear her voice come from the kitchen. "I'm just gonna run up to get my stuff. Thanks, Mr. Irving."

There's a sort of unfamiliar desperation in my father's voice when he says, "Are you sure you won't stay?"

I wish she would stay as much as he seems to. Partly because I want to know what she means, whether she thinks I don't know about James's dad being dead, whether he has a girlfriend I don't know about. I want her to know that I know about his dad, that he confides things in me he may not confide in her. But mostly I want her to stay because there'd be something new for my family to talk about at dinner, something to take our minds off the empty seat where Mom used to be.

The second Liza leaves, my father's out the door and then back in twenty minutes with a bucket of chicken from KFC.

"I thought we were gonna have spaghetti and meatballs," Ben says when he comes into the kitchen, sounding entirely brokenhearted.

"It's too hot to cook pasta," my father says as he bites into a drumstick, but we all know it's more than that. Liza's worthy of home cooking, would have probably offered to set the table. Ben and I, ungrateful brats that we are, are not.

That night, I take a pair of tiny scissors from the medicine cabinet and go to my room. I set the picture of Ben up in front of me and imagine a graph on top of it. My brain is breaking the lines of his profile into tiny boxes and then I let the lines in my mind disappear back into the photo and I start to cut a profile. I force myself to relax—if such a thing is possible—and to just go for it. To keep it fluid and free. In an instant, I'm done. I've cut out the whole of Ben's head and shoulders in black paper; to my complete astonishment it's the best cut yet. There was something wooden and choppy about the profiles I tried to cut more slowly, more deliberately. This one just flows, and the miracle is that it looks like Ben: pointy nose, firm chin, high cheekbones.

The house phone rings. It sort of shocks me because it hasn't been ringing much at all since my mother died. She was the keeper of the family friends and their silence has been deafening. It's like we're bad luck or something. People don't want to call or stop by and be reminded of what happened. She died, and we're all living proof that they're going to die, too, that bad things happen to good people.

"Betsy!" I hear my father call. "It's for you. A gentleman caller!"

I groan and hope he's covered the mouth of the receiver but doubt he has. He thinks he's being witty and has no idea he's humiliating me.

"Hello?" I say. I probably sound puzzled because I have no idea who it could possibly be. If it were Brandon, my dad would've said so.

"Hey." A pause. "It's James."

"Hey," I say. "What's up?"

"Nothing, what are you doing?"

"Um." I can't think of a good way to describe it. "Sort of an art project."

"Cool. Think you can tear yourself away for a minute?"

My face is getting hot. "Depends," I say. "What for?"

"Does your bedroom face the street?"

"Yeah." I turn to the one window that faces the street, though the shades are down.

"Look out your window," he says.

I push one of the shades aside and peek out. He's leaning against his car and he waves. I step back from the window and let go of the shade, as if I've just been caught spying. I'm more than mildly freaking out.

"Just come downstairs for a minute, okay?"

I say "okay" and he hangs up.

I check my face in the mirror and decide to put my hair up. I let it dry on its own after the swim and it looks awful, like a bird's nest. I put on some lipgloss, ditch my fuzzy slippers for flip-flops, and head down the stairs. I've never seen James off the village grounds—never even seen him in twenty-first-century clothes, and the idea fills me with anticipatory thrill. I open the screen door and step outside just as James's car pulls away. What the . . . ?

As I turn to go back inside, I see a package wrapped in brown paper on the porch. I pick it up—it's no larger than a large TV remote—and take it up to my room. It's got twine tied around it to hold the paper on and not an inch of tape. I carefully untie the twine and set it aside—I already know that I'll save it—then open up the paper. Inside, there's a smooth piece of wood and as I turn it over in my hand, I see my name carved into one side: BETSY pops out from the otherwise smooth surface.

The phone rings again. I call out, "I got it!" then close my bedroom door. "Hello?" I say.

"You like it?"

"I do." I turn it around in my hands. "I don't know what to say."

"Say thanks."

"Okay, thanks." I peek out the window to see if maybe he's coming back. But he's not. No headlights coming down the street. No nothing.

"I gotta go," he says. "And I'm sorry about today. I know I said I'd give you a ride home. Something came up. It's kind of complicated."

"That's okay. I mean, I had my bike, but Liza drove me."

"Cool," he says. "I'll see you tomorrow. And you better have a story for me, something you want to remember."

I know he doesn't have a wife—that Will was just ad-libbing because "girlfriend" isn't an Early American word—but it had never even occurred to me before that day that he might have a girlfriend. Which is pretty stupid because why wouldn't he? *Something came up,* he'd said. And if it's not a girlfriend, why not tell me what it was? Then again, if it *is* a girlfriend, why not tell me *that?* The fact that he hasn't mentioned her means maybe he doesn't want me to know he has a girlfriend, if he does. Which is sleazy on the one hand, and something else entirely on the other.

Upstairs, I take Ben's profile and study it again, relieved to find it's as good as I thought it was. I glue-stick it to white paper, then go to his room and knock on the door. He's at his computer, playing a game.

I walk over and and say, "Turn your head."

He turns his head and I compare the silhouette to him and decide, yes, it's good. I hand him the silhouette and he looks at it and says, "Cool."

He gets up and pins it to a bulletin board over his desk. "How'd you do it?"

"Just did it, really. Looking at a picture."

"That's cool," he says. "You gonna make more?"

Like the idea of James having a girlfriend, this hadn't occurred to me. "Maybe," I say. "We'll see, I guess."

Back in my own room, I close the door and lock it and double-check it before going to my closet and taking out the dress. This is the story I want to tell James but won't—that my mother took me shopping for a wedding dress. That it was a sneak attack and I was already standing in Kleinfeld's—a huge, famous store in Brooklyn—before I even knew what we were doing there.

"We're not going to buy one," she said, when I complained that it was insane. "We're just going to have some fun. Here"—she took her diamond engagement ring off her finger and handed it to me—"just so they take us seriously."

I imagine now that my mother appeared sickly enough, with her gray skin and bad wig, that the saleswoman helping us had some clue as to what was going on but I'll never know for sure. For days afterward, I imagined the ladies who work there talking about us on their smoke breaks; the crazy lady with cancer and her no doubt knocked-up daughter. I tried on dress after dress before one fit perfectly and looked good. I stepped out into the mirrored room where my mother awaited and she gasped. "Oh my!" She put her hands to her mouth, then came forward and turned me so I was facing the mirrors. She gathered my long hair in her hands and twisted it, holding it in an updo position. "You'll be such a beautiful bride," she said. "Such a beautiful bride."

I cried then, and she did, too, and the saleswoman left us alone. "Can we go now?" I said, irritated by the whole scene. "Oh, honey," she said. "I wish you could know how this is as much for you as for me."

She left me in the fitting room, took the dress with her on a hanger, and it was only when I came out, having composed myself, that I realized what she'd done. She was holding a big white garment bag.

"You don't have to wear it," she said as I followed her to the car in a huff. "I just like knowing that you have it."

I'm too scared to put the dress on but I hold it up to the mirror with one hand and pull my hair up with the other. It's strapless with a sort of high waistline and I remember, in the store, loving its A-line shape, the way it fits nicely high up, then plunges toward the ground, getting wider as it goes. I try to imagine what I'd look like in the dress through James's eyes and wonder whether he ever even thinks about stuff like that, like getting married. I decide he would run for the hills if he could see me holding the dress, see into my mind, so I put the dress away and climb into bed, thinking that surely, surely, there are others stories—better, happier stories—to tell.

chapter 8

driver's ed starts the next morning and I have to drag my butt out of bed at 6:00 A.M. I'm getting my bike out of the shed in the backyard when a voice calls out, "Betsy! Betsy!"

I don't have to turn around to see who it is. It's my neighbor, Alex Elks. He's maybe ten years older than me and has Down's syndrome and I've known him as long as I've been alive. When I was little, I used to spend hours upon hours in his basement. He has a pool table and a Ping-Pong table and a couple of arcade games and, when I wasn't hanging out and doing girl things with Mary, I could think of no better way to spend my time. Alex is entirely responsible for the fact that I shoot pool pretty well, and can hold my own at Ping-Pong even if I only play once a year. Lately, though, I'm not around as much, and what with dating and all, I don't have as much time for Alex. I feel guilty about it but not guilty enough to make more time for him.

"Hey, Alex," I say. "How are you doing?"

"Good," he says. "That's a nice shirt." I say thanks but it

sort of creeps me out when Alex tells me I look nice or anything like that. I know he doesn't mean anything bad by it but it makes me squirm. I've never told anybody this—how when he tells me I'm beautiful or something I clamp up—because I know how it'll sound.

Alex says, "I'm making a new latch hook." A lot of people have a hard time understanding Alex—the way his words come out in a blurry burst—but I've never had a problem. "You want to see?"

We used to spend hours doing latch hook together, too. It's sort of a paint-by-numbers with yarn and a canvas mesh. You hook tiny pieces of yarn through a mesh to create a picture in rug form. I'd sit beside Alex with a picture already stained on my mesh—they sell them that way, in kits—and pull short, colored wool threads from tight bunches wrapped in a white plastic band, then hook them through squares stamped the same color. Alex has only ever worked with blank canvases, though. No kits for him. He can sit down with a white mesh—they vary in size depending on what he has in mind—and just start at the bottom left corner, doing horizontal row after horizontal row, changing colors with no apparent rhyme or reason, and at the end, there will be a picture of some kind. Usually flowers or fruit. Sometimes animals. Always great. My favorite one he ever made for me especially was a lion—a cute lion, like a cartoon—with a background of mint green. I had it made into a pillow—one that's now stuffed up in my closet somewhere.

"I can't now," I say, realizing that maybe all that latch hook was good training for silhouetting, practice working with a mental grid. "I have to go to school to learn how to drive, Alex. I'll see you later."

"Okay," he says. "Bu-bye Betsy."

"Bu-bye, Alex," I say.

Riding through the quiet streets, I try to appreciate the early morning light, the dewy smell of the air, but I'd rather be sleeping. My mother was a morning person and it nearly drove me crazy. She'd be all chirpy first thing, and of course she'd already been up for at least an hour by the time I joined her. "Wait'll you have kids," she'd say, whenever I said I'd never be a morning person. "The only way to get any peace is to get up before your kids do. Remember that."

"I'll be sure to do that," I'd usually say, dryly. Me! Having kids! I'm not even out of high school.

Thinking of her like that I try to open my mind and see if more details follow—like maybe the sound of her voice. I try to recall it, try to hear it in my head but it feels impossible, like trying to look inside your own ear.

I let go of the handlebars and think, Look, Ma. No hands, and then grab on even more tightly and pedal hard the rest of the way.

Sandra's in the back row of the driver's ed classroom at school. I rush over and give her a hug. "I'm so, so sorry I wasn't here," she says into my hair.

"I know," I say, because I do know and we both know that's all there is to say.

Sandra's parents got rich during the "dot-com boom," retired at the age of forty, and now spend most of their time trying to figure out how to spend their time. They usually opt for educational travel—a trip to Alaska to build an igloo, cruises with famous authors, most recently cooking classes in Tuscany—and take Sandra along. We usually only see each other with Mary as the third but I'm hoping maybe we'll get to know each other better now. Mary skipped fourth grade and won't be taking driver's ed for another year. This sad state of affairs for Mary is our first topic of conversation.

"It's just too bad she's not here with us," Sandra says. Her hair seems curlier, redder, and I wonder whether she's using some fancy European shampoo.

"Yeah, I know." I wonder whether she senses my ambivalence. I haven't missed hanging out with Mary nearly as much as I thought I would. I feel bad about it, but it's true. I'm happy she's not here. I'm happy that maybe I can get Sandra on my side since everyone else is on the other.

"But it gives us a chance to hang out, which is cool." Sandra puts her hair up in a ponytail and I figure it's because I was staring. She says that about her hair. That people seem to find it distracting when it's down. I've never really understood but now I do. "I heard about you and Brandon. What a jerk."

"Yeah, seriously." Being around Sandra always makes me feel so young and naïve. Like I have no idea what I'm talking about even if I do.

"I can't believe she knew and didn't tell you."

"Yeah, it's pretty unbelievable." So she *is* on my side!

"Are you two still not talking?"

"Pretty much." I wish I could just call Mary and be fine but I can't. I still feel like such an idiot whenever I think about it. Brandon. And Lauren. And the stuff they're doing together that I'm not doing with anyone. And all the people who *knew*.

"Well, it'll pass," Sandra says. "I mean, you can't not talk forever, right? And you can do better than Brandon anyway."

I think a part of me always thought so but the fact that Sandra thinks it astounds me. I want to shout, Why? Why can I do better? And how? I want to tell her every detail of James and get her expert opinion but I'm afraid that talking about it will jinx it somehow.

"You should see the guys in Italy." Sandra nods her head at the room. "They put these guys to shame." She leans in more excitedly now. "You can't tell anyone, okay?"

"Okay." I lean in closer.

"I did it." She raises her eyebrows to check whether I get her meaning and it's only because she does that that I do.

"You *did*?!?" I feel mortified. To think I was going to tell her about James when nothing has even happened at all. For a moment I actually regret not doing it with Brandon.

"His name is Marcelo and he's gorgeous." She pulls her hairband out now as if the word "gorgeous" made her want to look more gorgeous. "I'm hoping he'll come over and visit later this summer."

"That's amazing!"

"Yeah. He totally saved the trip for me. And hey, if you're still single, I'll tell him to bring a friend." She smiles and squeezes my arm.

"Okay, people," Mr. Pagano says. I had him for freshman year history. All my father did was complain about what he calls "the dumbing down" of the classwork and suggest supplementary reading that I never did.

"Some of you know me," he says. "I'm Mr. Pagano. Some of you don't! I'm Mr. Pagano. We've got a lot of material to get through these next four weeks, so let's get started. If you'll open your textbooks . . ."

Sandra looks at me and we both roll our eyes and then laugh.

*   *   *

The bike ride from school to Morrisville is even farther than the ride from home. Liza's already in costume, carrying a bucket of water in from the well, when I burst into the farmhouse. "Everything okay?" Loretta says, looking panicked.

"Yeah, sorry I'm late," I say. "I'll change fast, promise."

"We're fine," Liza says coolly. "Take your time."

When I come back downstairs in costume I see a bunch of kids wearing T-shirts from Camp Bay Cove piling into the front hallway. Brandon is a counselor at Camp Bay Cove and I knew they were coming today from way back when—Brandon and I were looking forward to it—but now the sight of them makes me want to run and hide. Right as I'm finishing greeting the group with "good days" and "welcomes"—where's Liza when I need her?—Brandon steps inside the house and says, "Hey." Running into him at the beach was bad enough. Now this. People should have to move to another town when they betray you, so you don't have to relive it every time you bump into them.

The kids are antsy, expectant, so I call them to attention and start going on about how the house was built in 1812, how we use the first room they see—the parlor—for formal entertaining and blah blah blah. I remember Loretta's plea that I spruce things up a bit but I don't care. I whip through the script as quickly as I can, without any flourish. Brandon's fellow counselor is a perky little blonde wearing short shorts and a Camp Bay Cove tank top and I feel ridiculously frumpy and ugly. It's hard to make a guy regret dumping you when you're wearing burlap.

After a quick stroll through the upstairs—replete with the spiel about how ceilings were lower to keep heat closer to where people live—I lead the tour into the kitchen, where Loretta pipes up and takes over. I step aside as she launches into her explanation of colonial cooking and authentic brick ovens and walk back into the parlor. I can't believe he turned up here, somehow, and feel like my stomach is slowly tying itself up in knots to rival the one Liza used on the hatchback.

"Hey." It's his voice. I turn around and see he's followed me into the parlor.

"Hay is for horses," I say. It's hard to ignore someone when you're the only two people in the room. I wonder where Liza has gone to and wish she'd barge in, maybe say something cool and scathing—something cooler than "hay is for horses."

"How are you?" Brandon says. I want to tell him it's none of his business how I am anymore, but I say, "Good. Great." I want to blurt out, "I'm over you, I like somebody else now, too," but I say, "How are you?" because that's what comes next when you make small talk.

"I don't know," he says. "It's complicated."

"Jesus Christ." That's Liza, who's apparently in the adjoining hallway eavesdropping. Not exactly cool and scathing, but it'll do.

"What was that?" Brandon asks.

"That was Liza."

"Liza *Henske*?"

"Yeah."

Liza steps into the room and says, "I don't believe we've ever been formally introduced." She's sweeping nonchalantly, pushing dust in the direction of Brandon's shoes.

From the other room, Loretta's voice gains volume. "Mind the step on your way out and thank you for visiting us today."

"I better go," Brandon says.

"Yeah," I say.

Just before he leaves the room he says, "Maybe I'll see you next Friday."

Liza sweeps for a few more seconds, then the swishing sound stops. "Not that it's any of my business." She plops herself down in a rocker. "But what's next Friday?"

I tell her the truth. "I have no idea."

I'm shucking corn in the rocker on the porch—Loretta's making vegetable barley soup today—when James strolls over. He only has one set of clothes for work and I'm starting to have a hard time imagining him ever wearing anything other than this ivory-colored frock and brown pants. "So I've been thinking," he says.

"Did you hurt yourself?" I smile.

"Very funny." He takes a seat in the other rocker.

"What about?"

"What exactly *is* a Yankee-Doodle dandy?"

I look at him, eyebrows raised, and then return to my shucking.

"I'm serious." He takes his own ear of corn and starts to shuck, too. His shirtsleeves are rolled up a bit and his arms look muscular. He could arm wrestle Brandon in two seconds flat. "Answer the question."

I think of the song in my head and say, "A real live nephew of Uncle Sam."

"Mnn. Don't think so. The Yankee-Doodle dandy in the song might be a real live nephew of Uncle Sam but they can't *all* be. I mean, really, how many nephews can one man have?"

"Okay, well, what do you think a Yankee-Doodle dandy is then?"

"Maybe a gay patriot?" he says.

I smile but don't look up. "Who draws flags when he's bored."

It takes him a second to get this. The doodling bit.

"You're funny," he says.

"You think?"

"Yeah."

I study him in profile and wonder whether I could cut a silhouette of him from this one memory of him right here and now. Whether Ben's was easy because I've known him as long as he's been alive. I think that if I had a silhouette of James, I'd hang it where those pictures of Brandon used to be—at least until there were pictures of James and me together, until we had memories that we shared.

He says, "So do you have a story for me yet? Something you don't want to forget?"

I put an ear of corn on a clay pottery platter and then take another one out of the basket. "I can't think of anything."

"You're not trying hard enough." He picks silky strings off his corn. "Either that, or you're trying too hard."

"Why don't you tell *me* one?" I have to work really hard with this latest ear of corn; my nails start to hurt. "Maybe it'll inspire me."

"Okay." He takes another ear of corn and goes to work. "Let me see. Let me see." He looks like he's thinking, eyebrows all serious, and then says, "Okay, I got one." He seems to relax into his rocker. "When we moved into the house we live in now, there was this really ugly toilet. The lady who owned the house before had painted it red. Not the inside of the bowl, but the whole outside."

"Sounds kind of funky." I slow my shucking, wishing we could stay here all day.

"Trust me," he says. "It wasn't. Or at least my mother didn't think so. She was always nagging my father to put a new toilet in. You know, just go to Home Depot and get one." He looks up to make sure I'm following. "So this one night they're talking about it and my mother's nagging my father about it, and then also about how he never brings her roses anymore, the way he used to. So the next day, she goes to the mall for something. And my father takes me with him to Home Depot and has his friend over who's good with stuff like that and he replaces the toilet."

I'm waiting and hoping the story gets better. A family of four arrives at the house and James says, "Good day." Liza comes to the door to greet them and begin their tour.

James puts his corncob on the platter and, silly as it sounds, I wonder how and when he learned how to shuck corn, whether his father showed him how to do it, or his mother, whether he'd remember a detail about his own life so small as that. "So then he takes the red toilet out to the backyard and I'm figuring he's going to put it in a bag and break it up for trash or whatever, but he doesn't. He puts it in the center of my mother's flower garden, and puts some soil in it. Then he goes back out to the car and comes in with a rose bush and he plants it right in the center of the red toilet."

I stop shucking. "You're making this up."

"Nope." He sneezes and I say, "Bless you." I take a moment to process his physical presence again. This is James. This is James's body. He has a body. And it sneezed. Then: "What did your mother do?"

"Well, she laughed." He's so at ease sitting here, so oblivious to the fact that I'm studying him, that he's my new favorite subject. "And I guess he somehow knew that she would. And then he told me that I should always try to give a woman what she wants, but that I should remember that I don't have to do it exactly the *way* she wants."

"That's a great story," I say. I know I'll never be able to think of any as funny and charming. Loretta calls me from the kitchen. "How's that corn coming?"

"Saved by the bell," James says, getting up. I've just finished the last of the corn. "But don't think you're off the hook. You owe me one."

Things never felt like this with Brandon. Never felt this natural. Like so much was already understood.

"Okay, okay." I pick up the platter and head inside.

Liza's fifty paces ahead of me on Main Street when I'm leaving for the day and I break into a jog to catch up. "Hey," I say, falling into step beside her.

"Oh, hey," she says.

"Everything okay?" I ask.

"Yeah, why?"

"I don't know. You just seemed quiet today."

"Just tired." A car horn beeps a few times.

"Okay." I don't feel okay, though. "You're not mad at me for some reason, are you?" I'm fishing around in my backpack, looking for my bike lock.

She says, "Why would I be mad at you?" and that doesn't make me feel any better, either. I'd have preferred a "no" or an "of course not, stupid." I feel like I'm being punished for something, but I don't know what. Maybe setting foot in Liza's house and discovering her deep dark cheerleading past? Or maybe she's jealous of me and James? Why else would she warn me to stay away? I keep wanting to ask James if he has a girlfriend but it doesn't feel right. I want to make it clear that I don't have a boyfriend anymore, either, but there's no way to say that without it sounding like "I'm available."

The car horn beeps again and I look up and realize it's my father. He pulls up in front of us and the passenger side window buzzes down. "Hello, ladies," he says. "Liza, can we give you a ride anywhere?"

"She has a car, Dad," I say. "What are you doing here? Is everything okay?" We hadn't talked about him picking me up.

"Yes, everything's fine. You have an orthodontist's appointment. We almost forgot." Ben's in the passenger seat; we always go to the orthodontist together. "Ben's braces are coming off today," my dad says. Ben grins wide with metal.

Liza looks at me perplexed.

"I have a retainer wire behind my bottom teeth."

She nods and says, "Got it. Well, I'll see you tomorrow," and she walks off as my father and I heft my bike up onto the rack. We've got it down to a science now.

"How was your day?" my dad says, all bright and oblivious.

I'm reeling from the Brandon episode. Basically, my day sucked. Big time. "It was okay," I say, because it's easier that way. I guess I don't want him to worry.

"I know your mother usually went in with you but I thought I'd drop you two off and go pick up something for dinner," he says. "Is that okay?"

"Sure," I say as we pull into the parking lot. Ben and I get out and I say a quick prayer that my dad's going to the super-market and not visiting the colonel again.

The office smells sweet and waxy and since we're a tiny bit late, the receptionist takes us both straight into the room where Dr. Willis works. There are four chairs in one room and the other two are occupied. Ben and I climb into chairs beside each other. Linda, the doc's assistant, says hello and straps a paper bib around my neck, attaching it with a metal chain. She goes and does the same to Ben. It's a strange way to operate an office, all of us patients sharing the one room, but maybe it saves him a lot of walking around?

"That should do it," Dr. Willis says to the patient he's been working on. "I'll see you in another month."

I hear him go to wash his hands as his patient—a pimply boy from my school's marching band—heel-toes it out of the room. Dr. Willis starts working on the girl in the chair next to me, but when he sees me and Ben, he says, "How are you over there?"

"Okay," I say. Ben says the same.

"I think we'll take that wire off today," the doctor says to me. "What do you think of that?"

"I think that's a great idea," I say. It had been put there when I had my top braces put on but left alone when the top came off. Something about making sure my new bite wasn't going to move my lower teeth around.

A few minutes later, Dr. Willis is ready for Ben. He's washed his hands again, strapped on a new face mask, and he goes to Ben and says, "Open." He picks up a pliers-type instrument and says, "You'll feel some tugging, but that should be it. Okay?"

Ben nods, and Dr. Willis goes to work, plucking off braces one by one.

"Your mother's stuff still showing at that café in town?" he says to Ben. My brother turns his eyes to me, petrified. I've completely forgotten about the fact that some of my mother's photos are on display in my aunt's café. We all got so used to seeing her pictures pop up in unexpected places—on book covers, in magazines, in photo frames in stores—that the idea of actually going somewhere to see them, knowing ahead of time where they'd be, seems strange. The exhibit entirely slipped my mind.

I answer for Ben and say, "Yeah, they are."

"I'll have to check them out," Dr. Willis prattles on. "She come in with you today?"

"No," I say. "Not today."

There are two other patients and two assistants in the room. I can't bear to explain and Ben certainly can't, not with a mouthful of pliers and metal. How is it possible they don't know? In a town like this it seems like everybody always knows everything.

Finally, Dr. Willis decides to stop chitchatting and applies himself more aggressively to taking Ben's braces off. It looks like Ben's crying and Dr. Willis says, "Are you okay?"

Ben just nods.

Once he's done with Ben, the doctor comes over to work on me. Removing my retaining wire doesn't take nearly as much time. "Voilà!" he says, holding a wire with two molar-size clamps out in front of my face. "What do you think of that?"

"Pretty cool," I say dryly. I bet he says, "What do you think of that?" more times than any of his employees can stand, each and every day.

He gets up and looks at me, taking my chin in his hand. He says, "Smile," so I do. Then he says, "Keep wearing the retainer on top and I'll see you again in a month."

"Sounds good," I say.

"And tell your mother Ben should come back in a few weeks to get fit for a retainer, too."

"Okay," I say.

"All right, Ben?" he says.

Ben nods.

The receptionist stops us on the way out and asks me whether I want to schedule our next appointments before we go. "We better call," I say.

"Okeydokey," she trills. "Say hi to your mom."

"Betsy," Ben says, on our way out the door. He looks like he's going to cry for real now.

"I'll take care of it," I say.

In the car, my father has the A/C blasting and I realize how cold it was inside the doctor's office. "Can we turn this down?" I say, going for the fan switch after I've climbed into the passenger seat. Ben's quiet in the back.

"Sure," my father says. "How'd it go?"

"Great," I say.

My father looks in his rearview and says, "Let's see, Ben."

I turn and see Ben smile dutifully. I wonder whether my father can see the signs of trauma on my brother's face. I think of James and think, These are the kinds of stories I'm accumulating now. I wonder when James will tell me the next story he wants to remember, then wonder if he'll ever tell me any he wants to forget.

"They said we're done," I say to my dad, fake excited. "We don't have to go back."

"Really?"

"Yup." I look out the window. "They took the bottom wire off, so that's it. And Ben, too. Unless he has any discomfort, they said."

"Really, Ben?" my father says.

"Yup," he says. "All done."

"Well, that's good." We're stopped at a light and my dad attempts to rustle my hair, the way he does Ben's. "The end of an era, eh?"

My father opted for McDonald's and, while neither Ben nor I are entirely displeased, the whole thing just feels wrong. My mother would've never allowed us to have McDonald's for dinner. Pizza, sure. KFC, on occasion; she'd always get vegetable sides. But tonight, on account of lukewarm McNuggets, it really sinks in that our father hasn't cooked us a meal since the night of the cacciatore, the night we blew it. I wonder if I'll spend the rest of high school eating a fast-food diet, getting fat and unhealthy, and turning up at my prom all supersized. At least I'm getting a bit more exercise than usual, what with the bike ride.

We eat right out of the wrappers, dumping fries onto them and making piles of ketchup for dipping. Ben is quiet, still traumatized from today's orthodontic fiasco, so I overcompensate conversationally, telling my father about Liza's cheerleading past, the trophies. "She must be a very driven young lady," he says, completely missing the point.

That night in my room, I sign onto a site that sells some of my mother's photos and do a search using the keywords "girl" and "laughing." A bunch of photos appear and I flick through them until I find the one I'm looking for. It's a picture my mother took of me when I was about fourteen. Ben and I were her subjects for a shoot consisting entirely of stock photos of kids having fun. Ben's in the background of this one, all fuzzy, and I'm in the foreground in sharp focus, laughing with my eyes closed and head thrown back. There's a pink-and-green ice-cream cone in my hand. I click forward to another photo from the same shoot—one of me pushing Ben on a swing by the beach. He looks so young and I feel like I can barely remember him looking like that, being like that. I close my eyes and try to picture what my mother looked like that day, but I can't remember. And the problem with having a mother as a photographer is that she's never in any pictures. I click back to the picture of me with the ice-cream cone, then get up and look in the mirror. I try to picture myself laughing but can't.

Before going to bed I decide to check on Ben. I can't see any light underneath the door but I sense that he's awake, so I crack the door and stick my head in. "Ben?"

His reading lamp is on real low and he's got a hand-held mirror in his hand, which he tries to hide. "Whatcha doing?" I say.

"Looking at my teeth," he says.

"You okay?" I ask.

"Yeah," he says, all fourteen again. "I'm cool."

"Okay, good night," I say.

I go to leave and he says, "Bets?"

"Yeah?"

"You think Dad's ever gonna cook again?"

"It's been too hot to cook," I say, wondering whether Ben's smart enough to see through me, knowing for sure that he is.

chapter 9

My mother lived in fear of the infamous parties at Midland Beach. She imagined all manner of debauchery and drunkenness going on there, and feared I'd lose my innocence by simple virtue of attendance. On nights when there were reported to be big parties going on down there, which is most Fridays during summer, she'd barely let me out of the house. It was as if someone were putting out some high-pitched siren that only protective parents could hear. My father, however, is on a different frequency. . . . So when Liza asks me on Friday afternoon if I want to go to a party at Midland with her that night, I say, "Yeah, definitely." I pause and say, "So you're really not pissed at me."

"No, I'm not pissed at you." She says it like it's the most ridiculous idea ever. "I was pissed at James. But it's not important. It's over now."

"Oh," I say. "Okay." What the hell could that be about?

She says, "I'll pick you up around nine?"

Over dinner (Taco Bell), I tell my father that I'm going bowling again. It's one of the only legit things to do in town and it's easier than saying I'm going to the movies because he always wants to know what I think of the films I see. When he asks, "With whom?" I say, "Liza from work."

"She seemed like a nice enough girl," he says. "Odd but nice . . . not the usual for you." In the quiet kitchen, his voice sounds strained. Ben's sleeping over at a friend's tonight and I'm grateful he's not witnessing my deception.

"I take it she's picking you up?"

"Yes."

"Does she drink?" he asks.

"Dad," I moan. "No. And it's the bowling alley. They never serve anybody. Besides, Mary's coming, too."

It's an out-and-out lie but I know it'll put his mind at ease and then, miraculously, the fates help me out. The phone rings. My dad picks it up. He says, "Oh, hold on, Mary. She's right here." I haven't been answering her calls on my cell so I guess she figured this was the way to force the issue.

"I'll take it upstairs," I say, unable to believe my luck.

When my dad hangs up, I say, "Hey."

"Are you ever going to talk to me again?" Mary asks.

"I just need to cool down for a while."

"Well, do you want to come over? My mother rented *The Princess Diaries Two.*"

I'm looking through my closet for something remotely cool to wear to Midland Beach and I almost laugh. *The Princess Diaries*! I love Mary but sometimes I wonder whether she'll ever grow up, ever want to stop being a little girl who hangs out with her cat, Mittens. Of course, I adored the first movie when it came out. We've all had our share of princess fantasies, particularly if it means being swept away by a prince. I just feel disconnected now, like Mary and I have grown apart faster than you can say meow, like my own fairy tale has taken a particularly bad turn.

"Thanks," I say, "but I made plans."

"Oh," she says. I know she wants me to elaborate but I don't. Mary won't look kindly on my going out with Liza Henske and her reputation for cutting class and aborting babies. Least of all going to Midland Beach.

"I'll call you tomorrow," I say, throwing her a bone. "You can come over and we'll hang out by the pool."

"Sounds great," she says.

I say, "I better go."

I take a quick shower and blow out my hair superstraight. The fact that my father thinks I'm going bowling sort of eliminates the possibility of wearing a skirt, so I opt for jeans since I'm not sure I've ever seen Liza or any of her crew wear shorts. I put on my favorite T-shirt—it's black and says CONEY ISLAND in big block pink letters. My mother was born in Brooklyn—a fact she seemed to remind my Southern-bred father of at least once a day. She talked about Coney Island the way people talk about cities like Bethlehem or Jerusalem.

My parents used to take us there, but I was too young to remember. Still, I like the way the shirt makes me feel—like I've left this town more than I really have. It also fits really well, the letters positioned in such a way as to make my chest look nice. Not bigger, just nice. My hair looks really blah, though, no matter what I do to it. I try to wet it and dry it again but the results are even worse. My forehead looks big and oily and I can feel a pimple starting to form right above my nose. I know I might regret it but I decide to take some drastic measures. I dig around in my room for one of my mother's magazines and flip to a page highlighting "this summer's side-angle bangs." There are pictures of five or six A-list actresses, all sporting bangs angled across their foreheads. I wet the long strands at the crown of my head and start to cut, conservatively at first, then more confidently as I see the results. My eyes look brighter, a more vibrant brown. On the whole I look hipper, less bland. I decide not to bring a bag of any kind and put money, my phone, and lipstick in my pockets. I spritz on some Body Shop perfume, grab a zip-up, hooded sweatshirt, and head down to the foyer to wait for my ride.

When Liza pulls up in her car that, I now notice, looks like it's going to fall apart, I'm glad I'm right there waiting. "I'm leaving!" I call out to my father, again in front of the TV.

"Be home by eleven!" he says and I say, "Okay," though I haven't broached the subject of my curfew with Liza and don't imagine it'll go over too well. I have the number of a taxi company stored in my phone just in case.

I slide into the passenger seat and Liza turns down the radio. It's something I've never heard before: it sounds like cheerleaders and a bad marching band but with this sort of cool hip-hop beat. She looks much edgier and I realize it's because she's wearing a lot of black, and a lot of black eyeliner. I haven't seen Liza in makeup and jewelry for weeks now and I almost forgot that in school she's sort of a punk/Goth chick. Her ears are each holding about five hoops and clamps now and her fingers are loaded with heavy silver rings. It takes me a minute to process that this is the same person I've been sweeping out fireplaces with.

"What's different?" Liza studies me curiously.

"Oh." I comb my fingers through my bangs. "Bangs."

"Right." She nods. "They look good." She surveys me and I feel my face get hot.

"Thanks."

"And that's a cool shirt."

"Oh," I say, as in, *this old thing?* "Thanks." I think about telling her that my mother got it for me, but I'm afraid it'll trigger tears. I wonder sometimes how long it will be before I can talk about my mother without welling up or breaking down. I wonder how long it will be before nothing I own was around when my mother was alive.

"Okay," she says, putting the car into gear. "Love fest officially over."

We drive without talking—she turns up the radio again—and I feel like I've stepped out of my life. No one but Liza has any idea of what I'm up to tonight and I feel slightly sick with excitement . . . and maybe just a tinge of fear. What if Liza abandons me and I've got no one to talk to? What if none of her friends like me? What if I make a fool of myself? What if I get caught? There seem to be so many questions these days and so few answers. The one thing I do know is that it's the perfect night to spend at the beach. The sky is clear, the stars bright, and the air warm like a favorite fleece. Brandon and I would've driven down to the wall for sure on a night like this and I suddenly miss having a boyfriend, feel suddenly sad that I have no one to put his arms around me or to kiss me. I don't want Brandon back. I just want to know that there's someone else out there for me, someone who'll make it all feel better in a way he never could. I'm hoping that person will be James.

We pull into the parking lot at Midland Beach and I can see a handful of cars parked at the far end, near the boardwalk. Liza pulls into a spot on the opposite side of the lot and says, "Let's hang out for a little while. There aren't that many people over there yet." She reaches into the backseat, pulls up a plastic bag, and takes out two oversize beer cans. "You want one?" she says.

It feels like a defining moment. I knew there'd be drinking here, it's why my mother never allowed me to come. And it's not like I've never had a beer before. Brandon and I snuck a couple at his house once or twice, trying to get up the courage to actually remove clothing and not just push it aside—something we succeeded in only a handful of times. "Yeah, cool," I say. "I can give you money."

"Don't worry about it," she says. "It's on me."

We both snap our cans open and sip quietly. The beer's cold and sour tasting. I fear I like it too much already.

"So do you *really* actually like working at Morrisville?" Liza says. I'm relieved she's thought of something to say.

"I didn't at first," I say. "Loretta's a little hardcore. But I kind of like it more and more now. It's like an escape."

"Yeah," she says. "I know it's geeky and all but I like it. Beats being a cashier in a drugstore or being stuck in the mall all day or some other crap. I kind of like the acting. Everybody's acting all the time anyway."

"You're really good at it," I say. Then I realize it came out all wrong. "I don't mean that you're good at acting all the time. I don't even know if you do. I mean you're good at the acting part of the job. At Morrisville. You're way better than I am."

"You just can't take it too seriously."

"Loretta told me I need to take it *more* seriously."

"But she really means have fun and loosen up with it. It's not like anybody who's on a tour knows what colonial people talked like anyway. You kind of just have to go for it."

"But you really seem to know the history, too. My father would love that about you."

"Maybe, but I'm sure he wouldn't like that I just handed you a beer." She smiles supersweetly and bats her eyelashes.

"No," I admit. "Probably not. Where'd you get them anyway?" I've heard of people with fake IDs but don't actually know any.

"My dad lets me take them."

"Really?"

"Yeah." She looks serious for a minute. "He has this theory that the forbidden is more attractive than anything else. So if he lets me drink, it loses some of its appeal. And he says he wants me to make mistakes, the same kind he made, so I learn about life. It's sort of an interesting strategy."

I'm fascinated. "Does it work?"

She taps her can with mine—a hollow tinny sound—and says, "What do you think?" Then she reaches into the bag and pulls out two more beers for us.

By the time we drive across the parking lot to join the party, my head is buzzing from drink. Quite honestly, it's the best I've felt in weeks. When Liza introduces me to a posse of her friends—all of whom I've seen around school, none of whom I've ever spoken to—I feel rejuvenated and at ease. This is what they must mean when they talk about alcohol as a "social lubricant." I feel slippery, slick, relieved to be around people who either don't know about my mother or don't care. I discover how easy it is to hide behind a can of beer, to stand in a circle holding one and nod and laugh when everyone else does. How it makes you feel like you're part of something even if you're not participating. I know that Liza's friends are somehow different from mine, but maybe mine aren't as similar to me as I'd originally thought. I've been feeling so antsy, so misunderstood. Like maybe it's time to shake things up big time now that they've already been shaken up for me.

I've never talked the way Liza and her friends talk and all I can do is listen. They know about things I know nothing of, like world politics and alternative music and philosophy. Things we haven't learned much about in school because they don't teach it. I'm not dumb by any stretch of the imagination—I do well on tests—but I suddenly feel unintelligent. Like there's so much to this world that I'm completely ignorant of. Forget about naming the thirteen original colonies on command. I want to know how these kids—my peers—have learned how to have opinions, to pick up books I've never heard of, to read obscure British magazines and blogs. All this time I imagined them smoking in the boys' room, talking about foolish dreams they'd never accomplish—like being a poet or a rock star—and here they are, full of ideas and knowledge that puts me to shame. It's like they're speaking French or Swahili.

"You doing okay over here?" Liza asks. The group has broken down into smaller conversations and I notice a new car pulling up. It's Danny Mose's car. He and a guy I don't know get out and head over to a keg.

"Yeah, great," I say to Liza. "Your friends seem really cool."

She looks over my shoulder and her eyes light with recognition. "Oh, look who decided to turn up after all," she says.

I turn and see James walking toward us. Early American James is cute. Real-world James all but knocks the wind out of me. He's wearing jeans and a black T-shirt with a gold star high on the chest, and his hair is way more hip and funky, with actual product of some kind in it. He's older, sexier, and looks as surprised to see me as I must to see him.

"Hey," he says. "I would never have expected to see you here."

The drink has made me loose. "Why not? 'Cause you think I'm lame or something?"

He laughs at me. "No. I just didn't think you'd be allowed."

"I'm not." I'm full of fake confidence. "But you know, whatever."

"Are you okay?" he says.

"Yeah, why?"

"You're acting funny is all. And your hair is different or something?"

"Bangs." I teeter slightly as I run my fingers through them again.

"She's a lightweight." Liza hands James a beer.

"Nothing wrong with that." He snaps open his can.

I finish the last warm drip of beer from my current can and hold my hand out. Liza's got the remainder of a six-pack dangling from her fingers by its plastic. She looks at James, who shrugs, and hands me one. He says, "Anybody want to go sit on the beach?"

"Last one to the water's a rotten egg," Liza says, and we tear out of the parking lot and rush across the boardwalk. Suddenly we're all three on sand, struggling to kick off our shoes, and running toward the shore. I nearly fall down a few times and, at the water's edge, I'm winded from the run. The three of us start laughing as warm water brushes over our feet. The ocean looks like a big nothing past the tiny breakers. Like we would fall off the face of the earth if we waded out about twenty feet. I imagine what's lurking underneath the surface of the water in all this darkness and think of eels and sharks and seaweed the size of forests. My stomach flips at the thought and I walk back up the beach a few yards and sit down.

We're an awkward threesome. I wish Liza had stayed with her friends in the parking lot and left me and James alone. I feel like there's something I want to say to him—or that he's got something he wants to say to me—and instead he's talking to Liza. He keeps looking at me funny, but then something she says makes him laugh and I lose his attention. Then she jumps up on his back and he carries her around piggyback, runs a circle around me in a motion that makes me dizzy. I feel a little dumb because I didn't even know they were friends . . . and now it's like I'm seeing some special bond between them. It makes me think they're dating or hooking up. There's a physical ease between them as they joke around and I feel my stomach twist up. Headlights from the parking lot shine our way and I see the party—cars, kegs, surfboards, people laughing, talking on cell phones, holding beers, holding hands—like it's a silhouette. Liza and James run past—caught between me and the headlights—and I see them, too, as if cut out of black paper. It dawns on me that they've had sex.

"I should probably get going," I say.

James bends his knees and Liza slides off his back, then

sprawls out on the sand. She says, "But it's so beautiful here."

"You stay," I say. "I'll call a cab. It's no big deal."

"I can take you," James says.

Liza sits up and looks at him askance. "You just got here."

"Yeah." He smacks his hands together a few times, trying to get rid of sand. "I'm gonna get up early, though. Surf's supposed to be pretty decent down near Seaside Heights so I'm gonna drive down." Seaside Heights is a beach and amusement park about twenty miles south of us. There are rides and games and that's where my mother took the series of photos in the café right now.

"You surf?" I ask, not wanting to think about my mom.

"Sure do," James says with a smile, and I think that that's the coolest thing ever, even though I already knew that about him. I live in a beach town. Practically every guy I've ever known (except Brandon) has surfed at some point and still, I'm blown away.

"Fine." Liza lies back. "I think I'll just sleep here."

"Liiiiza," James moans.

"I'm only kidding," she says. "Fucking hell. You two really know how to ruin a party."

I feel lame for having to go home but I'm also reeling over the fact that James is going to drive me.

"You ready?" he says to me.

"Yeah," I say.

"Adios!" Liza says.

"You okay to drive?" James asks her.

"Hunky-dory," she says.

He marches back over to her, pulls her up by an arm, and says, "Come on. I'll drop you off. You can come get your car in the morning."

We say good night to Liza's crew and pile into James's car. I get to ride shotgun since Liza lives only a few blocks from Midland and is getting dropped off first. I'm thrilled and nervous but also convinced there's something between them that I'll never be able to compete with. Here, with his jeans—faded from wear in at least one place I dare not look—and his T-shirt stretched across his lean chest, James kind of scares me. It's like he and Liza are somehow more worldly. I'm just a naïve little virgin with an eleven o'clock curfew. I thought about having sex with Brandon just to get it out of the way but when push came to shove, I could just never go through with it; there was always something about the moment—the way his hair looked or the way his breath smelled like milk—that made me think, No, not now, not him. When I hear about girls at school who are giving boys oral sex in the third-floor AV equipment closet I can't quite get my head around the concept and I'm not sure I want to. Most of the time it feels like a good thing that I've waited.

I'm filterless after the beers I drank and I can't help myself. The second Liza's out of the car, I say, "So are you two seeing each other or something?"

He looks at me but I can't look at him for more than a second.

"Me and Liza?" he says, almost laughing.

"Yeah." I fidget with my phone.

"No," he says. "We're not."

"Did you used to?" I've never been so bold in my life. I'm not sure I like it.

"Let's just say that we got close enough to dating to realize we shouldn't date."

There's no way of asking him what I really want to know,

whether they've done it. The idea that James may have already had sex—probably has—makes my head spin. Even the idea that he has a penis is too much.

"I was happy to see you tonight," he says, and it's like the butterflies in my stomach flutter madly.

"You were?"

"Yeah. But you really shouldn't hang out down there at night."

"Why not?"

"Trust me, it's not your scene."

"But it's yours?"

"It's complicated."

And suddenly I'm so sick and tired of everyone wanting me to be something I'm not. My father wishes I were some brainy history buff. My mother wanted me to be *passionate*. Mary wants me to never change. Brandon wanted me to be somehow simpler. And now James wants me to stay a goody two-shoes because that's all he thinks I am. With all these new feelings swirling inside me I feel like this new, indefinable person, like my spirit is somehow rising up in rebellion, starting a civil war of the heart. Because as much as I wish that I could have my perfect family back, I also wouldn't trade what I'm feeling deep inside right now for the world. It's a growing feeling of power, of the power of experience, and what freedoms and rewards that grants you in life. Because no, I haven't had sex, or swiped beers from my father's liquor stash, or even gotten my dumb driver's license, but I know things Liza and Lauren Janey and Mary don't know. Like what it feels like to have your world turned upside down, what loss really feels like, and how completely terrifying our existence is each and every day.

"Have fun tomorrow," I say. "I've always wanted to learn how to surf."

"Maybe I'll teach you someday," he says. Then he reaches over and squeezes my arm. He says, "You're going to have to start doing push-ups first, though—or churn more butter."

I look down at his faintly hairy hand on my arm and feel slightly dizzy again. "Why?"

He says, "Surfing's all about upper body strength."

"It is?"

"Well, yeah. And balance."

I say, "Obviously," a bit too eagerly, and he laughs.

"What?"

"Nothing."

There's silence for a few seconds, both of us looking straight ahead. Then I look out at my house—we've stopped in front—and I'm filled with dread.

"How are you holding up in there?" he says. It's like he's reading my mind.

"I feel guilty when I'm not there and miserable when I am." I start crying again and suddenly, I don't know how, his arms are around me and it feels so wonderful that it makes me cry even harder. I wish none of this had happened, that I could walk through that front door straight into the fifth-degree routine my mother always gave me when I came in. She'd come close enough to smell for smoke and liquor and she'd ask just enough detailed questions to confirm I'd been where I'd really been.

"I'm sorry," I say to James. I pull away from him and he leans over and pulls a packet of tissues out of the glove compartment.

"Don't be sorry," he says. "There's nothing to be sorry for."

I blow my nose and feel wildly unattractive.

He says, "Tell me a story."

I sniffle and say, "I'm really not in the mood."

"I don't care. Tell me one anyway."

I puff my cheeks up as I exhale a deep breath. "I just can't seem to get past all the ugly stuff."

"Like . . . ?"

"Like how my boyfriend was seeing someone else behind my back—a girl who actually had the nerve to come to my mother's wake."

"You mean, you're not going out with him anymore?" There's a look on his face that I can't read and his body seems suddenly tense, ready to pounce.

"No." I try to find a dry spot on my tissue.

"What else?" He puts his hands on the steering wheel, holds on tight. "More of the bad stuff."

I look straight ahead out the windshield. The streetlights are reflecting strange patterns, like stars that are melting. "My brother and I were at the orthodontist's the other day and no one there knew she died so we were talking about her like everything was peachy. Oh, and this is the best. We pissed my dad off one night by not helping out with dinner and we've been eating fast food ever since."

"Okay. Asshole boyfriend. Asshole orthodontist. Crap food. Anything else?"

"That's the big stuff." I cry a tiny bit more and he takes my hand and says, "Look at me," and I do and there's this look in his eyes that says I can tell him anything and then there it is, just like that. A story. I take a deep breath: "Okay, so me and my mom are in the car." I look down at his hand in mine, trying to process the fact of skin on skin, and he releases it, which isn't what I wanted at all. "She's driving me to a friend's birthday party." I blow my nose. "And I'm already late and it's a surprise party, and we're stopped at a red light and she sees these two people—a guy and a girl, probably in college—holding a table. They're carrying it somewhere, obviously, and they're struggling with it. They're resting and shaking out their arms. And my mother always talked to strangers, so she said, 'Looks heavy,' and the girl says, 'You have no idea,' so my mother says, 'How far are you going?' and the girl says, 'Just a few blocks.' So my mother pops the back of the car—this is when we had a station wagon—and says, 'Hop in.' So she's talking to them the whole way and I'm fuming because I'm just late enough now for the party that I can't show up until much later when I know the coast is clear, and when she drops them off with the table I say something like, 'Thanks, Mom. Now I missed the surprise,' and she reaches over and messes up my hair and says, 'Well, wasn't that a surprise, too?' "

James nods his head and smiles. "I have a feeling you're going to be very good at this remembering stuff."

"Now you."

"We don't have to."

"No, I want to hear another one. We made a deal."

He exhales loudly and thinks for a second. "It's not a story so much as something I want to remember. A moment. Is that okay?"

"Sure."

He smiles sort of shyly and says, "You ever tell anyone I told you this and I'll have to kill you. It'd ruin my reputation as a man's man."

I try to keep a straight face. "You have a reputation as a man's man?"

"You haven't heard?" He smiles.

"Well, get on with it."

"It was maybe only a week before the accident. We were at my cousin's wedding. This big mansion down on the water, I forget the name of it. They didn't know I was watching them. My mother was standing on this porch looking out at the water, and she had this shawl that was sort of hooked around her arms but not around her shoulders. And my father walked up behind her and bent and kissed her on the shoulder and then pulled the shawl around her and put his arms around her like a shawl, too. It may have been the first time I thought of him as something other than my father. That he was a person. And I realized that I wanted to be the kind of man he was, and have that kind of love. That's it. It was just a moment. A good one." He grabs the steering wheel again. "Like this one."

I look at his profile and study it again, feeling an idea taking shape in the far corners of my mind. He turns and seems to look at my mouth and I feel all snotty and weird and then he turns away and sighs like he's being tortured or something and says, "You should probably go."

"Yeah," I say, sort of startled that I'm being dismissed. "Thanks for the ride." I get out of the car as fast as I can, teetering just slightly when I stand, still buzzed. I walk to the front door and don't look back.

chapter 10

"What's wrong with you today?" Mary asks. We've been lounging around on inflatable floats in the pool for about a half hour and I'd love for her to just shut up. I'm firmly in the clutches of my first-ever hangover and I swear it'll be my last.

"Nothing," I say, willing my stomach to settle, hoping the fog will lift from my head.

"If I didn't know better"—Mary's voice is all teacher's pet—"I'd guess that you had a hangover."

I pinch my nose with my thumb and index finger and roll over into the water. The bracing cold seems to help my headache, if only through shocking my system anew. I don't resurface until my lungs ache from the strain of not breathing.

I hear Mary say, "Isn't it?" when I resurface.

"Isn't it what?" I wipe some stray hairs out of my face, brushing them back against my head and getting back up on my float.

"I *said*"—she's gritting her teeth—"it's Liza Henske, isn't it?"

I knock water out of my ear. "What about her?"

"That's who you went out with last night?"

"Oh, so what if I did, Mary? What exactly am I supposed to do?" I've sort of had it with her.

"Well, not drink, for starters. And I thought you thought she was a freak."

"Well, she's proven me wrong."

"Yeah, and how exactly did she do that?"

"She told me about Brandon and Lauren Janey, that she saw them at the movies together and thought I should know. This was *before* she knew he dumped me."

Mary looks like she's going to cry and a part of me feels awful, but it also feels good to make her feel so bad. A part of me wants to say all is forgiven and tell Mary every detail of last night, especially those that involve James, like the moment he realized I didn't have a boyfriend anymore, the way his body seemed somehow altered on a molecular level. But I can't help but think she'd ruin it for me by not understanding. I don't even think I understand it myself.

"I feel like I don't even know you anymore," Mary says.

"Yeah, well, maybe I don't know me, either," I say.

My father steps out onto the deck. "Mary," he calls out, "your mother's on the phone."

Mary steps out of the pool and my father hands the phone down to her over the deck railing. She holds it carefully between two wet fingers, as far from her ear as she can while still hearing. "What do you mean?" she cries, standing there in her pink-and-purple flowered one-piece. And then she actually starts crying. "Okay," she whimpers. "I'll ask."

I can't imagine what it could be. My mind goes to the worst-case scenario and I wonder whether this is how it happens. Whether once one person dies they all start dying—whether there's such a thing as opening the flood gates on death.

She holds the phone away. "Mr. Irving, can you drive me home?"

"Of course," my father says. "Is everything okay?"

She says, "He's gonna drive me," into the phone, and ends the call. Then she wails, "Mittens got run over!" She's sobbing now and when she looks at me, I can't help it. I look at her bawling in her girlie-girl bathing suit and I laugh. This stops her crying in an instant and she looks at me like she's seen a ghost.

"For chrissakes," I say. "It's a cat."

I've crawled back into bed, wet hair and all, by the time my father gets back from driving Mary home. She lives close enough that she walked over here earlier but I guess her mother didn't want her bereaved daughter wandering the streets in distress. My dad knocks on my door, then opens it without my telling him to. "You awake?"

"Yeah." I curl up tighter.

"You coming down with something?"

"I don't know." A part of me is scared I've done some irreparable damage to my brain, which feels clamped and fuzzy, but of course I can't tell my father what I've done, that if I die here in my bed today it'll be all my own fault.

"Well, I'll tell you one thing," he says. "Go around treating people like that and you'll be out of friends before long."

He slams the door shut. He's never been so disgusted with me. I cry and cry but it only makes my headache worse. It's a miracle I'm able to fall asleep, but I do and I dream in vivid black and white.

My father and Ben have tickets to a baseball game on Sunday so when they leave I raid Ben's school supply stash and take all his black construction paper. My dream has rekindled an idea that flashed through my mind last night. I've got an image of the party at Midland emblazoned in my mind and I want to try to assemble it in silhouette—sort of a modern-day version of that group of aristocrats at a dinner party.

I start with a surfboard, which seems like it'll be easy enough, and it is. Except that it needs context for it to really look like a surfboard. I picture the party in my head and imagine a grid on top of it. I focus on one figure and decide to try to do a full body, not just a face in profile—a boy with his arm outstretched, holding the surfboard upright. I'm using the tiny curved scissors and they cut clean and sharp. Still, my first attempt is a disaster. My second attempt is better. The third time, I apply the lessons I've learned from Ben's profile, relaxing my arms and shoulders and going with the flow, and the result is nearly perfect. My silhouette of a boy actually looks like a boy—spiky hair and all. If there were a speech bubble over his head it would most definitely say, "Duuude!" In a weird way, he also kind of looks like James even though he's only six inches tall. I feel focused, excited, and then sad. Because there's no one to show my work to, no one who'll get it. With my father and Ben at a baseball game it hits me for the first time that I'm the lone girl in the family now. I wonder how many Sundays there will be like this, with them doing their thing and me doing mine, whatever mine is.

I decide to bike down to my aunt's café. But when I get there, she's not there. There's a girl working the counter who I've met a few times so I ask her where my aunt is. "The boys had a softball game or something so she took the day off," she says. My sadness returns and then I turn to leave and my mother's photos on the wall stop me. I can't bear to linger and look at them, though, not with this girl here watching. So I bike home and curl up in my window seat with Harry Potter again. I've started it maybe five times already but I can't seem to get into it the same way I did all the others. Maybe because I know there's no such thing as magic. If there were, my mother would still be alive. I set the book aside and close my eyes and try to imagine myself in a story—*Harry Potter and the Motherless Daughter.* It's the darkest tale yet in the series and my character is pure evil. She has scars that make Harry's lightning bolt look cute, and shape-shifting powers that make her impossible to seek out and destroy.

I hear my dad and Ben come in and, after a while, there's a knock on my door. I scurry to hide the paper clippings on the floor, then say, "Come in."

"Everything okay in here?" my father asks.

"Yup."

"It's dinnertime." He turns to head back downstairs.

I follow him into the kitchen where Ben is opening up a white pint of Chinese takeout. He looks up at me and raises his eyebrows as if to say, "Too hot to cook, my ass." The temperature didn't go above seventy-five all day.

chapter 11

Sandra and I are assigned the same car at driver's ed on Monday and I'm super-psyched, even though we're hitting the road the first time out with Mr. Pagano himself and not one of the assistant instructors—other teachers from school, all of whom are cooler than Mr. Pagano. Thankfully, they rotate cars, though, so we'll only have Mr. Pagano once or twice.

At the car, it turns out Mr. Pagano somehow took the wrong keys, so he leaves us in the parking lot with the other two people assigned to the car—Bobby Hopkins and David Leto, two bookish, track team types—while he goes back to get the right set.

"So." Sandra checks the car for dust with an index finger, then leans against it. "Are you going Friday?"

It takes me a minute to process the question. "Going where?"

Sandra's eyes bulge. "This is worse than I thought." Her hair is pulled back in a librarian's bun, stuck through with a pencil. Only someone with features like Sandra's could pull this off and still be popular. She says, "Mary's having a party."

Stunned, I say, "Haven't heard a thing about it." Then I realize I sort of have. Brandon must be invited.

Sandra sort of winces and says, "Maybe you'll get the invite in today's mail?"

"Doubt it." I'm chocking back tears on the one hand and fuming on the other. I can't believe Mary didn't invite me to her stupid fucking party.

"You think it's the cat thing?" Sandra says.

I guess it's a bigger deal than I thought. "She told you what I said?"

"Yeah." It's clear from her tone even Sandra's not impressed.

I lean against the car, too. "I don't mean to be this totally insensitive person. But . . ."

"No, totally. I know what you mean." Sandra crosses her arms and shakes her head. "She's such a freak."

"What do you mean?" I honestly don't know.

"I think she's jealous of you."

Mr. Pagano returns just then and we all pile in, him in the passenger seat—where he has his own set of controls—and Bobby Hopkins, the first guinea pig, in the driver's seat. Sandra, David, and I are in back.

"Jealous of what?" I whisper.

She shrugs and winces. "The attention, I guess?"

"Well, that's the stupidest thing I've ever heard."

"Ladies!" Mr. Pagano says. "We learn from each other here. Please pay attention."

"Sorry," I mutter.

Sandra looks up at Mr. Pagano all alert and takes out a notebook. "Sorry, Mr. Pagano," she says. "It won't happen again."

"Well, thank you, Sandra," Mr. Pagano says. "Betsy. John. You should have your notebooks out, too. Now, as I was saying . . ."

Sandra starts writing in her notebook and I look to see what she can possibly be taking notes on. *Things not so hot between BF and LJ.*

Brandon Fields and Lauren Janey.

I write in my own notebook, *Says who?*

Mr. Pagano is saying, "Signal, signal, signal." The wind is flipping up his hair, nipping at his toupee. For a second I imagine it flying out the window and causing the car behind us to swerve and crash.

Trevor. According to Mary.

Fascinating, I write.

Sandra nods and we sit quietly as Bobby drives for the first time. He seems like he's been doing it all his life.

When it's my time at the wheel, I'm giddy with nerves. The idea of being able to drive to school come September 30, the notion of being able to go wherever I want whenever I want—without having to huff and puff on my bike—thrills me to no end. We're driving on wide, mostly sleepy, residential streets behind the school.

I feel like you learn a certain amount about driving just from watching other people do it over the years, so I start out confident. But then it takes me a while to figure out the relationship between pressure on the gas pedal and the speed of the car. When I do, I like the feeling of control. At the first stop sign, I come to a nice neat stop and Mr. Pagano congratulates me. I start to roll forward, as we've been told to do, looking in both directions, and the coast is clear. So I give it some gas and head through the intersection. I wish I could just take off right then, hop on the highway and drive somewhere alone. I don't even know where I'd go but I like the idea that I can. Whenever my parents had a fight—and it wasn't that often that I knew of—one or the other of them would always head for the door, pick up their car keys, and say, "I'm going for a drive." I like the idea that I might soon be able to do that, too. Storm off somewhere in a huff.

I look at my hands on the wheel and feel like a foreigner to myself. I feel like changes are coming hard and fast now, like my mother would barely recognize me if she were suddenly alive again. I wonder for a second whether the fact that I even have a thought about her being alive again means that I've somehow reverted back to denial. I'm starting to become obsessed with that list on my wall, with whether I'm progressing properly through the stages of grief. I figure if I can get through them all this summer, then senior year won't suck so bad. But I haven't exactly been making progress.

Right then—and I'm barely doing thirty-five mph—a kid runs out in front of the car and I slam on the brakes. My body lurches forward and I see Mr. Pagano clutching his door's armrest, his foot on his own brakes. "Everyone okay?" he says.

"Yeah," Sandra says. "Fine."

The boys in the backseat mutter, "Fine." Then Bobby Hopkins says, "Fuckin' A," and Mr. Pagano doesn't even scold him.

In the meantime, I've put the car in park in the middle of the street. I'm out and I'm chasing after the kid. He's playing basketball in front of his house—right there—oblivious.

"What the hell are you thinking?" I scream at him. "You could've gotten killed! I could've killed you!" I'm shaking now and Mr. Pagano is standing there, too, looking as dumbfounded as the kid. He's about eight or nine and wearing a baseball hat while dribbling and I'm tempted to rip it off his head and stomp on it and scream, Wrong sport, kiddo!

"Bets," Sandra says. "Come on." She goes to put an arm around me but I snap away. "No," I say. "I'm serious. People get killed by cars. He should know that."

"You're scaring him," Sandra says.

"He *should* be scared!"

"Okay, babe," she says, now pulling me into a hug and this time I let her and I start to cry. "Okay," she says. "Okay. You're right."

Sandra and I get into the backseat and Mr. Pagano drives us back to school without a word. When we get out I hear Bobby Hopkins say, "What's her *deal?*"

I wipe my eyes again and Sandra rubs my arm. "You okay?"

"Yeah." I take a deep breath. "I honestly don't know why I freaked out."

"It was scary." She's rubbing my back now. "I would've freaked out."

I nod, knowing that if I try to talk I'll only start to cry again.

Liza and I lead a tour together at my suggestion. She does almost all the talking but I'm determined to learn from her, if only so that I don't spend my remaining days here feeling like an idiot. We step out onto the front porch after the group heads for Loretta in the kitchen and I'm immediately assaulted by a bee that's buzzing around my head. "Fucking hell," I say, swatting and then rushing away.

"What kind of bee is in your bonnet today, missy?" Liza takes a seat on a rocker, not minding the bee, still buzzing around.

"Having a bad day," I say from a safe distance.

"Taxation without representation got you down?" She doesn't rock but splays her legs out limp, like the Wicked Witch of the East.

"I had a freak-out in driver's ed this morning."

"What happened?"

The bee zips away so I step onto the porch and take the other rocker. "This kid ran out in front of the car and I had to stop really short and I sort of lost it. I yelled at him."

"Well, driver's ed is for pussies anyway." Liza reties her bonnet strings.

"Well, how'd *you* learn to drive?" It comes out with more attitude than I intend.

"My father." Between his beer policy and his personal driving school I'm increasingly intrigued by Liza's father.

"I thought it would be easier."

"You've got a lot going on. Maybe you're not ready."

"I'm ready," I say a bit too forcefully. Then I have an idea and I express it before I can decide whether I really want to. "Can you teach me, maybe? At least get me over the hump?"

Liza looks stunned, like I've just asked her on a date. "What's the hump? Do we know?"

"I'm afraid I'm going to hit someone, I guess."

She shoots me a look that tells me she knows everything, that of course this has something to do with James. That he's under my skin whether I admit it or not. "The odds of that are incredibly slim," she says. "You have to know that, rationally."

"I know a lot of things, rationally."

"Like what?"

The bee comes back, tormenting me in particular. I flee the porch again, swatting around my head. "Like that a bee sting doesn't really hurt all that badly." I was stung once last year, during soccer practice. "But I'm still scared out of my mind of bees." A story comes to me in a flash right then: about going to get my ears pierced with my mom. I file it away for James.

"All right," Liza says. "One lesson—tomorrow after work—and we'll see how you do. We'll start small, in a parking lot or something." She shakes her head at me as I run from another bee. "And we'll sweep it for beehives first."

Mrs. Rudolph comes by the farmhouse at about 11:00 A.M. and asks Loretta if she can borrow Liza and me for an hour or so before an expected afternoon rush. She's collecting the younger members of the staff in order to start getting us ready for the end-of-summer banquet.

We gather in the tavern—me, Liza, James, and Ian and Matthew, who work in the general store. I haven't spent much time in the tavern and I study it—wagon-wheel lanterns, a stone fireplace, thick, dark wood tables and benches, a corner bar stocked with pottery mugs—as Mrs. Rudolph explains why the banquet is so important, how crucial the donations of these wealthy benefactors are to the survival of Morrisville. Then she promises that the dinners will be fun, and more importantly, that we'll get paid twice our normal hourly wage.

I hear Liza say to James, in a fake surfer way, "What's up, dude? Ride any monster waves this weekend?"

James says, "Like, ohmigod, like totally."

"Now," Mrs. Rudolph says more loudly, clearly sensing she's losing the group's attention. "To get things started on the right note, we've got some music today—the likes of which might've been played in a tavern much like this one in the early 1800s—and we're going to let you loose on the dance floor and give you some pointers in period tavern dancing."

"Boys!" she calls out the window.

A few of the older employees of Morrisville come into the tavern. There's a man with a fiddle and another with a banjo-type thing—I'm pretty sure he's Loretta's real-life husband—and they're playing some wacky, fast song. Another man approaches me, slides a hand around my waist, and says, "May I have this dance, miss?" Then my right hand's clamped around his and, my feet barely touching the ground, we're skipping around the dance floor like a pair of idiots. I feel dumb and I'm getting dizzy but then I settle into a rhythm, following his lead, and soon I see that the whole room is on its feet. James is dancing with Mrs. Rudolph, and Liza—apparently an old pro at colonial dancing—is showing Ian some moves and I want to throw my head back and laugh at how ludicrous it is—it's 2005, for chris-sakes! I think of how my mother so loved to dance—even just around the house—and how maybe, just maybe, she'd be proud of me, or at least colonial me. Because when James cuts in and asks my partner, all polite, "May I have the lady's next dance, if she permits," and the two men bow and I nod and I think of the beach party and the way being alone with James in his car made me tingle and want to do things with him and to him that

I've never done with anyone—not even Brandon—I think my mother wouldn't be too proud at all. And as James takes me in his arms, I think I don't much care.

When Mrs. Rudolph dismisses us, Liza heads off to use the bathroom in the restaurant and James and I sprawl out on the grass next to the tavern, winded and sweaty. "How was the rest of your weekend?" he asks.

"Awful." I'm just now catching my breath.

He perches up on his elbows to show interest.

"My friend's cat died and I laughed."

He inhales sharply through his teeth, making a wincing kind of sound. "Ouch," he says.

"Yeah. I'm pretty evil." I can see tiny beads of sweat on his forehead and I swear I can still feel a patch of heat on my back, from where his hand held me.

"But I mean, come on—" he says, after a pause.

I look at him and he's sorta smiling.

He says, "It's a cat!"

"That's what *I* said." I sit up.

"No, wait." He's laughing. "You actually *said* that?"

"Yeah." I'm not feeling especially proud now. "I guess some things are better left unspoken."

"I've been wondering a lot about that very issue myself," he says. I don't know what he means but there's this new heaviness to the air around us.

"How about your weekend?" I say to shift the mood. "How was Seaside?"

"Good. We caught some good waves."

I catch on the "we" for a second but obviously it's him and his surfer pals.

"Listen," he says. "I want to explain to you something about the other night, why I was down at Midland."

"Okay . . ." I say.

"Betsy!" Loretta screams from the farmhouse down the way. "Incoming!" I see her pointing up Main Street where a gaggle of ladies and kids are heading her way.

I look at James and he looks at me seriously.

I start to get up. "I better go."

"Okay," he says. "I'll see you later."

I head toward the farmhouse, a pounding sensation in my ears. As I slide past Loretta to go greet a tour, she says, "Flirt on your own time, Irving."

Still, when the afternoon slows down and Loretta catches me looking out the kitchen window toward the carpenter's house one too many times, she takes a cloth out of the kitchen linen closet and loads a basket up with muffins she baked earlier in the day. As she does so, she says, "Do you think maybe Will and James would like some muffins?"

"I thought I was supposed to flirt on my own time," I say.

She just shrugs, smiles, and hands me the basket.

It's all I can do not to break into a run I'm so grateful for the excuse to go see James. It's funny because he used to stop by maybe once a day and nobody thought anything of it. I went by the carpenter's shop a couple of times before my mom died, too. But now, something feels different. Now he has something to tell me.

I step into the carpenter's shop and it's empty. Momentarily perplexed, I put the muffins down and then look around. Then I hear James's voice. It's coming from the shop's side window. "James?" I say, and stick my head out.

He's there all right, one hand on the wall, supporting him as he leans forward—and there's a girl there with him. She looks up at me and I think she looks familiar, but I'm not sure from where.

"What's up?" James says.

"I'm sorry." I'm sure I turn beet red. "I didn't mean to interrupt."

"It's okay," he says, but he looks uncomfortable. In my head I'm thinking, It's not okay. Who the hell is she? Then I remember where I recognize her from. The beach party. So this is what he's going to explain about the other night. He has a girlfriend. She was there.

"I brought you some muffins," I said. "I mean, for you and Will. Loretta sent me over. I'll leave them here. See you later." I duck my head back into the building and start to rush for the door. I can hear him call my name, hear him say "Wait," but I don't stop.

As soon as I get home, I go up to my room and cut the surfer dude and his board into tiny pieces—like black confetti—and have a quick cry. First Brandon dumps me for Lauren Janey and now this. I feel like such a fool for ever thinking anybody would want to be with me that way. Clearly, I'm cursed. I take the bits of paper and heft them in the air and watch them fall to the ground, all dark and funereal, a morbid celebration of the fact that my life is ruined.

My father comes home with Burger King and I'm tempted to scream, "What the fuck is your problem? Don't you know you're supposed to take care of us?" But of course I don't. We're not starving, after all. We're not wandering the streets barefoot. We've got a roof over our heads. It's just the inside that's neglected, being eaten away slowly by fat and grease and wilted lettuce and fake meat.

There's something chewy and hard in my chicken sandwich and I have to spit it out. I lose interest in the sandwich after that—grow preoccupied with how far removed from actual chicken it is—and eat only fries. "There's an extra burger in here," my father says, turning the mouth of a bag in my direction. But I've lost my appetite.

"I'm fine. You want it, Ben?"

"Yeah," he says. Ben seems to be getting taller by the minute these days. He needs the burger more than I do.

The doorbell rings as we're cleaning up. I look from the kitchen down the front hallway and see it's Mary standing just outside the screen door.

My father gets to the door first. "Oh, hello, Mary," he says. "Do you want to come in?"

"Can Betsy come out, Mr. Irving?" Her voice is polite, nothing more. "It'll only take a minute."

"Of course."

When he turns to get me I'm already there. "Hey," I say, stepping out onto the porch.

The front lawn is dotted with fireflies and I think back to the summers Mary and I spent catching them, and sucking on honeysuckle, and digging for buried treasure in the woods down the street; we once found a treasure map with burned edges and a bunch of Native American coins and discovered, a few hours later, that some of the neighborhood boys had planted them to trick us. A lot has changed and not all of it is good. We sit down beside each other on the top step and she hands me a small envelope.

"What's this?" I say, though I already have a good idea.

"An invitation."

I open the envelope and slide the invite out. It's for a pool party. On Friday night.

"My mother's idea. To cheer me up."

"I'll try to come." I notice that the envelope has a stamp on it.

"Well, why wouldn't you be able to?" Mary doesn't put her hands on her hips but she might as well have.

"I don't know." I'm fixating on the stamp, some kind of thirty-seven-cent tribute to Dr. Seuss. "I mean, you just gave it to me and the party's Friday. It's short notice." The stamp means she was going to mail it and then didn't. She could've at least peeled it off before handing it to me.

"Well, everyone's going to be there," she says.

"Well, maybe the fact that everyone's going to be there is part of the problem."

"I can't stop being friends with them," she snaps. "Trevor's best friends with Brandon and Trevor's my boyfriend, if you haven't forgotten. My whole life can't change just because . . . because of you."

I have a moment of clarity, a rush of understanding. Unless your mother dies when you're sixteen you have no idea what it's like to have your mother die when you're sixteen.

"God," she says. "I just wish everything could go back to how it was, with you and Brandon together and me and Trevor and us double-dating."

"I don't," I say without forethought. In a way I'm surprised I say it at all.

"You don't?"

I think of the picture of the four of us at Six Flags, the way I tore it to shreds. "I always felt there was something missing, like maybe he's too simple or something. I never felt taken care of, or like I could really be myself." And of course now I'm thinking of James, of the way I feel safe with him, safe just being me.

"You never said anything," Mary says. "You seemed happy."

"I guess I didn't know what to say. And I think I thought maybe that's how it felt, to be with a guy. That I built it up in my head to be something it wasn't. But I haven't, I don't think. I've been kind of hanging out with a guy from work."

She thinks for a second. "James?"

I nod. I'd practically forgotten that Mary ever worked at Morrisville and a part of me is actually glad now that she quit, that Morrisville and James and Liza are all mine. "I really felt like maybe something was happening and it all feels so right with him but then today I saw him with this girl and I don't know, Mare. I feel sick about it."

His car pulls up in front of the house as if on cue. "That's him," I say, completely wigging out inside but not wanting to seem that way outside.

"Do you have a date?"

"No. He just turns up sometimes." I figure that he really wants to explain whatever it was he said he wanted to explain about the other night. About Midland.

"Like a stalker?" Mary looks at his car distastefully.

"Not exactly."

"Well, don't jump to any conclusions." She gets up and brushes off the seat of her shorts. "I'd better go." She starts to walk away.

"Mare, I'm sorry about Muffin," I say. I know that things still aren't all quite right between us—I'm still conflicted about this party—but I want to at least say that.

She turns and smiles and says, "I know you are. Good luck."

Since James is showing no signs of turning off the engine and getting out of the car, I walk down the front walk to the curb and lean down to look through the open passenger side window. He says, "You wanna go for a ride?"

"Where to?" I keep a safe distance since I'm worried about my Burger King breath being less than royally wonderful.

"Anywhere." He smiles. "I was thinking . . . Montreal? California? Atlantic City?"

I smile, too. "I have to ask my dad."

He nods and I stand up and deliberately walk slowly back to the house. For reasons that are obvious, I'm hearing my mother's voice in my head: stuff about not going strange places with boys, and not being in their houses unchaperoned, for example, and how girls who do stuff like that get reputations. Bad ones.

"Dad?" He's in his office, on the Web. "A friend from work stopped by. Can I go out for a little while?"

"Is this friend from work Liza?"

"No."

"I thought not. Is it a male friend, mayhap?"

I roll my eyes. "Yes."

"Where to?"

"Ice cream." I figure it sounds innocent enough. "I swear I'll be home in an hour. Two hours, tops. It's only eight thirty."

"Okay." He looks at his wristwatch. "But one minute later than, say, eleven, and there'll be trouble."

"Thanks, Dad." I run upstairs to brush my teeth and spritz on some perfume. I put lipgloss on, too, but that's all.

"Where to?" James asks when I get into the car.

I shrug, wondering how long he can play this game of avoiding the fact that there's something between us. A wall we need to at least acknowledge if not take a wrecking ball to. The fact that he's here at all is proof that I'm not imagining it. That it's not all in my head.

"Beach?" he says.

"Sure." I wonder where people go when they live in towns that aren't by the water.

"Drive then talk?"

"Sure."

The windows are down and the wind blows a hair into my face and it tickles my nose before getting whipped back to where it belongs.

"I want to play you a song," James says. "But I'm kind of afraid it will upset you. Not that there's anything wrong with getting upset but I don't want to be the cause of it. It's just a song that makes me think of you. Is that okay?"

I nod and he pushes a CD in and goes to track number nine. It starts with a weird computer-voice countdown, then there's strumming guitars and strings and what sound like church bells and yet it's still totally rock.

Do you realize, the singer sings, *that you have the most beautiful face . . .*

I remind myself to not take this too literally. James doesn't necessarily think of the song because it's my face that's the most beautiful. While reminding myself of this, I miss some lyrics so try to concentrate again.

Do you realize that happiness makes you cry . . . which would be a corny line if the song weren't so goddamn beautiful, if I weren't with James in a car flying down a dark highway on a balmy summer night, feeling more alive than I've ever felt. And then the song says something about how we're all going to die someday and I feel strong, powerful, like I've glimpsed something sacred in life that most people have to wait longer to see, like maybe I'll be better for it, stronger, for having lost so much so young.

And then there's more, about life going fast, about the world spinning, and I can't help but look over at him. He looks over at me, too, and he's so serious I can barely stand to look in his eyes but I do, only for a millisecond—he's driving—but it feels like slow motion and I feel like I'm saying thank you without having to say it. The song goes on and now my head is spinning, because it's this amazing song and it's James playing it for me but I still don't know why we're here and what he wants and who she is. We're in a parking lot at the beach now, and when the song's over he cuts the engine and gets out. I get out and he nods his head toward the boardwalk and I follow. He sits down on a bench facing the water and so I do the same. The sea's calm, the sun just about set, and everything around that isn't pink from its dying rays is gray—water, birds, people in the distance—all muted, as if to make sure you notice how gorgeous the sky looks still just barely lit.

"So why'd you run off today?" He slides his hands into his jeans pockets, stretches long legs out in front of him. "I called your name. Didn't you hear me?"

"No," I say, then think of another lie. "I was afraid I'd miss my ride with Liza. And I interrupted you and your . . ." We're both looking out at the water while talking and I'm glad. I can't bear to look at him and I can't bring myself to say "girlfriend." Because I just can't believe it might be true.

"Girlfriend," he says, turning to me. "She's my girlfriend."

I feel like someone's standing on my chest. I say, "She was at the party. Midland Beach, the other night."

"Yeah, she was." He sounds more serious now. "I only really went down there to check on her. It's complicated, Betsy. I feel kind of weird talking about it. But I wanted you to know that . . . that I'm with her now."

"Okay." I don't know what else to say.

"After I dropped you off I went back and drove her home."

I don't even realize how mad I am until I snap, "Okay, why are we still talking about this?"

"I don't know." He looks at me sort of angry. "Because we're friends?"

I think, If we were friends, you would've mentioned that you had a girlfriend sooner.

Then there's this heaviness around us and we're staring at each other and then I say, "I thought of another story." I've been wanting to tell him and I don't feel like talking about him and his girlfriend anymore. In this case, I want to plant myself firmly in denial.

"I'm all ears." He rests his head back on the headrest and tilts it toward me.

"Funny you should say that: when I went to get my *ears* pierced"—he smiles—"there was a girl there before me, and she screamed her head off and I didn't want to do it anymore. But my mother really wanted me to have them done. So she sat down in the chair and she said, 'I'll do it, then you'll do it.' So I agreed. And her ears were already pierced. But she got a second hole put in on each ear, and she was all like, 'See, didn't hurt at all,' but then after I got mine done and it really didn't hurt that much, she told me that hers absolutely killed her. I guess the second hole hurts more or something."

James looks at me, expecting more.

"That's it," I say. "No witty punch line or anything. There's probably a better way to tell it."

"No, it's a good story." He nods his head. "She was teaching you to be brave."

We sit quietly for a minute—the ocean is dark and quiet, the air surprisingly still, the moon oddly low—and then he says, "What do you think is worse? Somebody dying suddenly or dying of a long illness?"

"I don't know." I think again of tufts of hair, and scars, and scarves and wigs, and can't imagine a fate worse than cancer. Then I think about a person walking on the side of the road. I think of the *bam!* "What's the worst part about how it happened to you?"

Without hesitation he says, "I never got to say good-bye."

I think back to the hospital room, to the smell of antiseptic and blood and Lord only knows what else. To my mother's skeletal arms, poked with an IV too many times, to the way she clutched my hand and rubbed one spot—repeatedly, too hard—and said, "Find something you're passionate about, Betsy. Everything else will follow. Don't worry about boys. Worry about passion."

James says, "What about you? What was the worst part for you?"

The nurse came in just then, and my mother introduced us.

The nurse said, "Your mom is one strong lady." And I believed it, but not really. She didn't look strong. She wasn't talking strong. She was talking like she knew it was over, and it was. The doctor's had given her maybe six months; she decided to take just a day.

I breathe deeply and will the tears pooling in my eyes to go back to where they came from. "I guess the worst part," I say, "was that I had to say good-bye."

We sit in silence for a while and then James says, "We're quite a pair, aren't we?"

"Yeah," I say. "The life of the party."

I want to be more mad at him, to scream at him that he should've told me, that he shouldn't be leading me on, that he should stop being so amazing in every way and leave me alone, but I don't want him to stop. I don't want him to leave me alone. I wish that he didn't have a girlfriend, the same way I wish my mother were still alive—no, that she'd never gotten cancer in the first place—but I know that there's something he and I have that's too precious to throw away. I took my mother, my easy breezy life, for granted, and I won't do it again. Not with him. Not with this. If friends is what we are, then so be it.

At home, I add a figure that looks like Liza to the beach party scene. She's got spiky hair that flips mostly over to one side and she's wearing heavy boots, even though it's the beach. Then I put in a girl who looks like Mary about six inches to the right of her. Mary's holding a cat and she seems to be looking at Liza antagonistically. I wonder where in the middle I would be.

chapter 12

tuesday is an almost painfully perfect summer day. Eighty degrees with low humidity and a breeze that feels like spring. It's the sort of day that makes me think people should only be allowed to die in the dead of winter. There's no dead of summer, no dead of spring or fall. I wish my mother had taken those six months that the doctors had given her, then think how weird that sounds. That the doctors "gave" her six months, like life—time—is theirs to take or give.

Biking to work I feel like I've woken up with the same kind of clarity I feel in the air today—like there's a low pollen count in my head. Friends don't cheat on each other. Friends don't break up. If I'm friends with James—and nothing more—then things can't go to shit. Friends are clear, simple. I could use a little bit of that in my life these days. I feel like I'm moving from denial—he can't possibly have a girlfriend!—to acceptance—we're just friends—and that seems like good progress to have made overnight. No doubt I'll make my end-of-summer grieving deadline after all.

Morrisville is hopping, between six busloads from some big Jersey historical society and tons of strays attracted by the prospect of a day mostly spent outdoors. The village has pulled out all stops in anticipation of the big day. The metalsmiths are working outside, banging hot iron into the shape of nails. We're gearing up to churn butter all day on the front porch and they're making ice cream over by the parsonage. James and some of the other young men have been recruited to take shifts pitching hay near a cow borrowed from the local zoo for the day. The idea is really that everywhere you look, there's someone involved in some colonial pursuit.

In addition to the three robberies of the general store, we've been told there's going to be a brawl outside the tavern, a small fire in the parsonage, and a rabble-rouser squawking in the main square about unfair taxation and the responsibilities of the citizenry to rise up. It's the first time that I feel something resembling genuine excitement on the job. There's a buzz in the air, a crackling sense of anticipation. Liza's so pumped up and giddy and restless, it's as if she's on drugs. She rubs her hands together excitedly and says, "I'm gonna have me some colonial fun today, you just watch."

She and I run a couple of tours together. We've realized it's more fun that way. In one of the upstairs bedrooms I'll lie down on the bed and she'll ask me if it's comfortable and I'll say, "Nay, not terribly." Then she'll tug on the ropes that support the mattress (such as it is) and she'll ask me if it's better, and I'll say, "Indeed, it is." I'll say, "You sleep tight, too!" and people's eyes will light with understanding. They've witnessed—in the tugging of these ropes—the origin of the phrase "sleep tight."

After we finish with a big group, I duck across the street into the restaurant to use the restroom. When I come back, I hear the manager of the general store shout, "Help!" Surprise, surprise, he's been robbed. A crowd of colonists and visitors has gathered and Mr. Martin's making his usual scene. Liza spies me in the crowd and points her finger at me and smiles and I think to myself, Oh. Shit.

"You!" she shouts.

Some members of the crowd turn and watch my approach.

"YOU!" she shouts again, gaining the attention of more visitors. "Where have you been?"

This is new. Completely off-script.

"Why," I say, "in the outhouse, of course!"

"Prove it!"

Loretta lives for this shit. "Liza!" she says. "How *could* you! Accusing your own sister!"

Liza reaches into her apron pocket and pulls out some unidentifiable old coins. "Then how do you explain these! I found them under her pillow!"

"Ladies! Ladies!" That's the sheriff, Mr. Hamner, a part-timer who thinks that Early American–speak is the same as putting on a Southern accent. "Calm yourselves. If y'all will come quietly with me, we'll get this sorted out down at the jail!"

Mr. Hamner walks up to me looking kind of scared and skeptical. We've never really improvised quite this much before. "Miss, if you'll kindly present your hands."

I decide I should resist arrest, beat Liza at her own game. "You wench!" I yell. I lunge toward her. "You greedy little wench! You think I don't know what you're up to! You and Billy!"

The sheriff manages to grab hold of me, and Loretta starts to cry. "Sheriff, please! Have mercy on my daughters!"

"Sorry, ma'am, but we're going to have to ask you to come down to the jailhouse, as well. Until this is sorted out." As he carts me off in the direction of the jailhouse, his deputy encourages the crowd to disperse. Just then Parson Joe comes out of the parsonage and screams, "Fire! Fire!"

I get thrown into a jail cell and stay put for a while. A couple of visitors come in to make sure I'm really in jail, that it wasn't some sort of act, and a few kids ask me whether I'm really a robber. Liza comes by to visit, presumably to gloat. I decide I'll make a scene since there are, at that moment, two families checking out the jailhouse.

"You wench!" I growl, clutching at the bars holding me in. "Get her out of here! Out! My own *sister* going about telling lies about me!" I pace around agitatedly and pull on the bars screaming, "Let me out! Let me out!" My outburst is driving the parentals—bemused but disinclined to engage—away but some kids hang around, intrigued.

I bend down to the ear level of a ten-year-old. "Hey, kid," I say. "See those keys over there?" I point at the big ring of keys hanging on the wall behind him and his gaze follows mine.

From outside a woman calls, "Clayton, come on!"

I say, "Help a girl out, will ya? I swear I'm innocent."

He runs out the door, screaming, "Mommy!"

James eventually stops in to see me. "Coming to bail me out?" I ask.

He takes the keys down off the wall and tries to figure out which one will open the cell door.

"To my own shock and dismay," he says, "the general store was just robbed again and they nabbed the guy, some trouble-maker up from Texas who has been wreaking havoc in these parts." There are some visitors milling about, thus the spiel. "The sheriff sent me ahead to let you out so the cell's free and clear for this bandito."

"And what of my sister?" I ask. "Will they arrest her for falsely accusing me?"

He lets me out and some kids run into the jail cell excitedly. "You'll have to talk to the sheriff about that."

We step out into the afternoon, the village still abuzz. "You and Liza plan that little routine?"

"Nope." Friends, I remind myself, when I catch myself looking at his butt for a second. Just friends.

"Not bad," he says. "And good day to you, ladies." He bows his hat at two young mothers and they smile. "I thought it was an elaborate ruse to get you out of churning butter all day."

"Hadn't even thought of that."

"She had a good time with the drunken brawl scene, too."

"What'd she do?"

"She said she was pregnant with the tavern owner's bastard child."

"Ohmigod, really?" Again, I feel like the naïve little girl to Liza's sexy sophisticate. Pretending she's pregnant!

"Yeah. Rudolph is having a chat with her right now. I think the suggestion of sex is a no-no."

The topic of sex seems to put a charge in the air. James shakes his head as if to shake it off. "So I want to ask you some-thing."

"Ask away," I say.

"I wanted to know . . ." He fidgets with his suspenders. "Would you want to come down to Seaside Heights on Saturday? We could go to the beach, maybe see if you can surf, then go to the pier, hit the rides and stuff at night."

I indulge a thought that the tides must be turning. He wouldn't ask me to spend a whole day with him if he wasn't going to dump her for me.

Things obviously aren't great between them or he wouldn't be carving me things out of wood and coming to my house at odd hours. Then I remind myself again that friends is good. Friends is simple. I don't want to be the kind of girl whose boyfriend goes from one girl to the next without batting an eye. If he dumps her for me, who's to say he won't dump me for someone else?

"That'd be fun," I say. Friends do things like go to the beach together, and go to amusement parks. "I'll ask my father."

I add, "But I know what he's gonna say."

"What's he gonna say?"

Dread stabs my heart. "He's gonna want to meet you."

"Well, we can do that, can't we?"

"I feel dumb." My father will say something idiotic, probably grill James about where he's going to college, what he's going to major in. He'll make it feel like a date when it's not.

"Don't feel dumb. I wouldn't let my daughter go off in a car with me, either."

I look at him funny.

"I mean, not without having met me and seen what an upstanding kind of guy I am, you know. And Liza's coming, too. He knows her, right?"

Of course he'd ask Liza—he has a girlfriend, this isn't a date, he's involved in a situation and it's complicated, whatever that means—but I feel my heart drop and think, Friends, shmends. Who am I kidding? "Yeah," I say. "Then it won't be a problem."

"Hey," I say, when he starts to walk off. "What are you going to major in anyway?" I feel foolish thinking my father will probably ask him that when I've never thought to.

"What else?" He walks off.

"What?" I call after him. "I don't know! Carpentry?" I know it's a ridiculous guess; they don't teach carpentry at Princeton.

"You idiot." He shakes his head and calls back over his shoulder. "History!"

After work, Liza takes me down to Midland Beach, where the parking lot is empty. "Okay." She puts the car in park and leaves it running for me. "You're up."

I climb out of my side and get in the driver's seat and I want, right then, to grill her about James, to see what she knows, to find out what's so complicated. But at the same time I don't want to know. Or at least I don't want to hear it from Liza. He has a girlfriend. We're going to Seaside as friends, just the three of us. That's all I need to know.

"Okay." I take a deep breath, put my hands on the wheel. "Where to?"

"Let's go up and down the aisles and see how that goes."

I put the car in drive and it rolls and then I press on the gas and we're off. My heart tightens in my chest and I get an instant headache. I hit the brake.

"Take it easy, babe." Liza turns the radio on low. "Look around you."

I look around. There are no people. Hardly any other cars—and all of them are parked, not moving. There's nothing to be afraid of. I tap the gas again and then we're off again. I slow down to make a left turn at the end of the lot and Liza compliments its smoothness.

"How do you feel?" she says.

"Good." I nod. "Pretty good."

I go up and down four parking lanes—there are maybe three cars in the lot in total—and then Liza says to do it again, so I do. The clamp on my heart seems to ease and I'm able to take a deep breath.

"You seem fine!" she says, when I come to a gentle stop and put the car in park after the second round. "I don't see what the problem is."

"Yeah," I say. "But it's a parking lot."

"All right." She gets out of the car, so I do, too. "That was your first lesson," she says as we pass behind the car. "Let the master contemplate the apprentice's next lesson."

"You're not going to let this go to your head, are you?" We get back into the car.

"But of course!" She starts the engine, puts the car in drive.

"How'd you get to be like this?"

"Like what?' Liza snorts and turns the radio off. She pulls out of the lot.

"I don't know. Everything seems easy for you."

"First of all, you're weird. People don't go around asking people how they got to be like how they are. Just FYI. But now that you asked, you freak, I think it's because I spent so many years trying so hard at one thing. How'd you get to be like *this?*"

"Like what?"

She studies me for a second and says, "Good question."

At home I've almost run out of room for the beach party on my wall. There's a couple holding hands in between the Liza type and the Mary type and her cat. There are two guys talking and a few girls giggling, and I know I should put the surfer back in but I don't. Wanting now to add even more—like a car and maybe a keg—I look around the room but none of the walls here are big enough. So I decide that I'll move it to the basement. The room is only semifinished—no one ever goes down there—and one whole wall is cement painted white. It'll be perfect.

"Whatcha doing down there?" my father calls down the stairs at one point after dinner (Wendy's).

I've just taped the scene I have so far onto the wall.

"I'll show you when it's done," I say. "It's sort of an art project."

"Oh." He sounds surprised. "Okay then."

"Actually, Dad?" I move to the bottom of the staircase and look up. "Can I go to Seaside on Saturday? James from work is driving."

"Is this like a date?"

"No." I'm about to choke on my words but I spit them out anyway. "Liza's going. Besides, James has a girlfriend."

My father takes off his reading glasses like this is a twist he wasn't exactly expecting, either, like he's as surprised as I was when I heard. Like he's wondering, But how could that be? "Is his girlfriend going, too?"

"No," I say. "I don't think so."

"No? Or no, you don't think so?"

"No."

"I'm not sure I like the sound of this guy."

"We're all just friends."

"Fine," he says. "But I want to meet this fellow."

"Fine," I say. "You'll like him. He's going to Princeton."

I start to move away and wait for the sound of the basement door clicking shut, then decide to add a bonfire to the scene. I've concentrated mostly on people up to this point—except for the surfboard, which I ripped up, and which any idiot could probably do. I find the prospect of cutting an image of flames out of paper exciting. Maybe Liza's right. Maybe I am a freak. I'm not even sure I care.

chapter 13

On Friday night, before hitting another party at Midland, I pack a bag for the next day at Seaside, bemoaning the fact that I don't have a cooler bathing suit to bring and didn't think to go shopping. I lay out what I'll wear over my suit in the morning. James said we can all shower and change at his uncle's place after we go to the beach and before we hit the rides and boardwalk games. It's a lot of pressure, like three dates in one. Except that none of them are dates at all, I keep reminding myself. Liza's coming, too. Still, I pack a black silky tank top and jeans for the evening portion and a necklace—a simple silver circle on a thin black leather strand—that sort of calls attention to my chest. I have a designer rip-off perfume in a spray can and I toss that in, too.

Then, after dinner (back to KFC; we've run out of new options and have started to repeat), I use the invitation from Mary to get out of the house, though I've no intention of going to the party. She texts me a few times—"R U coming?"—and I finally write back, "No. Sorry. Can't." I feel sort of bad about it but I just can't bring myself to go to a party where Lauren Janey and Brandon will be when I can hang out with Liza and knock back a few beers. I don't know if James is going to come by but I think that's a good thing: it's probably time for me to start checking out some of the other boys there.

I tell my father I'm walking over to Mary's—the invitation on the kitchen table is as bulletproof as an alibi can get—and I've told Liza to pick me up a block away. My mother never would've fallen for it but my father trusts me in a way I think only fathers trust daughters. My mother was endlessly suspicious of me, like I might be a spy or some imposter, and she had good reason. People my age are so full of deceit and secrets, so good at looking you in the eyes and saying "I'm not lying!" that they should restaff the CIA and FBI with us. My mom was our house's Central Intelligence and now that she's gone it's like I'm first in command. My dad just doesn't know it.

When I turn the corner, Liza gets out of her car and tosses me the keys. "You're up, freak."

"What do you mean?"

"It's only a couple of miles," she says. "We'll go slow."

I just stand there, stunned by the suggestion.

"Come on." She opens the passenger side door. "No time like the present."

"Okay." I climb into the driver's seat.

I can feel my chest tense up, like there's a column of steel inside my rib cage. My heart is beating fast against it and I have to take a few calming breaths. I feel like an idiot that this happens to me, that I panic like this in the face of something so simple, so common. Something practically every idiot on the planet can do.

Like she's reading my mind, Liza says, "It's easy. You know that."

With each block that goes by I start to feel more at ease; my grip relaxes on the wheel. Liza fusses with the radio and puts music on and then I really relax. I'm alert, on guard, of course. But I realize it's only driving. That it's not a matter of life and death any more than crossing a street or riding a bike and I do those things all the time. When we arrive at Midland Beach successfully, Liza points to the far end of the parking lot and I go there and turn the car around, so we're facing the party as it starts to take shape. Again, there are a few cars near the board-walk, a few people huddled around a keg. On the beach, I can just make out the shape of the lifeguard chair, tipped over, and think maybe I'll add one to my scene.

"So." Liza pulls a bag of beers from the backseat; she hands me one and I quickly snap it open. I confess I've been looking forward to it all day. "James putting it to you yet?"

She's caught me midswig and I nearly spit out my beer. I can feel bubbles come up and tease my nose's innards, like they might seek escape that way if I don't spit them out. I swallow hard and they go away. "What?" I finally say.

"James," she says. "Is he, you know, putting it to you?"

"Yeah," I say, "I heard you. 'Putting it to you?' What the hell is that?"

"It's an expression."

"Okay." I take another sip. "Well, he's not. Okay. I don't do that." I wish I could pull the words back into my mouth.

She raises her eyebrows at me.

"I mean, it's not that . . . well, I just mean that I haven't."

Now it's Liza's chance to nearly spit her drink out. "You're a *virgin?*"

"Yeah, so what," I say.

"No, man," she says. "That's cool. Just don't go giving it up for James."

"Why not?"

"Well, I take it he finally told you about Nora."

Hearing her name opens up the wound anew. He has a girlfriend. Her name is Nora. "Yeah."

"That's why I was pissed at him last week or whenever. I knew about her and knew the crappy shit your ex did and I didn't want you to be fucked over again and I also didn't want to be put in a weird position again. I made him promise he'd tell you so I didn't have to."

She's talking so fast I can't get a word in, not that I even know what I'd say.

"Anyway, so now you know why I told you not to get involved, I mean, she is one screwed-up chick and he totally lets himself get sucked into it. If somebody I was dating threatened to kill himself if I dumped him, I think I'd do the job for him. I mean, get real. 'I can't live without you?' That's pathetic."

I'm having a hard time comprehending what I'm hearing. This is why it's complicated. This is what James didn't mention.

"I'm not sure if she's a cutter or a sniffer or if she's a pill popper who's just incredibly hypermanipulative but—"

I cut in, "Has she ever actually *done* anything? Like to hurt herself?" I've never known anyone who has committed suicide or even tried to. There was a boy from my high school—when I was a freshman—but I didn't know him. Even that freaked me out to no end. He'd left the car running in the garage of his house and his mother found him. She tried to join him but then the mailman came and smelled the carbon monoxide. She lived; he didn't. That's one of the things I figure is worse than losing your mother. Losing your child.

"Not that I'm aware of," Liza says. "But James just can't seem to cut her loose. I mean, he's cool and stuff, don't get me wrong. And it seems pretty obvious he's into you and wants to be with you. But, I don't now. It's a pretty fucked-up situation. If I were you, I'd steer clear."

I don't like having this conversation. I don't want Liza giving me advice about James. I don't want to know things about him, about *her*, that I'm not supposed to know. "We're just friends," I say.

"Right." She looks at me skeptically.

"What? *You* guys are friends."

"Yeah, but I don't want to jump his bones and he doesn't want to jump mine."

"It's not like that with us." It feels like a lie. "Anyway, you'll see tomorrow. At Seaside."

"Yeah. It'll be fun! We're all pals. No tension whatsoever."

Someone knocks on her window. Five times, in the "shave 'n' a haircut, two bits" rhythm. "Yo, Liza," he says. I recognize him from the last party; he was hanging out with Danny Mose. She rolls the window down an inch and says, "That's original, Doyle."

I notice her friend has a friend with him but I can't see his face. Doyle bends down to look in at me and he says, "You guys coming to hang out?"

His friend bends down and it's Danny Mose. I take an enormous swig of beer.

"Yeah," Liza says. "Hop in. We'll drive you over."

The party's maybe one hundred yards away but the guys seem eternally grateful for the lift. "I'm Johnny," says the one she called Doyle. "And this here's Moses."

"Betsy and I know each other," he says. "Hey, Betsy."

It's established that Liza's never met Danny and that he and Doyle work together. Doyle's a lifeguard, too.

"Why do they call you Moses?" Liza says.

"Last name," he says.

"Which is . . . ?"

"Mose," he says. It's pronounced like "mo's" and I guess it's odd when you hear it for the first time.

When we get out of the car, I can't get over how hot he is. He's too-hot-for-me hot. And something about guys who are "hot" or even using the word "hot" makes me feel kind of strange and weird. People talk about "hot sex" and stuff but I can't entirely imagine how it ever happens or how it could ever possibly involve me.

We're near a keg and the boys immediately go for drinks.

"Hey," I say to Liza. "Do you know if James is coming by tonight?"

"Wouldn't know," she says, handing me a beer can. Liza thinks kegs are for losers. "Why?"

I shrug and say, "No reason," but even I'm not convinced.

Danny and I are drinking a beer together and he seems really into me. I can't imagine I'm his type at all, he's so good looking, but I like the idea that I might be. Boys like Danny Mose rule the school and there's something about just being with him that feels different. The air around him seems charged with confidence and it's catching.

"So what's your deal?" he says.

I see James's car pull up to the gathering and he and the girl—Nora—get out of it. She looks pale and frail as she pulls on a cardigan and her hair is wild and dark. I note that it's not especially cold out at all.

"My deal?" I honestly don't know how to answer.

"Yeah." I swear he checks out my chest. I'm wearing a tank top and jeans and I'm not cold. "I mean, like, you have a boyfriend?"

"No." I can't believe he's asking me this. This is Danny Mose!

"Girlfriend?"

"No," I say. "Don't be stupid."

"Never know these days." He blatantly looks at my breasts then says, "I think you're hot."

I nearly choke on my own saliva. "You do?"

"Big time," he says. And in that moment I don't care that it's cheesy or whatever to tell people that. 'Cause no one's ever told me before. Cute, sure. Pretty, maybe. Beautiful, only Alex Elks and my mother. Hot? Never. At least never before. "So," he says, "some of us are gonna check out this party over in Belmar." It's a few towns away. "You want to come?"

"Maybe," I say. "I mean, I don't know." I bite my lip to buy some time because he's looking at me so intensely.

"Hey kids," comes a voice from behind me.

I turn and see that it's James; Nora is a few feet behind him, talking to a group of girls. The sight of her—the reality that she's here with James, that he brought her here to a place he knew I'd be—sets in and I feel my jaw clench. This is no better than going to Mary's. Because he's never going to break up with her. We can't be just friends. I've been deluding myself. James says to me, "Who's your friend?"

I wonder if he and Nora have sex, whether he's ever left me and gone right to her to be with her that way. I wonder where they do it, how often, and whether he ever thinks about me during it. I wonder if he's ever gone home in his Morrisville gear, whether she's ever undressed colonial James, suspenders and all, and played the part of the pastor's daughter or let out a rebel yell.

"This is Danny," I say.

James holds out his hand to Danny, who just stares at the hand for a second, then realizes he's supposed to shake it. "Hey, what's up, man?" he finally says.

"This is James," I say. "We work together."

"We do more than work together, Betsy." There's this weird edge to his voice; we all hear it. He sounds cocky, arrogant, and it makes me want to smack him.

Danny's interest in me is cooling by the second. He says, "I need a beer," and shakes his cup; a tiny bit of liquid flops around. "Let me know what you want to do, okay?"

"Okay." I'm sorry to see him go, annoyed that James drove him away, shocked that Danny Mose invited me to a party, and scared and desperate to go.

"Aren't you going to thank me?" James says when Danny's gone.

"What for?" I take a sip of warm beer.

"I was saving you from that guy." I like to think he likes defending my honor but I'm also feeling like who the hell is he to scare guys off of me when he has a girlfriend?

"Who says I needed to be saved?" The feisty me always seems to control the vocal cords these days. I'm getting tired of feeling like Jekyll and Hyde and am starting to wonder which one of me is the monster—the me who doesn't give a shit about dead cats or the me who wants to go off with Danny Mose and do things I've never done just to show James what he's missing.

"Oh, come on," he says.

"I know him from school. He's nice."

"Nice?" He lets out a "Ha!"

"Yeah." I toss my beer at a garbage can and miss.

"That guy had one thing on his mind and one thing only."

"Yeah, and what's that?'

"Getting in your pants."

"I can't believe you just said that." I pick up my can and put it in the garbage. "I need a beer."

"Yeah?" James says, kind of fake-cheesy. "You feeling wild tonight, party girl?"

"Oh, give me a break. It's just a couple of beers."

"Whatever. But I'm picking Liza up at nine forty-five and getting you at ten."

I look over toward his girlfriend. "Why don't you bring Nora," I say.

He looks at me seriously. "What are you trying to prove, Betsy?"

I want to tell him that I could threaten to hurt myself, too, if that's what it takes. That I've got as many reasons to kill myself as she does, when you think about it. But I know I won't say it. I know a part of me knows it isn't true, that I'd never do it. No matter how bad things got.

"I don't know what you're talking about," I say, but I do. I head toward the keg, looking around for Danny, but he's already gone.

chapter 14

James rings the doorbell at 10:00 A.M. and I'm in the living room, pretending to read Harry Potter. I'm feeling dry in the mouth and pulsing in the head but I put on a brave, who-me-hungover? face when I open the door. "Hey." I close my book and put it down on a small table in the foyer.

"Hey." He's wearing long, wet cement-colored shorts and a T-shirt with some surfing logo on it. He whips off his sunglasses when my father comes to the foyer.

"You must be James," my father says.

"Yes, Mr. Irving. Nice to meet you."

They shake hands.

"Betsy tells me you're going to Princeton in the fall."

"Yes, sir." He actually says "sir"! It's all too cute.

"What will you be studying there? Do you know?"

"I'm thinking history," James says, and I say, "My dad's a history professor," so my dad knows I haven't been coaching James.

"Really?" James sounds surprised, impressed.

"One of my former colleagues is at Princeton now. Max Lowenberg. Keep an eye out for him when you're selecting your courses."

James says, "I most certainly will."

We all three stand there, not sure what to do next. I think it's funny that James and Liza and I are sort of forgetting how to talk like normal teenagers.

"We shouldn't keep Liza waiting in the car," I say to the room.

"Well, drive safe," my father says—as if anyone has ever really set out somewhere thinking they're driving unsafely. I wonder in a flash whether the words "drive safe" have a weird resonance for James, whether he catches on them the way I've started to catch on the words "my parents."

"Home by eleven," my father says. "And have fun. And nice to meet you, James."

"You, too," James says.

My father disappears down the hall and then I grab my bag and we leave. At the car, I see it's empty. "I thought you were getting Liza first."

We get in.

"She called me this morning." James starts the car and pulls away real quick, like he's excited that's over with. "She said she wasn't feeling so hot."

"She's not *coming*?"

"Nope." He looks over at me. "Are you okay with that?"

"Yeah," I say. "I guess."

We ride in silence for a minute and it's an awkward one. I don't know how you can tell the difference between a comfortable one and an awkward one but I just can. I also suspect that Liza—*yeah, we're all just pals*—never planned on coming at all.

"So, tell me something," James says, once we've hit the highway. "What is it about guys like that?"

"Guys like who?"

"Don't play dumb, Betsy. It doesn't suit you."

I think of Danny Mose and his movie star hair and white, white teeth. "He's cute."

James looks at me with a grimace. *"Cute?"*

"Cute. Hot. Whatever."

"You don't want to be with a guy like that, trust me." He shifts his butt around on the car seat as he changes lanes again. I feel my stomach react as if it were a roller coaster.

I want to say, *"You're* what I want, you idiot." I say, "You have no idea what I want." All feisty, no honesty. All Jekyll, no Hyde.

He's not even looking at me but it feels like he's staring into my soul when he says, "I think maybe I do."

We stop at a surf shop and rent me a long board and wet suit and I start practicing trying to stand on it on dry ground. Over and over, I lie down on the board and then grip it and push up to try to plant my feet and stand. My balance is pretty good— "You're a natural," James says—but like he warned, my arms start to feel like jellyfish.

"I think you're ready to try it out for real," James says, when we've been at this for almost an hour. I'm coated in sunscreen and wearing a sturdy one-piece that won't fall down no matter what the ocean pulls. James says it's time to slip into wet suits so we walk off the sand, rinse off, and get suited up. It's a weird feeling, a second skin, like masquerading as a seal.

The water's refreshing, cool on my feet. We paddle out together, James leading the way, and I'm afraid my arms are going to fall off, they're so tired. Then I think of that surfer girl in Hawaii, the one whose arm got bit off by a shark, and I paddle faster and faster, trying to keep my arms out of the water as much as possible, which proves impossible. James looks so cute and boyish in his surf gear. The more time I spend with him the more he seems in my mind's eye like a dress-up boyfriend. His paper doll clothes involve everything from surf gear to colonial carpenter clothes. It scares me to think what he'd look like stripped bare.

We lie on our boards, bobbing and waiting, and I remind myself he's not my boyfriend. I see a jellyfish in the water—big, pulsing, and red—and shift away. I notice its outline, barely a hint of an edge to define it, and realize I've started to see everything this way, in its most basic form. Maybe it'd help if I saw me and James that way, too. Two figures—boy and girl—close, as close as you can be, but not touching. Never ever touching.

"There's something people don't realize about surfing," James says.

"What?"

"It's boring," he says. "The waiting, I mean. Though it's not like this on better beaches. Like in Hawaii. When there's a good set."

"Have you been there?"

"No," he says. "But I want to go. My parents went there for their honeymoon."

I nod, and we wait and wait. I'm still looking out for the jellyfish, making sure it doesn't pulse back my way.

"This is a secondhand story," James finally says. "Is that okay?"

He crosses his arms and it seems funny to me—that we're out here just chatting, in the ocean. I really would just talk to him anywhere—anytime—I like the feeling of being with him so much, and for a second I envision us traveling through space and time, talking our hearts out in Las Vegas—by the roulette wheels—and in California—on some gold rush dig—and in Salem, while a witch is tried in the town square. I try to imagine us in these waters during the American Revolution—because they were *here,* these same waters—and then in Hawaii, in the water there, so wrapped up in our conversation that we don't even see the wave coming. It's huge and perfectly curled, and it carries us both on to shore, where we lie on the beach and sip mai tais and talk some more.

"I think secondhand is fine," I say. I tuck my feet up so that they're touching the underside of the board.

"My parents were on their honeymoon," he begins. "And they went on a whale-watching tour. And it was early in the season, so they weren't having much luck. They saw a bunch of dolphins and sea turtles but no joy with the whales. So my father starts complaining that he wants his forty dollars back, and my mother's mortified. So right then someone yells out, 'There's one,' and my father turns around and loses his balance and falls off the boat, and meanwhile my mother is watching him but also watching this whale leaping out of the water and my poor father resurfaces right as the whale disappears back into the water."

"He never saw it?" We both bob sort of high on a swell but still nothing's breaking.

"Nope." James sticks his hands in the water and splashes them around a bit. "So they help him back up on the boat and he takes out his wallet and it's soaking wet and he hands the guide forty bucks. So the guide says, 'What's this for?' and my father says, 'They forgot to charge me the surcharge for assholes.' "

"Ohmigod, you just reminded me of something. A story. I haven't thought about it in years, I don't think."

"What is it?"

I take a breath or two as the details start to come back, as a part of my brain springs to life, as a memory crosses some synapses. "My mother took me and Ben into New York, to the Museum of Natural History, when we were little."

I know what I wore that day. We have pictures. It was a matching shorts-and-top set. Turquoise with white trim. The shorts were shorter than any I'd ever wear now. Before I had any kind of meat on me whatsoever.

"And we were excited to see dinosaurs—that was mostly Ben; he was in his dinosaur phase—and the whale. She'd been hyping the whale. But then when we got there, we found out that the whale display was closed down. There was some private party going on in there that night and they were setting up, so my mother asked if the guard could just let us in, and he insisted there could be no exceptions . . . and everyone's children are disappointed and blah blah blah. So my mother went down to this other area, where the caterers were bringing stuff in and got this older man's attention and started talking to him the way she always did with strangers and sure enough, the guy brings us in with him, so we're all three standing there looking up at this whale, and I can't get over how big it is and Ben's even more excited than he was about the dinosaurs, and then up on this terrace around the room, the security guard who wouldn't let us in appears. And he looks at us, and I look at my mom, and she smiles down at me, then she turns and waves at the security guard, and then she says, 'We should go.' "

"That's another good one. But we should actually go, too." He points out at the sea and I see what he's talking about. "You see it?"

"I see it, yeah."

"Okay, do what I do."

I follow his lead and paddle with one arm so that my board turns and points toward the shore. "Okay, start paddling," he says. With the wave coming closer—its white top dancing toward me, its roar getting louder—I can't hear James anymore, but I know what I'm supposed to do. I've watched surfers do it a hundred times or more, but the wave sneaks up on me and it catches the backside of the board and I feel myself flipping, teetering, and there's no way I can stand and then I'm underwater and I'm thinking, Please, God. Not my neck. Please don't break my neck. There's water swirling around me and I'm holding my breath but I don't know how long it'll last, and then the roar ceases and I surface and James is right there. "Are you okay?" He sounds panicky.

I wipe water from my eyes and plant my feet on the ocean floor. I say, "Yeah. I think so." But I feel kind of off. "I need to sit down," I say. Only then do I think of my board—but James has somehow reeled it in and pushes it ahead of us toward the shore.

"You're fine," he says. "Come on." And as we're struggling against the weight of water to walk onto dry sand, he puts his arm around me and laughs into my ear, "Wipeout!"

I smile but I'm shaken.

*   *   *

On the beach, I lie back on a towel and close my eyes.

"You sure you're okay?" James says.

"Yeah." I cough and taste saltwater. "I thought I was gonna break my neck, though. I think I did a full backflip. But I'm okay."

"You poor thing," James says. "Now you'll never want to try again."

"No," I say. "I will."

"You will?"

"Yeah," I say. "I think so. But definitely here and not Hawaii." I picture myself skimming the surface of a massive glassy tower of Hawaiian water and then being swallowed up by a rumbling, crashing curl of white while people on the beach gasp. "Just give me a couple minutes," I say, grateful that I live in New Jersey.

I lie back and feel the fading warmth of the afternoon sun on my face; it's tingly—warm and cool at the same time. James takes my hand and squeezes it and I breath hard and almost laugh, thinking how ridiculous I must've looked from the shore, this tiny body being tossed aside by the ocean, and I feel, somehow, that I've cheated death.

James says, "Man, did you get your ass kicked," and I laugh and he laughs and I think that life is good, even when it's bad.

I sit up and say, "Let's try again," and so we do.

We try and try and I don't get my ass kicked again but I don't catch any waves, either, and then finally James says, "We should get your gear back," and I feel like I've let him down. Or maybe it's just myself I've disappointed.

chapter 15

James's uncle's house is a small bungalow about ten houses down from the beach and set back from the road more than other houses, like a secret. James leads me around to the back of the house where we rinse off the sand from our feet with a hose before returning to the front porch, which is carpeted in Astroturf. He introduces me to his uncle, his uncle's new wife, and her two kids—girls about eight years old, who are busy playing cat's cradle on the floor.

"Okay if we hit the shower?" James says.

"Sure thing," his Uncle Joe says. "Just not together."

James actually blushes. "It wouldn't feel like a complete visit if you didn't humiliate me once," James says. He turns to me and says, "I guess we can go home now."

"Oh," his uncle says, "you're not children. Do whatever you want. Hell, there's even beers in the fridge."

"Jo-oe," his wife scolds in a singsong, but she's half smiling.

"Come on, Bets," James says and he turns to leave the

porch. He's never dropped the "y" before and it makes me happy.

"It's nice to meet you," I say. The adults just nod.

Out back James tosses his stuff down on the patio and says, "You want to hop in? I'll grab us some towels inside."

I'm confused and I look it.

"The shower's here." James leads me over to a wooden shower stall attached to the side of the house.

"Oh!" I say. "Okay." I wish he'd grab us some beers, too, though I'm not even sure why. Maybe just because he can. I wonder if this is how it starts, the slow decline into alcoholism, whether it starts with the slight craving for a beer over a Coke or glass of water or iced tea. Whether before I know it I'll be going off to college and doing keg stands and turning up on Montel Williams to discuss why I'm suing the makers of some *Girls Gone Wild* video in which I'm dancing on bars and yanking off my bikini top.

James goes into the house through a back door and I quickly strip off my shorts and T-shirt and hang them over the shower door. The water comes out warm, having been sunned in the pipes, then turns quickly cold and I have to step back against the wooden slats while it gets hot again. I step under and get everything wet, then start to strip off my suit. I'm determined to shower as fast as I can because I'd swear people can see in through the spaces between the wood panels of the door. But then, as I'm lathering up my hair with Suave in some berry scent, I look up and see nothing but shower mist and blue skies and it's so wonderful I want to stay there forever. A breeze blows up from under the shower doors and I make the water hotter and wish we had a shower like this at our house—or at

Morrisville. I'd take showers and pretend I'd never even imagined such a thing as indoor plumbing all day for tour groups without a care.

"Here you go." James's voice comes from outside the stall and a towel appears over the door. I take it and secure it there, and say thanks. I can see a slice of red between the slats and realize James is sitting on the back patio. I hurry up and condition and soap up my body so that I can get out. Only when I turn off the water and dry myself off do I realize I left my change of clothes out on the patio.

"James?"

"Yo," he says. "What's up?"

"Where can I get dressed?"

"I'll show you. You can go right up the back stairs into a spare room."

"Okay," I say. Then I imagine how I look right then and use my towel to mess my hair up and pull some stray bangs down onto my forehead. I wrap the towel around me and hold on tight, then grab my wet bathing suit, something you never want to leave lying around for a guy to see, not with those awful-looking beige liner bits. Still, there's no way around the fact that I'm practically naked. I mean, I'm technically showing less skin than when wearing my suit, but there's something more intimate about this—especially when you consider that James is used to seeing me in burlap skirts and bonnets and two layers of shifts. If this towel were to drop or get sucked up by a random tornado, I'd be naked. James seems to sense it, too. When I step out onto the patio, he jumps up, opens the door to the house, and points straight up the back stairs. "First door on the right," he says, averting his gaze fairly unsuccessfully.

I grab my bag, slip in under his arm, and scurry up the stairs, hoping I don't look like too much of an idiot. Upstairs, in what seems to me to be a pretty typical beach house spare room—big shell on the dresser, framed starfish on the wall—I turn on my phone and see I've missed three calls from Mary, who hasn't left a message. Which can only mean one thing. She's mad. I scroll to her number and send the call through and hold the phone to my ear. Spying the oversize seashell again, I hang up the phone and turn it off. Holding my towel secure with one hand, I pick up the shell and hold it up to my ear. I swear I hear the ocean, but know it's a trick of physics. I wish there was a shell I could listen to for my mother's voice. She could tell me things, like how to explain to Mary why I couldn't go to her party, or whether I'm supposed to be here with James at all, or what it really feels like to know that you're going to die.

In the car James and I look clean and refreshed and slightly sunned. The sky over the bay is pink like a baby shower and I feel like I've never quite seen that particular shade before. Everything feels so new lately and I wonder how much is James, how much is my mom, and how much is me.

"Shit," he says, feeling the back pocket of his jeans. "Left my wallet inside. Be right back."

His phone is on the front seat and it rings once, then stops. I flip it open and see he has a text message. It says, "Where R U?" It's from Nora.

I snap the phone shut when I see James coming out of the bungalow.

"Your phone beeped," I say, when he gets back in. He opens it, reads, closes it, and we drive in silence.

"You okay?" he says.

"Yeah," I say. "Fine."

"You're not still freaked out about your wipeout, are you?" I wish he knew what was really bothering me—the feeling that I shouldn't be here with him when he's not really free, when we're not really friends—but I don't want to tell him.

"No." I watch out the window as beach bungalows make way for ice-cream parlors and bakeries and pizzerias and minigolf courses and arcades. "I'm fine."

"You look amazing."

"Thanks," I say. "But you really shouldn't say stuff like that."

"I didn't know there were rules."

I just look out the window.

"Listen," James says. "I know it's sort of weird, but can we pretend it's not? Can you believe me when I say I'm really trying to do the right thing and that if you knew the whole story, you'd understand?"

"I feel like we're doing something wrong," I say.

"But we're not."

"But she wouldn't see it that way."

"But she's not here."

"Well, maybe you should tell me the whole story then."

"I'm sorry, Betsy. But I can't. I promised someone I wouldn't."

We park in the shadow of a water park with a slide so high it makes my stomach flip. I imagine climbing up the hill to the top and plugging my nose and letting my body go and then bumping up against the grainy turquoise siding, maybe hitting my head on the way and getting a wedgie to boot and ending up in the receiving pool unconscious or dead.

The air is full of salt and grease and sausages and something sweet, as we walk up onto the boardwalk. There are game stands and arcades stretching in both directions and a pier to our left boasts rides, their every inch covered in light. Different top forty music blasts from each stand; we walk through Blink 182 and Black Eyed Peas and Queens of the Stone Age. I wonder whether James will try to win me something, like a stuffed Shrek or a Tasmanian Devil or a packet of cigarettes or a TV.

We start out small, going on the merry-go-round. We pick horses side by side, and he has to help me up on mine—a white horse with gold reins and an elaborate saddle of pink jewels—since it stopped in an up position. His hands on my waist make me think of our silhouettes moving closer together—of black arms reaching out to touch my black waistline. Our horses—his is black without a saddle—travel up and down on their poles so that he's always on his way up when I'm on my way down, and vice versa. We don't talk much; the music—some old-time instrument—is too loud, and James tries to grab onto a ring dangling from the top of the ride each time we pass it. He can never quite reach and so we don't win a free ride.

We move on to the Ferris wheel. From the line, I mostly study the wheel to see how hard it'd be to make one in silhouette. In the car, it's just the two of us—dangling over the ocean and pier—and I think how weird it is to be so alone with him. How if we wanted to do anything we shouldn't be doing, this would be the place to do it. No one would ever have to know.

"What are you thinking?" he says.

"Nothing," I say. I look at his lips, then back at his eyes.

"Why won't you tell me?"

"I did," I say. "I wasn't thinking of anything."

"I don't believe you."

When we get off the ride, James seems antsy, irritated. He says he wants us to kick it up a notch, so he tries to convince me to go on the Mousetrap, a small roller coaster that sticks out over the ocean and looks so old it might topple into the sea. "Come on," he says. "It's tiny. It's nothing compared to the beating you got in the water today anyway."

I've never much liked roller coasters. A precancer trip to Disney with my family had left me traumatized by Space Mountain (an even earlier trip had left me terrified of Winnie the Pooh, whom I encountered on Main Street; I guess I never thought he'd be so big). But you can't see anything on Space Mountain—the entire ride is shrouded in darkness—so I figure this can't be any worse. What I can see can't hurt me. It's the things I haven't been able to see with my own eyes—Brandon's interest in Lauren Janey, dark impulses in Nora's mind, my mother's cancer cells replicating themselves—that hurt.

The Mousetrap's cars hold two people. James has to climb in first and slide to the back and then I have to sit in between his legs. Too fast, before I'm ready, we're climbing the first hill in a herky-jerky motion and I'm holding onto the rail in front of me, desperately trying not to lean back on James. My arms are already shot from all the fake surfing; they feel like they're going to implode. "It's okay," James says. "Lean back."

I do, and my arms and neck and heart relax and I feel the heat of his body through the back of my top, and then we're at the top of the hill but there's no drop. I'm momentarily relieved. We creep along a curve looking out at the ocean, black like gasoline, and at the moon—a white silhouette waiting for the sun to finish setting—and it's beautiful and scary all at once. Then the car hesitates for a second at the top of the first drop-off and I picture the entire coaster plunging into the sea and then we're gone into wind and power and chaos, and when it's over the relief almost feels like elation. I wonder if maybe it's good to torture yourself sometimes, so that everyday things feel better by contrast. Maybe if I went on a roller coaster every morning—shower, brush teeth, scare the shit out of myself—things would feel almost normal again.

"So what's it going to be?" James says. We're sitting on a bench now, eating sausage and pepper sandwiches, and I feel like my body is saying, Where the hell are we, what the hell is going on, how come we don't do this all the time?

"How am I going to win your respect?" James says. "Frog Bog or magnet fishing?"

We've walked past both games. We've watched people put rubber frogs on launch pads and try to bang them into a pond so that they land on a rotating lily pad. We've watched magnet fishers hover their fishing lines baited with magnets over a pool of circulating magnetic fish and try to catch a red one, not a green one. I opt for frogs for the fanfare, for the look of satisfaction on people's faces as they take a wooden hammer and bang the shit out of the frog launching button. The prizes are crappy—misshapen Barneys, inbred-looking pandas—but I don't care. Magnet fishing doesn't look much more lucrative.

James pays for three frogs and fails to land any of them on a lily pad, despite much bravado in his efforts. He slips his wallet out of his back pocket and says, "I just needed to warm up." He indicates he wants three more frogs and a kid who looks about our age pulls three slick, wet rubber toads from the pond. I pull money out of my pocket, having left my bags in James's car, and get three frogs of my own. I set up on the launch pad next to James and line up my first frog. It's bent over its long rubbery legs, facing the lily pads—straight as it can be. I hold the mallet in my hand and watch the round-and-round flow of the lily pads, gauging their speed. My first frog lands just shy of a white lily target. James has gone through two frogs of his own unsuccessfully.

I hit my second frog too softly and it goes nowhere near a lily and yet I feel I'm learning how the game works, feeling confident about my third frog. James lets his final frog fly and it goes way high but totally misses the pond. "Shit!" he yells, disproportionately loudly. There are, obviously, kids around. "Sorry," he mutters to a woman beside him.

I watch and wait for a lily pad to come near my frog's trajectory and let her rip. My frog leaps for its life and lands right smack dab in the middle of a lily pad. "And a winner here!" says the Frog Bog attendant.

I look at James, smug in my victory, but he's turning red. "Nice one," he says. "Guess it's not my game."

I select the inbred panda and the frog game guy makes a big deal of handing it to me. "A winner here, folks! Step right up!"

"Thanks," I say. James and I buy a funnel cake and sit on a bench and eat its warm sugary softness, then when we're done, he says, "Let's try magnet fishing!"

And so we do. And James fails miserably and I don't try very hard for fear it'll upset him further. He's getting more and more aggravated by his losing and finally I say, "James. It's not important. Can we just go?"

He throws his rod in the pond and says, "Goddammit."

"James!"

"I'm sorry." He storms off and I follow.

"What's your problem?" I say.

"I wanted to win you something," he says.

"It's not a big deal. It's all stupid," I say. "I mean, look at this thing." I hold the panda up and he kind of laughs.

"I'm sorry. I didn't realize I could be such a macho asshole."

"Yeah," I say, "well, me, neither. And I mean, I sucked at surfing but I didn't turn into some psycho about it."

"No," he says. "You were amazing."

I feel like he wants to kiss me and I know I want to kiss him but I know he won't do it. I clutch the panda in my hand tighter, and it dawns on me how it seems somehow fitting that I won it myself. A seagull flies low over our heads and lands on a perch near the magnet fishing stand. I look at it and it seems to be staring at me. I feel like I should take it as a sign, but I'm not sure what it's a sign of. I think of my mother's photographs—the ones hanging in the café right now—and for a second, I actually wonder whether my mother has been reincarnated as a seagull. I try to imagine what she'd be trying to tell me but I come up with only two things: this is exactly where I should be or the exact opposite.

We don't talk much in the car and then his phone beeps again. Without knowing I'm going to do it, I snap. "Did you call her back? Or at least text her?"

"Of course."

I'm surprised by this. We've been together all night. "When?"

"When I was in the bathroom. How'd you know it was her?"

"I just knew." I look out the window and shake my head. "We shouldn't have done this."

"We didn't *do* anything." He turns the air-conditioning on high. "I'm allowed to have friends. I'm allowed to have a life."

"But what if she *does* something?" I should have kept my mouth shut.

Anger floods his features; I can even see it in the dark. It's like he's turning into the Hulk, the way his brow seems to throb. "Liza told you?"

"Yeah," I say. "She told me I should steer clear of the situation."

"Now I'm a 'situation'?" His voice is all wrong, all defensive.

I'm saying all the wrong things. "You know what I mean."

"Do you think she's right?" He stops at a light and looks at me. "Do you think you should steer clear of me?"

"I don't know." I look away. "Maybe."

"Yeah." He starts driving again. "Maybe she's right. Maybe I'm this total player."

"Nobody's saying you're a player. I just don't think it's right to stay with someone if you're not—" I can't possibly say the words "in love" out loud. "If you don't really want to be with them anymore."

"It's not that simple." He gets on the highway that will take us home and I feel my body tense with the idea of the upcoming merge.

When we're safely cruising, I say, "It should be."

At home in bed, I replay scenes from the day but they all end differently. In one, James follows me up to the room in his uncle's house after my shower and I drop my towel and we silently make love; I'm aware that we're doing something horribly wrong but I don't care. It almost makes it more intense, more frenzied. I like the idea of his wanting to be with me so badly that he can't do the right thing anymore, can't wait a second longer. His aunt and uncle are downstairs.

In another, he slips his arms around me on the roller coaster, brushing the skin near the side of my breasts. It's an accident— or it feels that way to me—but then he does it again, then slides his hand down my belly as I turn my head to meet his mouth.

And in another still, my favorite one, we're back up on the Ferris wheel, high above everyone we know. He puts his arm around me and tells me he's broken up with Nora for good, that it's over, that I'm the one. We kiss and he tells me he wants me and it doesn't feel weird for him to say that, it feels good, because I want him, too. When it's time for us to get off, he slips the guy working the loading area a twenty and says we need another go-round. I climb on top of him, straddling him, and this time it's me who's doing the touching, it's me who's in control. We're high above the world and no one can touch us. No one even dares to try.

One scene I replay doesn't have to change at all, though. We've just finished our funnel cake and I'm holding a plate loaded with powdered sugar. The trashcan seems like it's miles away and the wind seems to kick up mightily right then. James looks at the plate and says, "Good luck with that," smiling. I get up and start to walk toward the garbage and the wind seems to grow more determined to blow sugar all over me but I surf the air with the plate—tilting it this way and that—and dump it in the trash without so much as a particle of sugar escaping into the night. I thrust my fists into the air—victorious, laughing—and feel like I've caught a wave after all.

chapter 16

When I wake up on Sunday morning, I've still got that Ferris wheel on my mind, but for different reasons. I want to make one out of black paper. There's only one problem. The only paper I have isn't big enough. After a quick bowl of cereal, I bike to the art supply store downtown to buy more paper and to look at scissors. A bell over the door tinkles when I enter and I stop short when I see that the girl behind the counter is *her*. James's girlfriend. Nora. Her hair is pulled into a tight ponytail and she looks more girlie than wild.

She looks up for a second, then goes back to reading the book in her hand. She's sitting on a high stool behind the cash register. I slip into an aisle and find the paper section. I find the construction paper but realize it's a waste of money since there are only a few sheets of black in the mix and I'd need them all—pasted together somehow—to make the wheel big enough. It'd feel like cheating that way. I find a section with some black oaktag but the texture doesn't feel right. I've grown accustomed to the grainy feel of construction paper. The oaktag feels too smooth, too clinical. Too, I don't know, processed? Modern? I'm caught between a rock and a hard place. Then I think things through: If I buy either the construction paper or the oaktag, I have to go to the cashier. If I want to ask about different paper, I have to go to the cashier.

I figure if I'm going to have to face her either way, I might as well leave the store with what I want. I take a deep breath and step back out into the aisle where she can see me. "Excuse me?"

She looks up and I decide to move closer. There's no need to shout. "I'm interested in paper like this"—I hold up the construction paper—"but bigger. Does it come bigger? Like oaktag size—or even bigger than that?"

She climbs down off her stool and says, "By special order." She puts her book down and reaches up to a shelf where she takes down a catalogue. "It comes on rolls." She flips through a few pages and says, "Here it is. It's a roll that's three feet wide and a hundred feet long."

Without even realizing it, I've moved much closer than I planned. She turns the catalogue around so it's facing me but there aren't any good pictures. There are too many product numbers and dimensions for me to process so I just say, "How much is it?"

"Thirty-four, looks like. Plus tax, and then shipping, which'll be maybe four?"

"I probably don't need that much." It's just a Ferris wheel. For a second, I figure I just won't make the damn thing; the whole idea's pretty stupid and meaningless anyway. But then I make a split-second decision. "I want it."

"Okay." She picks up a pen and a pad and asks me my name. When I say it, she cocks her head and says, "I know who you are."

My heart starts racing. I've been caught. Only I haven't really done anything. She can't possibly know I'm falling for her boyfriend. Can't possibly know that I think he's falling for me, too. That we were together all day yesterday.

"Your mother's that photographer whose stuff is next door."

"Yeah." On the one hand relieved but on the other I'm even more on edge now.

"I like her stuff a lot. I like the one of the seagull and the Frog Bog."

It's a funny shot of a seagull perched on a fake lily pad in the middle of all these floating rubber frogs. It surprises me that Nora likes this one, that she has a sense of humor at all.

"She died, didn't she? Your mother?"

"Yeah," I say.

"Your aunt told me." She's holding her pen really tight, writing hard to transfer through carbon. "Sorry about that."

"Thanks." I wonder how chummy she is with my aunt. I picture them having coffee together during off-peak hours and talking about stuff my aunt should be talking to me about. I wonder what my aunt knows about her and James, whether she's ever confessed her dark urges, whether she's ever told my aunt, "I can't live without him."

"So," she says, with an air of finality. "It should be a couple of weeks. I can call you when it comes in if you want."

"That'd be great," I say, and we add my cell number to the order form. She rips a copy off and hands it to me.

There's a guy with a laptop at a table in a far corner of my aunt's café but the rest of the place is empty, eager. "Hey, look who it is," my aunt says warmly. "My favorite niece."

"I'm your only niece." I approach the counter.

"All the same." She comes around front and gives me a hug. It feels different from other hugs I've gotten recently—like it means she's happy to see me, not just that she's sorry for me. "What brings you around these parts?"

"I just came to see you," I say.

She looks at me, eyebrows raised, still holding me near the shoulders.

"I was in the art supply store."

"Oh!" She lets go. "I should introduce you to Nora."

She goes back behind the counter and I say, "We sort of met." I step up to the seagull/Frog Bog picture and look at my mother's signature on the matting of the frame. *Kelly Irving* in a tight, neat row slanted heavily to the right on top. It's weird to think of her having a first name. "She said she likes the photos."

"I hope you don't mind, honey." My aunt's rearranging coffee cups. "We talk sometimes. I told her about your mom."

"No," I say. "It's okay."

She stops what she's doing and looks up. "So what brings you to the art store anyway?"

"Just this project I'm working on."

This seems to put a shine in her eyes. "Want to tell me about it?"

I consider this seriously for a moment. "No, not yet, sorry."

"That's okay." She's out from behind the counter again, rearranging some chairs near me. "Secrets are good, too."

I move on to the next picture of the sequence: a seagull in profile in front of a clam shack advertising clams and oysters. The bird almost looks ready to order up his dinner of clams casino or oysters on the half shell.

"I was with her that day," my aunt says from over my shoulder. "I thought she was joking, taking all these shots. It all sounded so ridiculous. But I didn't see what she was setting up through that lens of hers. Come 'ere." She squeezes my shoulders. "Sit. What can I get you?"

"I'm okay."

"Come on. It's on the house."

"Iced tea, I guess."

"One iced tea, coming up."

I sit at the table she points to and wait and am surprised by how familiar the store feels, how familiar it *is*. We used to come here all the time when my mother was alive, mostly when I was younger, before I started being embarrassed by being seen with her. I spot a stack of fliers with a photo of my mother's on the front and pick it up and read the information. "It says here that the exhibit was supposed to be over a week ago."

"I know." My aunt sighs and sits down at the table with me with my iced tea and a half-empty one that's hers. "But the next artist fell through." She looks around the room at the photographs. "And I just can't bring myself to take them down." She seems to shiver, like she's had a chill, then, more brightly, she says, "So how's life as a farm girl?"

"It's okay, I guess. Not as bad as I thought it would be."

"And the boyfriend?"

"Gone. Moved on to somebody else."

"Your father mentioned something about that." She sips her tea through a straw. "I hope you're not too, too brokenhearted."

"No." I play with the straw in my tea and look away from her. "So you've been talking to my dad?"

She realizes we've changed topics and sort of shakes the last one off. "As much as he'll let me, yeah." She looks a lot like my mother—blond and angular and freckly—and it starts to freak me out so I concentrate on her voice, which doesn't sound like my mother's at all. "He returns maybe one call out of every three that I make. How's he doing?"

"Good," I say, because it feels like somehow snitching on him would be wrong. A part of me wants to tell her about McDonald's and Taco Bell and White Castle but I don't want my dad to know I told her. I want to tell her he's leaning more toward perishing than publishing but I don't want her to worry, too.

"And Ben?"

"He's Ben. He's busy with basketball camp and his friends and stuff. And he got his braces off." I don't tell her about Dr. Willis, about the appointments we're supposed to make but never will.

"I wish you'd stay in better touch, Betsy." She grabs my hand and the momness of the gesture makes me bristle. I think, You're not my mother. Don't even *think* about trying to replace her. "The boys miss you, too. Maybe Uncle Steve and I will have you all over for a barbecue. Wouldn't that be fun?"

"It would," I say. And I mean it. Sort of. My father doesn't get out and it would be some semblance of normalcy. If that's possible. I hate to think we're all avoiding one another just because we all remind one another too much of what happened, because we're all imagining how awful it is for each of us: what it's like to lose a sister, or a mother, or a spouse. It's like we're too busy feeling sorry for ourselves—and each other—to even have a conversation or a meal.

"But you, you specifically"—she grabs my arm and squeezes it—"need to stay in better touch. They're men. I'm not as worried about them."

I want to tell her she should be. That if anybody's going to be fine it'll be me, but I say, "I'm just really busy, you know. With work and driver's ed, and—" I want to tell her about James, maybe ask for advice, but I'm afraid her advice will be tainted by the fact that she knows Nora. "Stuff."

"Stuff, huh?" She's a mother. She's no fool.

"There's a boy," I blurt before I even know I'm going to. It feels so good to confess considering all I'm holding back from her but also sort of scary.

"Ooooh." She takes a sip of her drink. "Who is he?"

"You have to promise not to say anything." I play with the straw again, then put my hand on my chair—under my leg—so I'll stop fidgeting so much.

"Of course, honey. Spill it."

"Well—" Now that I've brought it up I don't know how to say it. "Do you ever see Nora with a guy?"

She thinks for a moment. "Tall, blondish. Really cute."

I nod. "We work together. And I mean, we're really just friends, but . . ." I don't want to tell her *everything* and am suddenly embarrassed that I'm pining after someone else's boyfriend. But I have to ask: "She ever talk about him?"

"No." My aunt shakes her head, sort of sad. "She's a tough nut to crack, that Nora. But be careful, honey. Sometimes just friends is better."

"I know, I know." I couldn't explain why this is different to her if I tried. "Anyway, I should get going."

"Okay," she says, "but if you ever want to talk, you know where to find me." She looks around the café as if I didn't already know.

chapter 17

Mr. Pagano is saying, "Signal, signal, signal" for the millionth time as Bobby Hopkins—the star pupil of our car—merges onto a local expressway for the first time. It's our first venture off local roads and it's kind of exciting. Sandra keeps whispering stuff to me, though, and I'm sure we're going to get in trouble. Then again, after my little meltdown, Mr. Pagano has started to treat me with kid gloves. I haven't been behind the wheel again yet. Not in driver's ed anyway.

"Where were you on Friday?" Sandra says.

Then a little later, "Mary's pissed."

I try to shush her but she takes out her phone and soon my phone buzzes a text message.

"I thought I told you to turn those things off," Mr. Pagano says.

"Sorry," I say, but I read the message before turning off the phone. It says, "She got dumped." I can only look at Sandra wide-eyed.

After Sandra and David take their turn at highway driving—Sandra's a natural; she could probably drive on the other side of the road if she needed to, too—Mr. Pagano looks at his watch. "I'm afraid we're out of time, Betsy."

"Oh," I say. "Okay." I look at my watch and he's sort of right but we could probably fit me in.

"We'll start off with you next time," he says. Then we return the car to the school grounds. When we're out of the car and dismissed, and able to talk, Sandra doesn't seem to think that Mr. Pagano's skipping me is a worthy topic compared to Mary's breakup.

"Everybody was having a great time." She seems about to burst with the news. "But then we were playing Marco Polo and Trevor was it and he seemed to be going after Lauren Janey and no one else, and then Mary got out of the pool and started stewing. So then when the game was over she pulls him away from everybody and they go around the side of the house, and when they come back it's clear she's been crying and he says his good-byes and leaves. So the rest of the guys decide they should go, too, and then most of the girls, too, especially Lauren, and then Mary spills it. He said she's too jealous and it freaks him out and he wasn't focused on Lauren Janey for any other reason than her voice seemed the closest and the clearest and no, he wasn't trying to grope her, and whatever."

I feel awful that I wasn't there. I also feel glad that I'm not the only one who got dumped this summer, that the perfect little friend group isn't so perfect anymore. "Is she really upset?"

"Well, uh, yeah! I mean, you know Mary. She was kind of overdoing it in the drama department, I think. I swear there's something else going on with her. But I guess they *have* been going out for, like, ever!"

I just soak it all in.

"You should really call her," Sandra says.

But just talking about the party, the party Mary invited my nemesis to, makes me angry all over again. "She should really call *me*," I say, wondering how you're supposed to know when to stay mad and when to give in.

"Well, the Italians are coming," Sandra says with a sigh. "And my parents are letting me have a party when they're here. So you should try to sort it out before then because I want you both to be there." She runs an arm under the back of her hair, lifting it off her neck and holding it up in the air for a second, elbow pointed out. "Marco's bringing a friend"—she lets her hair go—"and you've got first dibs. Brandon'll be so jealous he won't be able to stand it."

"But if you invite Brandon—"

"Honey, don't even think about it. I'd never do that to you." She leans in conspiratorially. "She thinks I'm her best friend. She told me she's breaking up with him this week."

I don't see James at all at work and it infuriates me that he's avoiding me. I haven't done anything wrong. I'm the one who should be avoiding him and maybe I am.

Liza senses I'm in a funk. "What's the matter," she says. "Finally growing weary of the heavy hand of the king?"

The middle of summer has Liza bored with our usual scripts. She's taken to actually reading about early America and text-messaging me and James random messages like, "George cannot prevail" and "The sun never shined on a cause of greater worth." She has also started a campaign to change Morrisville policy: she thinks we should all be speaking in British accents if we're supposed to be English colonials.

"I haven't seen James all day." We're on the porch of the farmhouse; I'm keeping an eye on the carpenter's shop.

"And . . . ?"

"We sort of had a fight on the way back from Seaside."

"Well, I hate to say I told you so, but he's off all week."

"He is?"

"Yeah."

He could have at least told me. "Why?"

"If I tell you, you can't be mad, okay? No shooting the messenger."

"Tell me."

"Her family has a house down by Cape May. He's there with her on a sort of family vacation."

My shoulders tense, my abdomen tightens. "How do you know this?"

"He told Ian he was going away with his girlfriend's family."

Ian who works in the general store knew this and I didn't. I feel like I'm going to cry. A small group is walking up the front path—they look like a family of Germans—and Liza says, "I'll take this one."

"Good day!" she says to the visitors. "Please, come in!"

She opens the bottom half of the door for them and follows them into the house after muttering to me, "Don't say I didn't warn you, kiddo."

That night, I can barely eat. My father and Ben are shoveling turkey and stuffing and mashed potatoes down their throats at a pace I can barely comprehend. It's all from Boston Market—an option that had escaped my and obviously my father's minds up to this point—but it's as close to a home-cooked meal as we've seen in weeks.

I want to eat it. I really do. But the way it's all pooling together on my plate is grossing me out. I will myself to eat, and still I can't.

James. On vacation. With his girlfriend.

The words, the reality of it, rattle around in my brain. I picture them walking on the beach holding hands, having big, happy family dinners at night, doing jigsaw puzzles—of medieval castles or autumnal forests or Dalí paintings, where things are melting—into the late evening, sneaking around at night so they can make out. Or make love.

"Everything okay?" my father asks.

"Yeah." I take a plastic forkful of mashed potatoes and wash it down with water. "We ate a lot at work today."

"Okay," he says skeptically.

"Can I be excused?" I put my fork down. "Mary and her boyfriend broke up and I want to go see how she's doing."

"Seems to be a lot of that going around," my father says and I think, Not nearly enough of it.

Standing on the porch at Mary's house, I'm tempted to turn around and run. I haven't been there in so long that I feel like a trespasser, unwelcome. I can already see the disapproving look her mother will give me if she opens the door, cut with a tiny bit of pity. Because yes, I said awful things about Mittens and haven't been a great friend of late, but my mother's dead. Mrs.

Giacomo can only be so mean to me. It's like my "get out of bitch free" card. At least that's what I hope.

I ring the doorbell and wait, fidgeting, hoping Mary—not her mother—will come to the door, which she does. "Oh, hello," she says through the screen door. She looks kind of pale and sad.

"You want to go for a walk or something?" I ask.

"Okay." She looks back over her shoulder. "Let me just tell my mom."

I know it's not meant to stab me in the heart but just thinking of her going inside again to talk to her mom makes me sad, jealous, awkward. I don't have a mother anymore. No one to tell the things that matter. Of course, for the last year or so I never wanted to tell my mother anything. Now I wish I had. And I wish I'd asked her more, too. I'm embarrassed by how little of her I remember already, how hard it's been to think of stories to tell James. You'd think that if you spend sixteen years with someone, you'd be able to conjure in your head every detail, every story, every joke she ever told—at the very least the sound of her voice. But nobody ever told me I should be paying attention. Nobody told me she wouldn't always be there to remind me.

Mary is coming down the hall when her mother yells, "Bring a sweater!" from a faraway room. "Just in case."

Mary grabs a sweater off a hook in the foyer and steps out onto the porch. It's still about seventy-five degrees out—I'm in shorts and a tank top—but that's Mary for you. I secretly wish my dad had told me to bring a sweater, even if I didn't need it. That was mom's job—the "just in case."

We walk in the street since so few cars come down the cul-de-sac that Mary lives in. We walk in silence as she ties her sweater around her waist, and I realize it's my turn to talk. I've called the meeting, after all.

"Sandra told me about you and Trevor," I say. "I'm sorry."

"Oh, screw Trevor," Mary says, startling me. "He's an asshole who was only after one thing."

"Oh," I say. "Okay." I can see that she's crying. She's wiping a tear away every couple of seconds so I try not to look at her. Then she says, "All men are assholes" and starts to cry harder, cupping her face with her hands.

I'm tempted to agree with her given my own circumstances. *James. On vacation. With his girlfriend.* The words keep running through my head one after the other.

But I don't think it'll make her feel any better.

"Mary." I rub her back. "Come on. He's a jerk. They're not all assholes. You'll find somebody else who's great in no time."

She's crying so hard she's breathing in hiccups. "My. Father," she manages in bursts. "Is. Leaving. He's been having an affair."

I've never heard her voice sound so cold.

"The fucking bitch is pregnant."

I've never heard her curse for real.

"So he's leaving to marry her and raise the baby."

Oh, great, I think. First Mittens. Then Trevor. Now this. I want to just hug her and cry with her about how it's all gone to shit this summer but at the same time, a part of me resents Mary. Because she'll get another cat. She'll find another boyfriend before I do. She'll end up thinking her new stepmother and stepsibling are super and will totally land on her feet. She always does. Besides, I'm the one who's supposed to be being comforted and taken care of this summer. Not her.

"I'm so sorry," I manage, wanting to be a good friend. "But you'll still be able to see him, right?"

"I knew I shouldn't have told you," Mary snaps. "It's not like he's dead, is that it?" She stops walking and glares at me. "Isn't that what you mean?"

"Well, that's *not* what I meant." Or maybe it was—*it's just a cat, it's just a divorce.* "But now that you mention it—"

"Well, *excuse me* for being upset," Mary says. "I guess I just can't compete."

"It's not a competition," I say.

"Well, you sure act like it is."

"I do not!" I'm so mad now I'm shaking. "My mother is *dead*."

"I know!"

We're both shouting now. "You can't possibly know what it's like!"

"And you can't know what *this* is like!" she yells. "My father is *choosing* to leave me. Your mother would've chopped an arm off if it meant she could stay with you."

She's right. My mother set out to live to see me get married. Then to live to see me graduate high school. Then to make it to my sweet sixteen, the only goal she achieved. Still, I can't help but think that what Mary's feeling can't possibly hurt as much as what I'm feeling and I'm too sunk into my anger to come out of it. So yeah, maybe it is a competition. Or maybe it's *no* competition, because death wins hands down.

"I should go home," Mary says. "My mother's alone and that can't be good." She wipes tears from her eyes with both hands. "He dropped this bomb over the dinner table tonight."

We walk back to the house in silence and Mary says, "I guess I'll see you around." I know she's expecting more from me, but I can't give it right now. I can't stop being angry. That list on my wall hasn't helped me at all.

Mrs. Giacomo is at the door when we stop in front of the house. "I froze that lasagna, Betsy. I really wish you'd take it."

I think of KFC and Mickey D's and Taco Bell and Boston Market and think, Something's gotta give. Mary looks at me with a combination of shock and disgust when I say, "That'd be great," and follow her inside to claim the cold, aluminum tray.

chapter 18

danny Mose asks me to go for a walk on the beach at the party at Midland that Friday night and I say yes, then down my beer so he can get me a new one. Then I down most of that in one go, too. I'm feeling buzzed and energized and this time, when he says he thinks I'm hot, I feel hot. When he asks me if I want to stop and sit on the beach, I say yes. When he goes to kiss me, I let him.

His kisses are different than Brandon's—the only guy I've ever really kissed. More confident, more rushed. More swirling and wet. He kisses like he's popular. He quickly pushes me so that I'm laying down in the sand. He's perched on an elbow and his other hand finds my stomach. His touch is ticklish at first, then he moves his hand up, pushing my bra away and grabbing me not so tenderly. It's not entirely unpleasant, just different. Before I know what's happening, his mouth is there, too, flicking and teasing, his head in my hands. I'm dizzy from beer and arousal and shock. It took me and Brandon weeks just to get this far. When Danny takes my hand and pushes it down towards his groin, I resist.

Someone clears his throat nearby. "Hey, Moses." It's a male voice, pretty close by. "We're going to a party. Wanna come?"

He lifts his head and calls out, "Yeah," while I rush to pull my top down. "You coming this time?" he says to me.

"Sure." I feel like I've stepped off a cliff. At the top of it is my father, who thinks I'm at Sandra's studying for a driver's ed test. Standing next to him is James, who can go to Cape May or hell for all I care. Mary's up there, too, a few steps back. She's shaking her head and saying, "What are you doing?" but I don't answer.

"All right," he says. "Let's go."

He gets up and starts to walk away and I follow a few paces behind him. I see Liza and tell her what I'm doing.

"Are you sure this is a good idea?" she says.

"Yeah," I say. "I'm having fun."

"Okay," she says. "Don't do anything I wouldn't do."

I say, "That leaves me a lot of options," then head off after Danny.

The party's at the house of a girl I've never met who goes to a private high school in town. Her parents are away and her house is huge and swarming with people I've never seen before in my life. The music is fast, like ska but cooler sounding, and the air smells of some weird combination of Axe body spray, sunscreen, and sweat.

Danny leads me into the kitchen and makes us a cocktail of vodka and a couple of different fruit juices. "Follow me." He hands me a drink, leads me upstairs, and opens a bedroom door. He peeks in and says, "All clear. Come on."

He's barely closed the door before he's kissing me again, even more aggressively than before. I feel kind of fuzzy and scared and wonder whether this is what it feels like to be wanted. In a minute, we're on the bed and he's back under my shirt again, groping and sucking. It feels good but it'd feel better if he were gentler, if he took his time. This room smells like Nivea and potpourri.

"Hey." I feel a wave of dizziness crash over my head. "We should probably go downstairs."

He all but groans and I take the opportunity to fix my bra and shirt and roll away from him.

"No," he says. "Let's stay. Come on." He kisses me sweetly. "We don't have to do that yet. I want to make you feel good, though. Don't you want me to make you feel good?"

We start making out again, and soon we're back to where we were, him kissing his way up from my belly button to my breasts. I want to stop him again and at the same time I don't. He's on top of me again and I can feel he's turned on and he's grinding against my left leg. Then he's fussing with his zipper and then he takes my hand and I feel a flash of hard warmth before I push him off me again. "Hey," I say. "Let's take things slow."

"No," he groans. "Let's take things fast." He takes my hand again. "Don't you want to touch it?"

"No," I finally say, but that sounds mean and I don't want to piss him off. "I mean, it's getting kind of late."

He breathes hard and says, "Are you kidding me? I thought you were up for a good time. 'Cause I'm just getting started." He puts himself away, gets up, and downs his drink. "I'm getting another one."

He leaves the room, leaving me to compose myself. I follow him downstairs and look around and realize I don't know anybody else in my range of vision. I take out my phone and look at the time, though it takes me a minute to focus on it. I'm already fifteen minutes past curfew.

"Shit." I push my way through the crowd and go out the front door. I sit down on the front porch—not feeling so well—and try to figure out what to do. I only really have one choice: I call Liza.

"Yello!" she says.

"It's Betsy," I say.

"You okay?"

"I fucked up." I look at my feet and for a second it looks like I have twenty toes. "Can you come get me?"

"Of course." she says. "Where are you?"

I start crying. "I don't know. It wasn't far, though."

"Well, can you ask somebody? Or find a piece of mail or something."

I turn around and the front door says 22. A group of guys walks by and I say, "What street are we on?" and they look at me and laugh like I'm a fool and the last one to go in the door says, "Preston Avenue."

"Twenty-two Preston Avenue," I tell Liza. "Do you know where that is?"

"Yeah," she says. "Chill out, babe. I'm on my way."

I go to call my father to tell him I'm sorry I'm late and that I'm on my way but I remember he thinks I'm at Sandra's. I'm caught if he thought to call there. And likely in serious trouble.

Unless he's fallen asleep. Unless he buys that Sandra and I just lost track of time.

When Liza pulls up I get into the car and say, "You're saving my life."

"What were you *thinking*?"

"He's cute." I'm still clinging to the idea that this Danny thing might pan out, that I'm the idiot who freaked out, that he likes me and I might like him.

"He's an asshole. You know that as well as I do. What did he do to you?"

"Nothing," I say. "We were just talking."

She looks me over closely and says, "Bullshit. What happened?"

"Nothing. I'm serious," I say. I'm afraid she'll say something to James if I let on that anything at all happened with Danny. That wouldn't be good. Or maybe it would. Maybe he should know what it feels like.

Liza is studying me for clues the way a mother would. "You *so* hooked up with him."

I can't bring myself to deny it and she mercifully drops the subject.

When we pull away from 22 Preston Avenue she says, "So what did you mean before, when I said 'Don't do anything I wouldn't do' and you said 'That leaves me a lot of options'?"

I barely remember saying that. "I didn't mean anything."

"No, I want to know what you've heard about me."

"You know what the rumors are."

"I want to hear you say it."

"You got pregnant and had an abortion."

"I can't believe you said it." She stops at a light and I hear the engine idling. Our brains are idling, too.

"You said you wanted me to say it," I say. The traffic lights seem to be swaying. I'm drunker than I thought.

"I should make you get out of the car." Liza's voice is tinged with outrage, hurt. "I should leave your sorry drunken ass here and let whatever is gonna happen to you happen."

"I didn't believe it!" I protest. "The abortion stuff."

"I've never even had sex, you asshole."

My head jolts with surprise.

"I was out of school because of my mother, okay? She wigged out and we all went away for a while. To get shit sorted out."

"Okay," I said. "I'm sorry. I mean it. I didn't believe it."

"Whatever."

"No. Not whatever. Really. I didn't believe it. You have to tell me you believe me."

"All right, all right." She looks at me like I'm crazy. "I believe you."

We drive for a bit and she puts the radio on and the mood shifts. When we're getting close to my house, I say, "I mean, I didn't think you were a *virgin*." I reach over and poke her and she laughs.

"I'm not." She puts the car in park in front of my house and pokes me back. "I'm just fucking with you."

My father is sitting at the kitchen table with a glass of something gold on ice when I skulk through the door. If he's drinking, that means it's bad. I sway slightly when I say, "I'm sorry I'm late," and he says, "If you think you're getting your driver's

license in September, missy, you've got another thing coming."
He gets up and dumps his drink out in the sink.

"It wasn't my fault," I try.

"It wasn't your fault you lied about where you were going,
and with whom?"

"I'm sorry."

He comes closer and I try to back away. His eyes look
bloodshot, like he's tired or he's been crying or both. "And
you've obviously been drinking."

I look away, playing the part of remorseful daughter while
inside I'm thinking, That makes two of us. I'm just wishing
he'd hurry up and say what he's going to say so I can go to bed.
He takes a step back and says, "You would've never tried to pull
something like that with your mother."

I feel my body teeter slightly in the face of this, the ultimate
guilt trip.

"Who were you with, that James character?"

"No."

"You know what?" He throws his hands in the air. "I can't
even look at you right now. Go to bed. I'll deal with you in the
morning. Your brother's in the doghouse, too."

My father raps on my door in the morning and it's as if he's
knocking directly on my skull. I feel a sharp pain shoot
through my brain and figure this is really it. I've gone too far.
I'm dying.

"Time to get up," he says. "You have a lot to do today."

I know that if I know what's good for me I'll get up, even
though I feel like death.

"There's a list there," my father says. Ben is already at the kitchen table, eating cereal, and I can see why he's in trouble. There's a shocking streak of blue in his hair. "And your names are next to different jobs."

I shuffle over to the list in my slippers and look at what he has in store for me. I see "skim and vacuum pool" and decide I might as well get started before it gets hot out. I go upstairs and put on shorts and a T-shirt and a baseball cap and sunglasses, then go back through the kitchen without a word.

The pool hasn't been getting that much use these last couple of days—or weeks, even—and it shows. There's a ton of leaves and propeller-shaped seeds floating on the surface and a few have sunk to the bottom and settled in a slightly brown coat of slime. I go around to the side of the house and turn on the filter, then lift the lid of a basket at the pool's edge where I'm supposed to screw in the vacuum hose. There are about thirty or forty bugs of varying shapes, colors, and scariness whirling around in there and I have to stick a hand in to pull out a basket full of them. I dump it out in the garden and thread the hose into the chamber and tighten it.

"You should test the water, too," my father yells out the kitchen window.

I don't say anything, and he says, "Did you hear me?"

"Yes," I say. "I heard you."

I feel far away in moments like this, because yes, this is my life. But it's not a part of my life that I've chosen. Sometimes it feels like my life is moving away from here, from this house, from my family. Lately, I prefer being anywhere but here—prefer churning butter to this—and I wonder whether that's normal.

I hear the house phone ring at one point and my father says,

"I'm sorry, Betsy can't come to the phone right now." He seems to be talking extra loudly, facing the window, for my benefit. "Can I take a message? No? Okay then." He hangs up.

"Who was that?" I call out.

"He didn't say."

James is due back at work tomorrow so that must have been him. He must be back in town. And as much as I'm pissed my father didn't let me take the call, I'm relieved. I don't know how to act.

I test the water of the pool and it's way low on chlorine and then I go into the shed and realize we're out. I go inside to relay this discovery to my father. "Come on, Ben," he says; Ben is dusting the living room. "Let's go to the pool store."

"Okay," Ben says.

My dad picks up his keys.

"What about me?" I say, and my father says, "There's plenty more on that list."

The house phone rings again as soon as my father leaves and my stomach clenches with the thought that it's not a coincidence, that James is parked down the street watching, and waiting for a chance just like this. He wants to come over to talk, to explain how it's all over with now. How at long last he's free.

I pick up and say, "Hello?"

"Is this Betsy?"

"Yes." I don't immediately recognize the voice.

"It's Danny." Danny Mose.

"Oh, hey."

"So what are you, like, in trouble?"

"Ohmigod, totally." I plop down in a chair, ready to chat. I can't believe he's calling me. Is it possible he actually likes me?

"So listen," he says. "About last night. I don't think it's a good idea to tell anybody about that."

"Okay." I'm completely confused about what's going on.

"I mean, it's not like we're going to start going out or anything and I have a girlfriend anyway. She's just away for a couple of weeks."

"Oh," I say. "Yeah, well, that's cool."

"All right. So we're agreed?"

My only response is silence.

He says, " 'Cause I'll know it was you."

Something in his voice actually scares me. I want to ask, "Is that a threat?" but I already know. I mutter, "Agreed."

"Good," he says. "See you around." He hangs up.

I say, "Fucking asshole" into the phone and throw it, too hard, on the floor. The battery pops out, bounces on the rug, and smacks into my toe—"Ow!" I sit down on the floor and grab my toe. Tears come with the force of a hurricane and, for the first time in what feels like a long time, I let myself sob. Again, though, I feel dumb, and I wonder where that comes from. Whether we all know too much about everyone else in the world, their suffering. When I'm done with that, I get up and look at the list, and go to get out the vacuum.

The afternoon is a blur of chores and smells . . . dust, Pledge, Windex . . . and of flashes of last night . . . *Don't you want to feel good* . . . and guilt. When I'm finally done with everything on my list, I go upstairs and let myself wallow. I'm a good-for-nothing whore who no one will ever love. I have a dead mother and I'm damaged goods and I'm killing any brain cells worth having with beer. I close my eyes and imagine my brain, imagine the edges of it all withered up and blackened from too much Bud and Miller High Life.

High life. What a crock.

Later, my father knocks on my door. "Ben and I are going to Pizza Hut. Do you want to come?"

"No," I say. "Thanks."

"Fine," he says. "Don't go anywhere."

"I won't."

I wait until I hear the front door open and close and the car pull away, then get up and brush my teeth and my hair and go down to the basement. I sit down on the cool floor, legs crossed, and study the beach party scene. There are a few spots where something seems to be missing but I'm not sure what, or whether I should just move the elements that are there. So I just sit there for a while, and think about the party on Friday. I look at two figures sort of inspired by Moses and Doyle and they look like assholes to me, though whether that's in the cut of the paper I can't be sure. I look at the couple holding hands and think of James. Of the whole "we're not doing anything wrong" line. I feel foolish for going to Seaside with him, and more foolish still for having so good a time. With someone else's boyfriend. I'm no better than Lauren Janey, really. I think of him and me out there in the water on surfboards and it seems so unlikely, such an impossible scene, that I wonder whether it ever happened at all.

Whether I want to admit it or not, I have to put the surfer and surfboard back into the scene. They belong there. So I start over, first with the board, then with the surfer dude. I make him thicker in the middle this time, with a bigger head. Less like James.

Then I think of Hawaii and whales and it dawns on me what the silhouette really needs. I take another sheet of paper and get to work. The scene needs a hint of a horizon, a line formed by the sea, and so I cut out three dolphins, in varying degrees of visibility, and together they create the illusion of a horizon. Once my paper comes in I can add the Ferris wheel and then I'll be done. The thought brings satisfaction and a bit of "so what?"

When I hear my father and Ben come home, I sit and wait with ears alert until I can tell that Ben's gone upstairs to his room and my father to his. I turn off the basement light and head upstairs and find a Pizza Hut box in the fridge. I pour myself a glass of water and sit at the table, relishing every cold, hard bite.

chapter 19

It's time for me to get back in the hot seat in driver's ed on Monday. Mr. Pagano is in a different car this morning and we've got Mr. Evans. He's a smallish, neat-looking guy—a teacher at school as of last year—and I'd guess he was gay if I didn't know he moved here from upstate New York with his wife and twin toddler girls. I'm sure he's been warned about me, told about my episode, but I just try to stay relaxed and remind myself that this isn't anything I haven't been doing with Liza.

I have a thought, when I'm making a left turn in a relatively big intersection, about my mother. In my head I tell her I'll never go down to Midland or hook up with an asshole again if she'll just watch over me and make sure I don't hurt myself or anyone else. But when I safely make the turn, I sort of go back on that in my head. I'm not sure I really meant it or whether I understand the bargaining phase of grief at all. What could I possibly offer when I know she'll never come back? I've started to wonder what kind of bargaining my mother did in her head, whether she promised to give more money to charity if she could live, or adopt a child in need, or stop eating meat, or gossiping about the other moms in the PTA.

"Nice job," Mr. Evans says, when I finish the circuit we've all been doing and pull into the school parking lot. Everyone in the backseat, Sandra included, seems to sigh with relief.

"You okay?" Sandra says. We're both walking toward our bikes.

"Yeah, fine."

"I mean, you did great. But I mean, in general, are you okay?"

"Um. Yeah." I have no idea what's going on. "Why?"

"You didn't hear? Church yesterday?"

I shake my head. My family doesn't go to church much anymore. The fact that Sandra hasn't noticed this, when we used to go all the time, sort of surprises me.

Right now, she just looks like she wishes she wasn't the person who had to tell me.

"Alex Elks," she says. "He made a big scene yesterday."

"What kind of scene?" Sometimes people think it's a scene when it's just Alex being Alex.

"He got up on the altar and started talking about your mom."

I feel a wave of heat or dizziness crash over my brain. I just look at her and wait for more.

"I couldn't understand a lot of it." Sandra's looking at me superintensely but I'm trying to act like everything's normal. "But he said she was his best friend. And how much he missed her."

We have our bikes unhooked now and I say, "That's sweet of him," but inside I don't know what I think or what I feel. I never even thought for a second that he'd think about her that way and it makes me sad for him and for myself—for everything about her that I'll never know. Still, I wish he hadn't done it, wish Sandra and I weren't having this conversation, wish we could all just go on pretending everything is fine. He has nerve, really, talking about her that way, when none of us can.

"I'm gonna be late for work." I straddle my bike.

"Okay." Sandra gets on her bike. We're heading in opposite directions and she knows this. "I'm sorry, Bets. It was really sweet, though."

"I'm sure it was," I say, and she starts to pedal away.

I love my job that morning more than ever. Life at Morrisville is so uncomplicated, so protected. I won't run into Danny Mose here. I don't see sad faces in the kitchen every day. The colonial version of me hasn't hooked up with an asshole, hasn't been threatened into secrecy. Colonial me has a mother in Loretta and a sister in Liza. Her life is cut and dry with chores and not much else to worry about.

As I help Loretta start up a fire in the oven, I wish I could disappear into this other version of me. I imagine myself actually living in colonial times, or, better yet, during the Revolutionary War. I imagine I've lost a mother and a husband to the cause, and that I've taken up arms in defense of my fledgling nation. I know how to pack gunpowder and fire cannons and how to dress wounds and sew skin. I know how to weather great losses every day, because that's what life is: bringing out your dead.

Mrs. Rudolph stops by with a few colonial puzzles that Liza and I are expected to master before the big patrons' dinner. One is made up of two large pieces of interlocking iron that you're supposed to try to separate. I puzzle over it for a while before Liza picks it up and makes a display of showing me each stage of breaking one of the pieces of iron free. It looks so easy, so obvious when she does it. I take it back from her, all confident, but I still can't do it. She rolls her eyes. "What?" I say. "It's hard!"

"Pay attention." She demonstrates again. "It's really not hard at all."

I think I really get it this time, and I gesture that I want her to pass it back. "It's easy once you know how to do it," I say. "Like most things."

I successfully separate iron from iron and hold the two pieces out.

Liza claps and says, "Bravo."

I hear James before I see him. He says, "Hey."

He looks at me but it's Liza who speaks first. "How was the beach?"

"Good," he says tentatively. He must know I'm pissed he didn't tell me. Must know I feel I've been had.

I can't bring myself to say anything because I don't know what tone to take. A friendly hello might let him off the hook before I want to, and still I'm not sure I want to sound pissy, either. I'm afraid, too, he might hear something else in whatever word I utter. Guilt. Shame. He and Liza are talking about something but I'm not following. When there's a pause he says, "What's the matter? Cat got your tongue?"

Liza skillfully leaves the room.

"Nothing to say." I shrug.

"You know what, Betsy? I really don't need this. Least of all today." He storms off and I can't believe his nerve.

I have a pit in my stomach the rest of the day. I don't see James again at all and I'm too mad at him and disgusted with myself to go over there but then I decide I can't go home and feel this bad all night and again tomorrow. Right before the end of the day, I finally go over to the carpenter's shop. Will's there alone and, thankfully, there are no tourists. I don't even have to ask; he knows why I'm there.

"Rudolph has him on maze duty." The lack of the "Mrs." startles me. I thought just we "kids" called her Rudolph.

"Maze duty?"

"Yeah, he and one of the other guys are learning the maze so they can rescue the rich folks' kids when they get lost at the big banquet."

"Okay," I say. "Thanks."

I ask Loretta if I can kick off a few minutes early and then walk across the grounds to the maze. I think of Julia and her ghost and her grand love affair and wonder why death is considered so romantic. I wonder if Nora will ever really hurt herself—fatally—on account of James and wonder if she thinks that's what love is, not being able to live without a person.

It's still pretty hot for five o'clock but the second I step into the maze the temperature seems to drop. The hedges are so high that I'm entirely in the shade. I know I should call out for James, follow his voice, but instead I just walk and walk, rounding corners cautiously, making arbitrary decisions in the hopes that I'm being guided by some other force without even knowing it. Here, in the maze, I actually feel as if I've traveled in time. There's just me and the sky and the ground beneath my feet, the hedges blocking out the real world. I think back to that day I barely remember, the day I got lost in here, and try to imagine my mother searching for me, the same way I'm searching for James. I round a corner and swear I see a shadow and I start to panic for a second, foolish as it sounds, and then I scream, "James!"

After a pause, he answers. "Betsy?" He sounds confused.

"I'm lost!"

"Stay where you are," he yells. "I'm coming."

"Hurry!" I catch a chill. I swear I hear a shushing sound, some ghostly whisper. I respond with my own hushed plea. "Hurry, James. Please, hurry."

I have the strangest sensation of not being alone and then James comes around a corner and I start to cry and he takes me in his arms and says, "It's okay. I'm here," but I wish it were my mother. I wish I could be close to her, hold her, even once more.

When he takes my hand and leads me back out into the world, I let him. "There's someplace I need to go," I say. "Can you take me?"

At first I'm afraid I won't be able to find the grave, and then when I do I'm guilty over having turned up empty-handed. I guess you're supposed to bring things—flowers, plants—but I didn't know. I'm new at this. Other people have been here, left their floral tokens of remembrance on my mother's stone. But the grass has yet to grow over the dirt patch into which the casket was lowered. I swear it's never like that on TV or in the movies. They never show you how ugly a new grave is, how cemeteries can look like construction sites.

James holds my hand but now that we're here I want to leave. I can't imagine what people do when they come to cemeteries to visit loved ones, unless they come for the gardening.

"I'm sorry I wasn't there—here—that day," James says. "I barely knew you. I thought it would be inappropriate but now I regret thinking that."

"It's okay." I step closer to the stone, to arrange some flowers better and that's when I see it. A wooden flower, like a daisy. My voice catches in my throat. I pick it up and turn to James. "You did this?"

He nods. He's so damn cute with his Roswell T-shirt and mussed-up hair and the light shine of sweat from the heat.

"But when?"

"Right before you came back to work. The duck wasn't enough to keep me busy."

I can't believe he did something so sweet for me, for her, and I didn't even know it. I examine the daisy. It's like a silhouette in 3-D. I place it back on top of the gravestone and wonder whether my father has been here since the funeral. Wonder whether it was my aunt who planted the pink flowering plant, the kind I know she has in her front yard. "Nobody even talks about her," I say. "It's like she never existed."

"Of course she did. And anyway, where did *that* come from?"

"I don't know. I was wondering who has and hasn't come here and it's weird to me that I have to wonder."

"I guess. But *we* talk about her."

I can't hold it in anymore. I have to tell someone. "She took me shopping a couple of months before she died . . ." Now that I've started talking I can't believe I'm telling anyone this, least of all James. ". . . for a wedding dress." I feel like it must sound so ridiculous that he'll have no choice but to laugh, but he doesn't. He smiles and says, "That's kind of cool."

"You think?"

"Well, strange but cool. I mean, considering the circumstances."

We stand there quietly and I try to think up a prayer or even a wish or something to say to my mother. I try to imagine what she'd have to say about James after meeting him but come up blank. "She's not here," I say, finally, and he pulls me into his arms. He says, "She's wherever you go, Betsy, wherever you go."

His embrace feels so wonderful that I don't want to let go. "Thanks for bringing me here," I say.

"Funnily enough, I was coming here anyway." He releases me but we stay close, hips sort of touching.

I'm confused for a second, then it hits me. Today of all days. "It's two years today, isn't it?"

He nods.

"Show me," I say.

He takes my hand and leads me through aisles of gravestones and I read the names and try to have a good thought for everyone here who's died. I have a flash of rotting corpses below our feet and try to imagine how much and how fast my mother's body has decomposed, whether there are worms slinking through her brown silk dress yet or bugs eating her eyes.

We stop, finally, in front of a gravestone that reads: TIMOTHY MANNING, LOVING HUSBAND AND FATHER, 1955–2004.

"He used to joke that he wanted his gravestone to say 'Evil never dies' or 'I'll be back.' "

I smile. "Do you come here a lot?"

"I used to come more." He brushes a couple of leaves off the stone. "Then I decided he'd probably be happier if I just lived my life. Besides, I'm like you. I never know what to do when I get here." He pats the stone for a second and he looks so amazing, so real, in his shorts with too many pockets. I've never wanted to be close to someone so badly, never felt so sure of anything. "Can I take you somewhere else?" I say.

"Um. Okay." We head for the car. "Like where?"

"Just a place I know," I say. "It's right near here."

"Okay." He sounds sort of hesitant but I like being in control. I feel bold, like I've surprised him. "Make a left," I say, then I direct him to the wall, in spite of the fact that it looks like it's going to thunderstorm any second. The sky can't handle the heat anymore. It's grown ominous and gloomy and I love it because there's a part of my heart that feels that way, too. All the time. Like there's something brewing inside me, too.

We get out of the car at the beach and James says, "This is cool." I feel flecks of water hitting me in the face, blowing off the ocean. Then large drops start pummeling my head so we duck back into the car. The rain is so heavy it's like we're in a car wash. James turns the key and turns on the CD player— "This is that band I played for you the other day"—and I hear the singer singing something about evil robots and a woman who has to kill them to save the world, which sounds really weird but I like the sound of it. He turns the wipers on, and they make a squeaky noise almost to the beat. We can see the ocean, which looks to be getting angrier by the minute; like it's mad it's getting assaulted from above, all rumbling and black and white. Through cracks in the window the air smells salty and somehow alive. The rain gets harder, heavier, like there are a million invisible drummers pounding on the car with their fists.

"Why did you bring me here?" James looks suddenly more serious than I've ever seen him.

"What do you mean?" I feel myself breathing heavily, as if I've been running, and then we're looking at each other hard and he says, "I know why people come down here."

I say, "You do?" all innocent but it's already happening. He's leaning over and sliding a hand up the back of my neck, cradling my head. He's kissing me, sweetly at first and then more fully, more forcefully. I want to melt into him and then he pulls away and rests his forehead on mine. "Wow," he says, when we're nose to nose. His breath is warm and sweet and I think, Yes. Wow.

This is what it's supposed to feel like. *This* is what the fuss is about.

We start kissing again and we're getting kind of hot and bothered together. I can feel the way his hands are pulling at my back and shoulders, clinging onto my neck more intently, twirling tight fingers in my hair. I've never kissed someone with so much hunger. I'm practically climbing on top of him and it makes me feel strong, powerful, because I know he likes it.

"Betsy," he says between kisses. "Hey." I'm still swirling my tongue around; he's still reciprocating, but more reluctantly. "Betsy." He stiffens and holds me away from him. "Hey. We should, you know . . ."

But I *don't* know. I don't know anything but this moment. I don't care about her or reason or Cape May or anything any-more. Not when it feels this good to be with him. "I'm sorry." I sink back into the passenger seat and brush off my mouth with the back of my hand. "I thought—"

He puts his hands on the steering wheel and takes a deep breath. "Don't be sorry," he says. "God, do not be sorry. I think you're amazing. You know that. I just—God! Why is this hap-pening to me! How did I even get in this situation?!" He looks like he's going to pull his hair out now. "I just need more time."

I look out the window, away from him.

"Hey. Don't do that. Look at me." He reaches out and touches my neck with his palm and it feels smooth and warm.

I look at him and I'd swear the look in his eyes is love.

"It's just time," he says. "That's all. I swear. Trust me."

And the miracle is that I do.

There's a message for my mother from Dr. Willis's office on the machine when I arrive home to an empty house. They're re-minding her to call to set up Ben's next appointment. I delete it without hesitation.

chapter 20

that week, I start to live for work—for every break on which I can pop by the carpenter's shop, for every visit from James, for every time we see each other walking across the village and wave and smile. Every interaction with him is more fun, more charged now, and I feel like I've changed, like I've become this confident, patient person who knows that whatever he's up to, whatever is going on, he's doing the right thing. I've decided that he's only trying to get out of a difficult situation without hurting someone unnecessarily. It strikes me then that that's what Brandon was trying to do with me, but that feels different. Still, I feel like it's only a matter of time before James and I are together for real. Him, I can wait for. I decide it's my penance for being so stupid as to hook up with Danny Mose.

When Mrs. Rudolph tells us all the village will be closed on Friday so that a few of the newer, administrative brick buildings can be power-cleaned, James suggests that he, Liza, and I go to the beach together. In that moment, I feel like I can't believe how lucky I am. How I've found these great new friends and how it's all going to work out perfectly in the end. Even the power-cleaning schedule seems to be working in my favor.

We're all three at the beach building a sandcastle when Danny Mose, in his lifeguard gear, walks by and gives me a look. It's a look that just indicates there's something between us, something not good. His eyes are like daggers, and then he says, "Look at the idiots in the sandbox" to the guy he's walking with. Liza just shakes her head then goes back to working on a turret. James has noticed the look, though. He says, "What's his deal with you anyway?"

"No deal," I say.

Liza looks at me like a disapproving mother.

"That guy's such an asshole." James shakes his head. "I can't believe you thought he was, what was the word again? Oh, yeah: hot."

I'm feeling so guilty that I can't speak.

"Hey." James nudges me. "I'm just joking."

I look at him and know that I have to tell him, and that he'll hate me but that I have to do it anyway. I look at Liza, eyes pleading, and she gets up and goes down to the surf. She starts rinsing sand off her hands.

"I hooked up with him," I say.

There's a moment of stunned silence before he says, "You *what*?" His lips appear to tremble. My ears are pounding.

I don't want to have to say it again so I just say, "It wasn't a big deal."

He takes a minute to absorb this, nodding his head and looking over at Danny, who is standing in front of the lifeguard chair, talking to another guard. "When?"

"James." I grab his arm. "It doesn't matter."

He slithers his arm away. "When." I can see his jaw clench.

I say, "When you were out of town with your girlfriend," a bit too snottily.

"For your information"—his voice is filled with venom, rage—"Nora's parents *begged* me to go. So they could talk to Nora about maybe going into some kind of clinic or getting some help. They thought it would help if I was there. A friendly face, or whatever. I couldn't exactly say no."

"Oh." He really was just trying to do the right thing. Meanwhile, I was acting out.

"So are you seeing him?" James says.

"No! God, no. He told me that if I even *told* anyone he'd . . ." I trail off. I've already said too much.

"He *threatened* you?" James's skin seems to pulse, like it can't contain his blood.

"Not exactly." I'm trying to sound nonchalant now, downplaying it all for his benefit and probably my own. "It really doesn't matter. I mean, it was just kissing."

He pushes up to his feet, brushes sand off his hands, and starts off in the direction of Danny Mose. "James!" I yell, struggling to get up off the sand. "James!"

I start to follow him and only then it dawns on me what he's going to do. I break into a run—my left knee sort of pops on the uneven sand—but I'm too late. James punches Danny Mose in the face.

In the car, I'm not sure whether we're mad at each other or not but either way James has to drive me home. In my head, I replay snippets of the scene: Danny and James wrestling in the sand. Two lifeguards breaking it up. James saying, "You're a fucking asshole" over and over. Danny threatening to call the cops, then, thankfully, deciding not to. The whole thing is so bizarre I can't really believe it happened.

When we're only a few blocks from my house, I figure I should say something. Unfortunately the first thing that comes out is, "You really shouldn't have done that."

James looks over at me and shakes his head, all disgusted. "I could say the same thing to you."

He's driving all herky-jerky. I keep getting jolted forward at stop signs and red lights, then smacked back onto the seat. "It's not like we were together," I say. "I'm not even sure what's going on with us now."

At the next stop, he looks at me like he's been stabbed in the heart. "If you don't know what this is, Betsy, I don't think I can explain it to you."

"Well, fucking break up with her!" I yell.

"I fucking *did*!" His voice cracks on the word. I've only heard him curse once before today.

"You did?" That sort of knocks the wind out of me.

"Yeah."

"When?"

"Last weekend. After I left you, after we—" I'm thinking back to the thunderstorm, to the way our bodies seemed to cling to each other like Velcro. He's thinking the same thing, I can tell. "—after we went to the beach. I knew I wanted to be with you. Now I'm not so sure."

"When were you going to tell me?"

"When I was sure it was gonna stick. And I wanted to go on the trip so she knew I meant it when I said that I still cared about her—plus her parents and stuff. And then there's the fact that if she did anything stupid I didn't want you to feel responsible."

Like he said several times. Complicated.

I'm still soaking it in. James is free. James wants to be with me. Or did. Until I went and screwed it up without even knowing it.

"Well, *I* did a stupid thing," I say. "But it doesn't change anything. And I wouldn't have done it if I'd known what was going on with you the whole time. You were so secretive. How was I supposed to know?"

He's not looking at me.

"James. Hey." I lean in to kiss him.

He shakes his head. "That's not gonna happen, Betsy."

He just stares straight ahead at another light. Both hands on the wheel.

I pull back and we sit there waiting for the light to change. I wish there were a light to tell me what to do next. Whether to stop or slow down or go full steam ahead. We're in front of my house after another long, torturous minute. "I'm sorry," I say. "I don't know what else you want me to say." After a pause, I say, "It's not like I slept with him."

"No, well, you may as well have." He's worked himself into a state.

"Don't be stupid."

"I just need some time." He nods his head, proud of his idea. "Some space. To think things through."

I try the dress on that night. I'm careful to wash my hands a few times on account of dinner: Chicken McNuggets and fries. I lock my bedroom door and step into the dress's silky shell. It's hard to close up the back of it by myself, but I'm determined; I nearly dislocate my arm in the process. I've picked a couple of flowers from the backyard. They've been in a vase since before dinner. Now I take them in a bunch in my hand and stand in front of the mirror. Unsatisfied with what I see, I put them down and try to wind my hair up into an updo. It's not super-tight—it'd never hold up to a first dance or last dance—but it'll do for now. My bangs have gotten long and, pushed to the side, they look sort of cool, dramatic. I take up the flowers again and look in the mirror. I'm trying to imagine what it'll feel like, to be done with all of this. To have met someone I want to spend the rest of my life with. I think maybe that person could be James—or could have been—but maybe I'm fooling myself. I'm only sixteen. I could go out with boys for the next sixteen years and still get married at a reasonable age. I wonder who I'll be when I walk down an aisle for real, whether the dress will even fit anymore, whether I'll still like it or whether I'll have thrown it out by then. I can't imagine ever wanting to part with it but maybe that'll all change. If, like James says, my mother is with me wherever I go, then it doesn't matter if there's nothing in my closet that she's ever touched, no physical reminder, if everything else about me changes except for the fact that she was my mother.

*   *   *

My father takes Ben and me to my aunt's house for a barbecue on Saturday afternoon. It's the first time we've seen a big group of family members and everyone of age who's not driving seems to cope by drinking heavily. When no one's looking I slip inside and open the fridge and take a beer into an upstairs bathroom. I sit on the toilet, lid down, twist off the cap, and take a sip. It tastes bitter but not entirely unpleasant. I look at the label and it's a beer I've never heard of, then I set about drinking it as fast as I can.

Somehow I can't believe it's all come to this: me with a dead mother and a fast-food family, sitting on a toilet and drinking a beer after screwing up the best thing that ever happened to me by hooking up with an asshole. Maybe I've hit the depression stage. The I-don't-care-anymore stage. Because no matter what I do, I still can't seem to get things right. Maybe I'll just stop caring so much. Eat fast food with abandon, go out and hook up with whoever/whenever. Make piles of black confetti out of my supposed art and call it a day. Call it a life.

I hide my empty under my T-shirt, flush the toilet, then head back downstairs and put the bottle on a counter in the kitchen. Right outside the door, my aunt is talking to my father. "How's the book coming?" she says.

"It's going well," he says. "Very well." I watch through the screen door as he nods, maybe even believing his own lie, and then he lifts his empty plate and says, "I'm going to get some more of that potato salad."

My aunt comes into the kitchen. "Everything okay?" She slides an arm around my shoulders.

"Yeah," I say. "Fine."

"Want to help me with the watermelon?"

"Sure," I say, excited by the prospect of putting actual fruit in my body.

I check my phone when we're in the car on the way home. There's a new message and I don't recognize the number. I hope maybe it's James calling from his house—not his cell—calling to say he wants to see me, can't bear to stay away. But it's not James. It's Nora, calling from the art supply store. My special order has come in. I click my phone shut after listening, and try to decide whether I care.

chapter 21

I wake up unusually early on Sunday morning and walk up to the beach. There's a coolness to the morning air—for the first time in weeks I can fathom the idea of wool sweaters—and it saddens me to think of summer ending in just a few weeks. I go down near the water and sit and dig my feet into the cold sand, thinking of the year ahead: My first birthday without my mom. The first Thanksgiving. Then Christmas. Then *her* birthday. Just thinking of it all is too much to bear. I'll be a senior. I'll graduate and she won't be there, then I'll go off to college who knows where.

I sit there looking out at blue-gray waters and a sky just beginning to let the sun turn it blue and fantasize about some great romantic end to the story of me and James. I imagine that a year goes by and I graduate and get into Princeton—meaning that a miracle occurred on SAT day—and I'm walking across campus and he sees me and I see him and he leaves the people he's with and walks over to me and says, "What are you doing here?" I'll say, "I go to school here now," and he'll say, "I'm sorry I left things the way I did." Then we'll go for coffee and it will all still be there. He'll come back to my dorm room and we'll pick up where we left off in the car that day, in the thunderstorm.

But I don't want to wait a year. I want to feel a tap on my shoulder and turn to see him right there, right here on the beach. He'll say, "I'm sorry. I overreacted." Or he won't say anything at all. It will all just be unspoken. He'll just take me in his arms and kiss me and I'll know that we're okay, that *everything* is going to be okay. Then Mary will have another party and James will come with me and everyone will be jealous—girls because he's older and cooler and cuter than any of the guys they know, boys because they wish they'd gotten to me first. But stuff like that only really happens in my head.

In reality, I turn and there's no one there but an old guy with a metal detector. I take it as a sign that I should give James the space, the time he asked for, and resist the urge to call him and beg forgiveness.

I think back to the first time I met him, to those stray raindrops that signaled the end of our conversation, to the fact that I claimed I only ever said one word at a time. If I could say one word to him now it would be "love."

When I walk into the art supply store, there's an eerie quiet. I look around at some notebooks and fancy boxes of cards but I have to talk to someone to pick up my order, and so I wait and hope it's someone other than Nora working today.

And still more silence. I tap my fingers on the counter.

I study pretty much every item for sale near the register—

pick up and put down at least ten different kinds of pens—before impatience gets the best of me. I walk down to the end of the counter where a burgundy curtain hangs in a doorway and I go to it and push it aside for a peek. I see Nora—some kind of shiny object held against her wrist—and gasp and step back and my shoe comes off and makes a snap on the floor.

I hear some commotion in the back room as I slip my foot back into my shoe and then Nora comes out, realizes it's me, and says, "You shouldn't snoop."

"And you shouldn't do what you were doing."

Our words seem to float over to each other, like we're in some bizarre time warp. She somehow forgot to drop her blade and she puts it down on the counter as she pushes past me, probably thinking I don't see.

"Oh, yeah?" She sounds hopeless, like there's barely enough air to power her words. "Why not?"

"You just shouldn't. It's not worth it."

She goes behind the counter and says, "You're here for your paper."

"Yeah. I got your message."

"What's it for anyway?" She wipes her nose and I get that she's been crying.

"I've been making a scene on a wall in my basement. It's a beach party cutout of black paper. I want to add a Ferris wheel," I say. "So I needed bigger paper."

We're both silent for a moment, then she says, "You work with James, don't you?"

"Yeah." I feel my throat close up.

"He broke up with me." She sighs heavily, loudly. "Again."

I realize we're not so different and my throat opens up wide.

"I got dumped at the beginning of summer. She was at my mother's wake. They started seeing each other behind my back." It's weird how long ago that all feels already. The funeral. The wake. The night out bowling with Brandon and Lauren Janey. I feel like I've lived a thousand summers in one; it's almost like it happened to someone else.

"Are you *serious*?" Nora's eyebrows shoot up.

"I wish I wasn't."

She shakes her head and I study her more closely: her long, thick eyelashes, her chapped bottom lip. She says, "How do you do it?"

"Do what?"

"I don't know . . . deal?"

"I don't have any choice."

"Sure you do." She looks toward the blade on the counter and almost laughs. I wonder for a second whether this is all a game to her, whether she has ever really meant to hurt herself or whether she's just toying with the idea . . . and James . . . and me . . . but it's not my call to make.

"No, I don't." I reach over and pick up the blade. "I've been using scissors but I should really be using one of these. Can I take this one?"

"Go for it," she says, like she really didn't need it anyway, like there are plenty more where that came from. "That's your paper over there."

There's a big roll in the corner near the burgundy drape. It's wrapped in brown paper and tied with twine and looks like a carpet—my magic carpet. My heart kind of sparks with excitement.

"Your project sounds cool," she says softly. "Where can I see it?"

"It's sort of just for me."

"That's too bad. Maybe you should rethink that."

"You might want to rethink a couple of things, too."

She nods her head but I just keep talking: "If you do something stupid, I'll never forgive you." I feel ballsy when I say what I say next. I say, "And neither would he."

"I know." She plays with the sleeve of her cardigan, then looks up at me. "Please don't tell anyone about this. Please don't tell James."

"I won't." I wish I could do more, say something to let her know that it's all going to be okay. But maybe it's not all going to be okay for her. I don't even know if it's going to be okay for me. I wish at the very least I could make her laugh, break this mood. Then an idea comes to me. "Actually, hold on," I say. "I'll be right back."

I walk next door to the café and my aunt's refilling sugar bowls. "I can't explain right now," I say to her, "but I need that photograph." I point to the gull and Frog Bog photo. Something about my face, my tone of voice must make it clear I mean business.

"Okay," she says.

I step around a chair and gingerly lift the photo off its hook. "Thanks," I say, and walk out the door and back to the art supply store. At the register, I hold the photo out to Nora.

"You don't have to do this," she says.

"I want to," I say, jerking the photo closer to her.

She takes it and starts to cry and laughs through her tears. "It's just so fucking sad."

The bike ride home is torturous as I'm doing it all one-armed, while holding the roll of paper under my left arm. I pass a

Dumpster at one point—it's in the parking lot of the 7-Eleven—and I'm tempted to just toss the paper in there and be done with it. I mean, a Ferris wheel? Who really cares? I even stop the bike, see if I have enough money in my pocket for a Big Gulp, but I don't. I'd already paid for the paper so I didn't bring my wallet. I find a better way. I prop one end of the paper roll on my pelvis, so the other end rests on the handlebars. It's not easy to pedal, but if I keep my knees close, the paper kind of shifts a little left and right. My arm is grateful for the break. But then my legs start to cramp. I'm using my muscles differently, I guess. So I stop again a few blocks from home and let out a few groans and curses. I put it back under my left arm and struggle the whole way home. It feels like my limb is going to fall off. I drop the paper in front of the house and go to put my bike in the shed. I come back out front for the paper and think again about just tossing it in the trash. But I don't. I bring it inside, open the basement door, and throw it down the stairs. It lands at the bottom with a thud.

I go to the party for the Italians that night—alone. Sandra stops me at the front door to tell me that Brandon's "quote-unquote not feeling so hot" and didn't come and that Lauren Janey showed up on Sandra's friend Carl Woodward's arm. "I had no idea he was bringing her," she said. "She's apparently jumped ship to him. I'll ask her to leave if you want me to. I'd have no problem with that."

"That's okay," I say, surprising myself, but for the first time it occurs to me that something must be wrong with Lauren Janey, going from boy to boy the way she does. There must be something she's missing in her life, something she's not getting at home and is looking for in boy after boy. "Find something you're passionate about," my mother said. "The rest will follow." It seems like as good a theory as any—and since they were her last words to me, they take on more weight somehow. I have to believe they were important, the most important thing she ever told me. I half want to walk over to Lauren Janey and whisper in her ear, "Don't worry about boys, worry about passion." I half want to walk over and slap her.

Sandra's parents have decided to test out the cooking skills they learned in Tuscany so there's a huge spread of Italian food on a buffet table on the deck by their pool. Trying to be discreet, I stuff myself silly. It all tastes so good I think maybe I'll have to move to Italy some day. I imagine myself bicycling through cobblestone squares and Roman ruins and buying Italian bread and saying "Buon giorno!" to everyone I pass. I imagine that when people ask me why I left America, I just shake my head and clutch a handkerchief to my chest and they all just accept that it was tragic and pass the pasta.

Mary isn't there and I'm sort of relieved. She's apparently having dinner with her father and the girlfriend. I'm sure she'd rather be here, even though I'm here.

Sandra introduces me to Marco, who is hanging on her every word, and then introduces me to his friend, Giovanni, with fanfare. "Giovanni is a painter," she says, and I think to myself, He's sixteen! But then I think of my basement wall and figure I'm no different. If he likes to think of himself as a painter, then so be it.

"I'm an artist, too," I say, trying it on for size with someone I know will soon be leaving the country.

"What is it that you do? You paint? Sculpt?"

"No, it's silhouette art."

"I don't know this word, 'silhouette'."

"I cut things out of paper. People. Scenes."

"Ah," he says, "very interesting." He's not wearing a shirt, having just come out of the pool, and he scratches a spot on his chest, then rubs his wet hair with a towel. His skin is dark, like creamy chocolate, and for no reason I can think of I think that he probably has a large penis. It's not a thought I've ever had about anyone before and I almost laugh out loud. "I find American girls to be very interesting." He smiles. "Very independent. Very sexy."

I don't know what to say to this so I nod.

"Do you know Sandra from working together?"

"No," I say. I've never talked to someone from Italy before and I find myself choosing my words carefully, making sure they're simple and clear; his vocabulary seems good but his syntax is screwy. "We go to school together."

"Do you work, as well? For the summer?"

"Yes."

"You need me to, ah, pull teeth?"

It takes me a second to get this and smile. "It's kind of hard to explain. I work as a farm girl at a colonial village."

"You farm the land?" He says it like he's completely perplexed. "In New Jersey?"

"No." I laugh. "I mean, there are farms in New Jersey. But I don't work there. It's like a museum. We dress up as Early American people and give tours."

He nods and absorbs this information. The job has never seemed quite so dumb to me. "You Americans. You are strange."

You would think that after spending a summer working as an

Early American/colonial farm girl that I'd identify myself even more than ever as American but I've never really thought of myself that way before. Probably because I've never left the country. I realize there are whole countries, whole worlds out there, that somewhere in Italy and in Greece and in China and in Iran there are girls like me whose mothers have died of cancer.

"You have no boyfriend?" Giaovanni says, and it sounds so easy that I can't imagine why I never had the courage to ask James point blank, "Do you have a girlfriend?" I think how it might have saved us a lot of trouble.

I shake my head—"No, I don't"—embarrassed. Giovanni's cute but in a sort of cartoon Italian way. I half expect him to drop his accent and confess to me he's an actor preparing to try out for a "Come to Italy!" commercial.

"But you are so beautiful! And an artist! These American boys. *Pfst!*"

He takes my hand and lifts it to his mouth and kisses it. I think how easy it would be to flirt with him, to hook up with him, even. And how wrong. "I think I'm gonna go home," I say.

"No!" he says. "You can't leave me! Who will I talk to?!" He leans in to me, trying to reel me in by my arm, and says, "There's no one else here as beautiful as you."

This makes me laugh and I lean back and say, "Sorry. I don't have a boyfriend but there's someone else."

"A great love! Are you star-crossed?! Like Romeo and Juliet!" The idea seems to excite him.

"Not exactly," I say. "I sort of screwed it up."

"Well, then you must fix it!"

This guy is too much. "How?"

"A grand gesture of some kind!"

"Like what?" He's kind of engaging but I get up to let him know I'm serious about leaving.

"Ah! Only you can know that!" He looks up at me.

"Well," I say, "I'll give it some thought."

Sandra comes over just then and says, "I hope you're not thinking about leaving."

"I am," I say, then turn to Giovanni. "It was nice to meet you."

"And you! A fellow artist." He takes my hand and kisses it again. Sandra looks at me funny then links her arm through mine and leads me to the gate of her yard. "How can you resist him? He's so cute; I wish I'd met *him* first."

"But Marco adores you," I say. "It's obvious." He hasn't left her side all night.

"Yeah," she says. "I'm thinking I'm over it."

"You're awful."

"Yeah. I know. And you're an artist?"

"Long story."

"Are you sure you won't stay?"

"Yeah, just not feeling in a Tuscan mood."

"All right." She opens the gate. "Arrivederci, then. I'll talk to you soon."

I get on my bike and start the ride home. It's only a mile or so and I start out slow, figuring what's the rush, really. I think about Giovanni and James and try to think up some grand gesture. Something to do to win James back. But then I think of Lauren Janey and girls giving guys blow jobs at school or at Midland Beach and decide that maybe if I make a grand gesture it should be on my own behalf, not on his. I think of Nora and her idea of a grand gesture—how different it is from mine—and then wonder what she's done with the photograph, whether right now she's got it perched up against a wall in her room while she's smoking a cigarette or doing something else that tortured people do. I wonder what it is that makes life much harder for some people to bear. I think how random it is that one of my mother's photographs now belongs to James's ex-girlfriend and wonder what my aunt must have made of my storming in there and yanking it off the wall. I think of the blank space of white where the gull used to be and an idea dawns on me. The more I think about it the more the idea gains power. It seems to travel down to my legs and they start pumping faster. I look at my watch, and decide it's almost too late to call but not quite. So I stop in the middle of the road and call my aunt.

"I think I have your next exhibit," I tell her.

"Really?" she says. "What? Who?"

I feel a strange calm come over me when I look around and listen close and it's just me and the crickets. I take a deep breath and say, "Me."

I unroll the black paper and cut off a sheet that will encompass the entire Ferris wheel. The people I've made are about six inches tall so I make the Ferris wheel three feet tall—the paper is only three feet wide and I need a circle. I figure I'll play with perspective, how far into the distance it'll be to look in proportion.

I begin with the outer circle. I take the lid off a plastic garbage can and trace it with my X-Acto blade. Then I fold the paper in half and neaten up the circle so it's perfect. Then I apply some skills I used making paper snowflakes when I was little: I fold the paper once more into quarters and then start cutting out shapes, careful not to cut where spokes are supposed to be. By necessity, I cut out little cars that dangle. Not bench seats. It'd be too hard to do each one individually, and they can't be mirror images or some passengers would be facing the wrong way. The cuts feel different, since I'm slicing through four folds of paper now and not just a single sheet. All the while I'm hoping, praying, that it's going to work. When I set the blade down and begin to unfold the paper, I'm excited but scared, too. I want it to be perfect. And it is. Or just about perfect. Close enough for me.

I think of grand gestures again. Of something I might do to win James back. But it's not a game. There's no winning or losing. I decide maybe James has had enough of grand gestures, of I-can't-live-without-yous. I decide to send him a signal instead. Nothing grand. Just a tiny scene within my scene. A scene just for him. I unroll some more paper and start cutting.

chapter 22

In the morning, I awake with purpose and get dressed and go right down to the basement. I take pictures of the beach party with my cell phone camera, so I'm sure I can reassemble it the same way in the café, then I start taking down the figures and stacking them one on top of the other. I fold the Ferris wheel again, then put everything in a folder in my backpack. I grab a roll of tape and set out on my bike.

The café is locked so I knock and my aunt comes out of a back room. She's still setting up for the day. Without more than a quick hug and a hi, I get busy. My aunt stays out of my way, mostly working in the kitchen, preparing baked goods and brewing tea. I don't even have to check the photos. I know the scene back to front, left to right, now. I like seeing it all come to life here again. In the café it seems more alive, more fun, than it did in my bedroom or basement. The black looks blacker, the lines sharper.

When I finally step back to take it all in, my aunt comes over. "Oh, Betsy," she says. "It's perfect. I've been hoping to get a younger crowd in here on weekends and this really might help."

I highly doubt that having a beach party on the wall is going to help business in her café. It's more likely to inspire people to go someplace else, like to an actual beach party.

"When?" She throws her hands in there air. "How long? How did you do it?"

"I just had an idea after I saw this exhibit at Morrisville." I look at the beach party again and admit it looks pretty freakin' cool.

My aunt smiles and turns to me. "Of course this party is imaginary, right?"

"Of course."

We sit there a minute and then she says, "She followed you once. Your mother."

"What? Where?"

"You were going to some pool party but she was sure you were trying to sneak off to a beach party. So she got in the car and followed you and whoever was driving you."

I'd never been down to Midland before she died. "But I wasn't lying."

"She found that out. And she felt horrible, just horrible, for not trusting you."

My aunt doesn't have to say anything else for me to know what she's getting at. Or maybe she has no idea what the effect of this story is on me now but I'm filled with remorse. I don't want to be the kind of person who lies about where I'm going. Who goes off with strange boys and comes home drunk and disgusted with herself. Who doesn't lift a finger around the house unless forced to. I'm better than that. So when I get home—my father and Ben have gone to another ball game—I take the lasagna out of the freezer and call Liza.

It feels weird to be in the supermarket without my mother. I half expect an alarm to sound when I step through the automatic doors, I haven't been here in so long. And clearly, I don't belong. I know it won't be long before I go away to college, before I have to buy some of my own food, but this just feels wrong, like I'm being dragged into adulthood kicking and screaming.

For as long as I can remember I was my mother's food-shopping assistant. In exchange for my "services"—which amounted, when I was little, to not throwing fits—I was allowed to pick tiny packs of Kool-Aid for tea parties I'd then host in the basement for my dolls. Thinking of that now, I'm amazed that I was ever that person. That throwing tea parties for dolls was a priority in my life, that I was ever so innocent, so carefree. In later years, I was given the job of holding my mother's coupon organizer and letting her know whether to buy Cascade or Electrosol, depending on what was in the folder marked "cleaning." In preparation for these trips, it was my job to clip from the Sunday papers coupons we might use and it strikes me as odd now, to think about that, to think how I spent the Sundays of my youth cutting paper.

I head for the produce aisle, already annoyed with my cart and its one wonky wheel. Just once I'd like to get a cart that's smooth, that doesn't give you a headache with each push.

"So what are we doing here, Betsy my darling?" Liza wants to know. I'd almost forgotten she was here.

"It's too embarrassing." I pick up a head of iceberg lettuce and head for the tomatoes.

"Well, I'm here, too, embarrassed right alongside you, so spill."

"My father hasn't cooked a meal since my brother and I pissed him off sometime last month. It feels like it's time for me to step up and put some decent food on the table."

"What have you been eating?"

"Name a fast-food chain." I can't believe how cold it is in the supermarket. Don't they realize people shop in their shorts when it's hot out?

"McDonald's," Liza says.

"You're starting with the easy ones," I say. "Check. Usually Mondays."

"Taco Bell?"

"Usually every other Tuesday or so."

"Burger King."

"Not as often as McDonald's but once every other week."

"Wendy's?"

"Too long of a drive. Only once in a month."

"KFC?"

"A particular favorite. Crispy style in particular."

"That is messed. Up. It's like that movie, where that guy ate nothing but McDonald's"

"Supersize Me."

"That's the one. Does he not know how to cook? Is that it?"

"No, he's a great cook." I have no idea how to buy tomatoes but I pick up a couple and examine them and put them back before deciding which ones I want. "I think we made him feel taken advantage of. He asked us for help one night and we blew it off. So he ate by himself and that was that. Fast food forever."

"So what's the plan exactly?"

"Mary's mother made a lasagna. It's defrosting in the

fridge." Mrs. Giacomo, bless her, put a Post-it with heating directions on the pan. "I'll just make a salad, set the table."

We're walking past the onions and garlic and Liza picks up some garlic and puts it in the cart. "You should make garlic bread, too. I'll tell you how."

I'm just finishing up making a big salad when my father and Ben come through the front door. They come into the kitchen and my father says, "Whatcha doing?" He looks around, puzzled, and inhales. "What's that smell?"

"I found a lasagna in the fridge so I made a salad and there's garlic bread in the oven."

"I'll set the table," Ben says.

My father's face looks like it's going to cave in on itself—wobbling under some unseen pressure—and he says, "Excuse me for a minute," then leaves the room. Without my really noticing it, Ben sets the table in the dining room instead of the one in the kitchen. He puts out a tablecloth, uses the fine china, even puts out two candlesticks.

My father comes back a few minutes later, having clearly thrown some cold water on his face. Bits of his hair near his forehead are wet and there are a couple of dark splatter dots on his shirt. He looks into the dining room and sees Ben lighting candles, the table in there set. I tense, not sure how he's going to react.

"Well, isn't this lovely," my father says. He pulls out his chair and puts his napkin on his lap and I can practically taste the lasagna already. It's fresh and warm and rich and cheesy, and even though it's Mrs. Giacomo's it tastes like home.

*   *   *

The doorbell rings when we're cleaning up and I expect it to be the paperboy but it's Brandon. The tiny squares of the screen door make him look like a silhouette but he looks all gray, his lines all blurred. It's somehow fitting. "Hey," he says.

"Hi," I say because it sounds less friendly, though I'm not feeling as mad at Brandon as I used to.

"Can we maybe go somewhere to talk?"

"I really don't think—"

"Please." He looks so desperate, so worn-out, that I can't say no.

I tell my father I'm going out with Brandon and that it won't be long, and he raises his eyebrows over his glasses but then says, "Fine."

We walk up to the beach and sit on a bench on the boardwalk. There are a lot of runners out. Couples with small babies, too.

Brandon's just looking at me and then looking away and I say, "This is *your* party, Brandon."

"I know, I know. I just wanted you to know that I made a mistake."

I look away so I can shake my head a tiny bit and roll my eyes. "Let me guess. She broke up with you."

"Yeah."

"What happened?"

"She met someone else."

"Sorry," I say. "But I think that's kind of funny. I mean—" I look away for a second, force the smile from my mouth, then look back.

"Yeah." I forgot how blue his eyes are, forgot how I used to think they were the most beautiful eyes I'd ever seen. "It pretty much serves me right. Anyway, um." He crosses and then uncrosses his legs, stuck out straight in front of him. "It's not like I think you'd take me back but—"

I study him and try to imagine being with him again. For a second I wish I could rewind the clock and be content with him, with what we had, which was fine, easy, comfortable. But I can't. Not now that I know there's so much more.

"Betsy?"

"Yeah."

He scrunches up his nose. "I mean, you wouldn't want to try again, would you?"

I shake my head.

"That's what I figured." He leans forward, elbows on knees. "It was worth a shot." He looks at me and smiles and I have a flash of remembering why I ever wanted to go out with him, why I ever felt compelled to kiss those lips or slide a hand down those pants. "But I really just wanted to say I'm sorry. And I hope you don't hate me. And maybe we can be friends?"

I picture the year ahead and the years after that. I know that we'll be pleasant to each other at school but that's about all. We'll say hi in the halls and maybe even sign each other's yearbook or snap a photo together at graduation. Then we'll go to different colleges and maybe bump into each other at the bowling alley when we're home for Thanksgiving and this will all seem like another lifetime ago, like a dream, or a soap opera we once saw.

"Of course we can be friends," I say, knowing there's no way to explain why we won't be. Why we never really were.

chapter 23

I'm dreading seeing James—or having to avoid him—on Monday but then it turns out he has some kind of orientation day at Princeton. I should be relieved—considering the dread—but I'm not. All morning I picture him walking around a beautiful old campus and meeting all sorts of fascinating girls from all over the country and the world; they're all wearing nametags and back-to-school miniskirts and he doesn't know anything about them, their baggage. They're happy and he likes that about them, wants to get some of it for himself.

Liza tries to snap me out of my bad mood by quoting from a book she's reading. She's hidden the paper jacket in the closet since it's too modern looking but without that it looks like any old hardcover they might've had back then, even.

"Check this out," she says to me as I'm dusting the parlor. "This is a quote from John Quincy Adams." She clears her throat: "'Wherever the standard of freedom and independence has been or shall be unfurled, there will her—meaning

America's—heart, her benedictions, and her prayers be. But she goes not abroad in search of monsters to destroy. . . . The fundamental maxims of her policy would insensibly change from liberty to force. . . . She might become the dictatress of the world: she would be no longer the ruler of her own spirit.'"

She looks up and says, "I want to rip that page out and send it to the White House."

But I'm caught on the phrase "the ruler of her own spirit." I'm turning it around in my head, wondering what it means, and whether it's possible to really be that. Not just for a country to be that but for an individual. For me. "What book is that?"

"It's James's. It's called *1776*. You can take it if you want. I'm done, really."

"Okay." I lift a lace doily off a table to dust underneath it and admit I should probably do at least a little bit more around the house, *my* house. Now that I'm in the habit of sweeping and dusting, it wouldn't kill me to help my father out. Making dinner was nice, sure, but I still wouldn't win any Daughter of the Year awards. I have tomorrow off and make a promise to myself to at least clean my room and the upstairs bathroom. I can't believe I'll have to wait until Wednesday to see James. Everything feels so wrong, so up in the air.

When I walk up to the bike rack at the end of the day, I see they're taking down "Profiles in History" and I'm sort of sad to see it go. The next exhibit has to do with quilting and I can't imagine I'll suddenly develop an interest in that. At least I hope not. Though at least I'd get a blanket out of the deal, something to keep me warm. I watch as a team of maybe three men takes down the framed portraits and wraps them carefully in bubble wrap before packing them up in boxes. I wonder what all those people from back then would think, if they knew their profiles were endlessly being shipped around the country to museums. I remember the day it went up, when James came over and I had a lot of attitude for a lowly farm wench. I was so full of hope back then—hope that he'd somehow save me from the misery of my life. I guess it wasn't up to him, though.

My father and Ben are playing cards at the kitchen table when I get home from work and I sense, somehow, that they've been waiting for me.

"What's going on?" I say.

"Grab a seat," my father says.

I slide my backpack off and slide into a chair.

"I spoke with Dr. Willis today."

Ben and I look at each other. We've been caught.

"He apologized profusely. He only found out about Mom last week. From his wife, who knew a friend of mom's."

I'm staring down at the queen of hearts, wondering whether we're in trouble or not. "I really wish that one of you had told me about the incident. I would've called and explained."

"We're sorry, Dad," Ben says.

"Yeah," I say.

"We need to talk to each other," my father says. "We three. We're all we have now. Okay?"

I want to scream, "No shit, Sherlock! Where the hell have you been?" but I'm too relieved, so I say, "Okay," and Ben does, too.

"Is there anything else on your minds? Any other things we should be talking about? Anything else you need from me?"

"No more McDonald's," I say.

My father nods. "You made your point last night. No more fast food. I swear."

"Where's mom's silhouette?" Ben says. "And yours, Dad? I think we should hang them up somewhere. All four of them. Where we can see them."

"I think they got ruined, when a hose burst in the basement one year. They weren't where yours were and I'm pretty sure we threw them out." I can tell he's barely holding it together but I don't care. I have to say it.

"I think we need to talk about her more. Tell stories. Talk about the good stuff. Even if it's hard at first."

"Agreed." My father gets up. "Everybody go change into something at least a little bit nicer. We're going out to dinner. To turn over a new leaf."

At Red Lobster, there's a short wait. The "Irving, party of three. Irving" sort of dampens our spirits but we all seem to recover pretty quickly. We hit the salad bar together, then return to a big, dark wood booth with plates overloaded. When we sit down, my father slathers butter on a breadstick, takes a loud, crunchy bite, and says, "Did I ever tell you about the time your mother woke up with a spider on her forehead?"

"Ohmigod." Ben bites a cherry tomato, with his hand in front of his mouth. "Did she flip out?"

I eat a forkful of chickpeas and just listen.

chapter 24

In the morning, I start a new project in the basement in an attempt to give Ben what he's looking for. But I can't really do this one from images in my mind. Finally, I go upstairs, where Ben is playing his video game. I say, "I need your help."

"I'm busy."

"Fine. Be that way." I go down the hall toward my father's office and knock on the door.

"Come in!"

I open the door and my father picks up a book, pretending to be busy. "I need your help."

"Now?" he says.

"Yes," I say. "Now. In the basement. It'll only take a few minutes."

My father follows me back through the kitchen and when Ben hears us going down into the basement, he decides to come, too. I've taped two huge pieces of black paper to the wall. "I need you to stand against the wall."

"Cool," Ben says. "Can I pose funny?"

"If you want."

"What is this, Bets?" my father says.

"It's an art project."

"For school?"

"No. Just for me. For us. You'll see."

When my dad and Ben go back upstairs, I set about cutting them out with the X-Acto blade. I take their big sheets of black down and lay them on the floor on cardboard from the recycling and start cutting. The trace is sort of crude, but I sharpen it as I go. Ben decided to pose with his knees slightly bent and his arms in the air as if he's just thrown a basketball. Adding the basketball afterward will be easy enough.

My father was more uncomfortable against the wall, couldn't figure out how to pose. First he stood with his arms crossed, one foot crossed over the other, toe tips down to the ground. In silhouette he'd have looked like he had no arms. He tried waving, but it looked too dorky. Finally I handed him a book and he held it in one hand, turned his head to the side as if to read from it, and put his other hand on his hip. While I was tracing him, he realized what book it was. "Where did you get this book?"

"It's James's," I said.

"Hmmph," he said. "Very impressive."

Working alone and confidently, I finish my father's and Ben's full-size silhouettes and contemplate the challenge ahead of me. I need to add my mother to the wall but I have no pictures of her in profile. I've looked and looked and have come up with nothing—not even in my parents' wedding album. I close my eyes and try to picture the lines of her face, try to imagine I'm in the passenger seat looking over at her and then impose my mental grid on her, but I can't get her image in my mind in sharp enough detail. My brain just isn't wired that way. Fortunately, I know someone whose brain is.

"Hi, Mrs. Elks." She seems so surprised to see me that I feel more guilty than ever about how much time I used to spend with Alex, how little time I have for him now. "Is Alex home?"

"Yes, Betsy." I hear no resentment in her voice. "He's in the dining room. Come in."

"Betsy!" Alex shouts when I peek my head into the dining room. He gets up to give me a hug. "Hi, Betsy," he says, and I say, "Hi, Alex."

"I miss Kelly," he says. The fact that he says my mother's name out loud shocks me. I'm not sure I've heard it said aloud since she died. It's been "your mother" this and "your mother" that, and I have to remind myself that she was something else. A person. Before she was my mother and even after.

"Alex got a little worked up in church last Sunday," Mrs. Elks says. "Didn't you, Alex?"

He just shrugs and picks up yarn and his hook and goes back to his picture. His breathing is heavy all the time. It sounds like he's constantly congested.

Mrs. Elks turns to me. "Alex got up during church and went up to the lectern so he could tell everyone how sad he was about losing his best friend."

I want to start sobbing right there on the spot because I remember my mother once telling me that she wanted to bring Alex to one of my soccer games. I threw a fit at the time—"Are you *trying* to ruin my life?"—and I feel so awful about it all now, about how I'm not nearly as good a friend to him as my mother was, that I'll lose it if I say anything other than what I say. "That was really nice of you, Alex."

"She was my best friend," he says again and I want to tell him I'll try harder, try to be more like her, but I don't and I'm not sure why.

"Hey, Alex." I pull out the framed silhouette of me. "Can you help me with something?"

I put it down in front of him and he looks at it from an odd angle. "It's you," he says.

"Yes," I say. "That's me when I was young. I was wondering, do you think you could make a rug like this? Only not me, my mother?"

He gets up and leaves the room without a word and Mrs. Elks says, "He's taken it very hard, Betsy. She was very good to him. It might be too much."

"I'm sorry I asked," I say. "I didn't mean to upset him."

"Of course not," she says. "Please tell your father if there's anything he needs. If he ever needs someone to watch Ben, anything."

"Thanks," I say, and as I do, Alex comes back into the room. He's carrying a smallish white mesh canvas and has two colors of yarn in his hands: black and white. He sits down at the dining room table and starts in with white in the bottom left corner and Mrs. Elks says, "I guess I'll make us some tea."

We sit there for an hour, just watching silently, sipping tea, as an image of my mother takes shape on Alex's canvas. It's like magic.

*　　　*　　　*

When Alex is finally done, I get up and go around to look at it from his side of the table. It's a perfect likeness of my mother. "It's perfect, Alex," I say. I kiss him on the cheek. "Can I borrow it?"

"You keep it," he says.

"Thank you," I say.

"You want to play pool?"

"Sure," I say. "Sounds fun."

A few hours later, when I'm out the door, I look at the flip-side of the mesh, where the knotted black threads form a clearer pattern than on the shag side. It's exactly what I need to add my mother's figure to the wall—a perfect blueprint for my silhouette. But it's only her face. I need something else, a body double.

I walk over to Mary's house and run up the steps and ring the doorbell as fast as I can so that I don't have a chance to stop myself. I don't know why but suddenly everything that's been keeping Mary and me at odds all summer seems to fall away. She's my oldest friend and that still has to mean something. Because in the end it's not about Brandon and Lauren Janey and the fact that Mary knew; it's not about her party or who's right or wrong or suffering more; it's about the fact that things are changing faster than we thought possible. But that doesn't mean there's no room at all for each other anymore. I just have to hope she feels the same. I have to hope that she cares that right now I need her.

She comes to the door, looking depressed, and I say, "Hey."

"What do you want?" she says and it sounds kind of harsh but I can tell from her face she's glad I'm here, glad I've taken the first step.

"I want to say I'm sorry," I say. "For everything."

She breathes hard, like she's not sure what to do, then opens the screen door and steps out onto the porch.

"I'm sorry I got so mad about the Brandon thing," I say. "I'm sure you thought you were doing the right thing."

She just watches me.

"And I'm sorry we had a fight when you told me about your parents. I should've been there for you more." Because I don't know what it's like to live through that, or to lose a cat, or to have the urge to cut myself because I think I can't live without someone. I'm not lucky that my mother died but I'm lucky that I've never had to deal with any of those things. Everybody has their own shit to slog through.

"I'm sorry, too," Mary says. "I should've told you and I shouldn't have invited her. And I just should've been there for you more. I guess I didn't know how."

"Well, now that you mention it—" I smile and Mary smiles hesitantly and says, "What?"

"Well, you know how we always used to joke how you and my mom were related? Because you're such similar body types and stuff?"

"Yeah?" She sounds confused, scared, and I guess I would, too.

"I need you to stand in for this thing I'm doing," I say. "It'll make more sense when you see it. Will you come?"

Mary is standing against the wall of the basement and I'm shining a light at her and tracing the shadow. "This is sort of freaking me out," she says.

"I know," I say, though it's not really freaking me out. "But you're the closest person I know to her size. She was tiny and compact, like you."

"I hope I'm still tiny and compact when I'm her age. I mean, when I'm older." This washes over me. I don't bristle. There will probably be a million things like this before I stop noticing them, stop feeling them like tiny pinpricks.

I work in silence for a minute. After some comfortable quiet, Mary says, "Remember how we used to play that game, Russia, when we were younger?"

"Ohmigod, yeah." I haven't thought of that in ages.

It's a game you play with a ball. You do one kind of toss once. Then a slightly harder toss—like letting it bounce once after it hits a wall—twice. Then a third, more difficult kind of toss—maybe one requiring you to clap you hands before you catch it—three times. And so on up to fourteen, at which point you have to toss the ball way high so you can clap your hands once in front, then once in back, then once in front again before catching it. If you drop the ball at any point you have to start over and the first person to finish the sequence wins.

"There was this one time," Mary says, "when your mother was watching us. And you were winning because you always did."

"I did not!"

"You did! Not the point. So I totally dropped the ball on, like, my ninth throw on something like thirteen, when you had to clap under your leg or something?"

I nod.

"Well, your mother saw me. You didn't. And she saw that I saw that she saw me. And she'd been keeping our tally and she was like, 'That's nine, going on ten' and winked at me. So I just kept going."

"Really?"

She nods.

"Huh," I say. I don't know what to make of it. My own mother helping my friend cheat? Against me? I wonder what James would make of this story, wonder if I'll ever have the chance to tell it to him. I think it says something new and complicated about her, I'm just not sure what it is.

"That always stuck with me. I mean, obviously it did. I'm talking about it now. But I thought of it a lot."

"Why?"

"Because neither of my parents would have ever done that. They always want me to win stuff, and be the best at stuff. Like this cheerleading thing? I mean, I like cheerleading. And maybe it's embarrassing that I haven't made a varsity team, but I really don't care. JV is fun. But God, there are tryouts in a few weeks and you'd think I was trying out for *Harvard*."

I think of trophies and plaques and ribbons and say, "I have someone you should see."

"Who?"

"It's a surprise."

"I've sort of had it up to here with surprises this summer."

"This is a good one, though. Trust me."

I work in silence a minute longer. "I heard you saw him last week. How was that?"

"It was fine," she says. "She's a ditz. Whatever. The weird thing, and please don't take this the wrong way, is that I really don't miss having him around the house as much as I thought I would. I mean, a part of me knows I'm probably doomed for life to have bad/needy relationships with men. But I'm sort of glad he's gone. It was too hard not knowing what kind of mood he'd be in when he came home from work. And my mom seems more relaxed without having to worry about that. She's gonna start dating soon."

I say, "God help her," and we laugh.

After Mary leaves I go to work giving my mother a life in paper. I work fast, with confidence. This is like second nature to me now. I feel like I could go to Disney World tomorrow and set up a cart and cut profiles for passersby in under a minute flat. I love the sound of the cut, the calluses that are starting to develop on my right middle finger, where the blade handle presses into my skin. I imagine this is how my mother felt when she looked through her lens, when she heard the click of her shutter. I wish she could've seen so many things—but most of all I wish she could have seen this. Me. Finally. Passionate about something.

My aunt calls later to tell me the beach party has been well received by her customers. "And Nora just adores it," she says. "We sat here and talked about every figure together. I love the little scene way over to the left—the man falling off the boat, and the woman with binoculars. And the whale? Just great. And the Ferris wheel. It's really quite extraordinary, Betsy."

"Thanks," I say. I wonder whether James ever told Nora that story. Whether she knows that scene is for him.

"You're an artist!" my aunt says, all cheesy like an adult. "Your mother would be so proud."

That I know this to be true is bittersweet.

"He was in here, too," she says, more confidentially, like she's keeping her voice down on account of customers. "You know, the tall blond. He demanded to know who the artist was. And if the way he tore out of here is any sign, I'd say he's coming your way soon."

I hear footsteps on the stairs and say, "Ben! How many times do I have to tell you! I'll tell you when it's ready."

"It's not Ben."

I turn and see James coming down the stairs. My first instinct is to try to somehow cover the scene taking shape on the wall. This isn't like the beach party. This is personal. Just for my family.

He steps down onto the cement floor and I can't believe he's here. It's almost as if he's died and has come back to life. He says, "Nora told me you talked her down off a cliff."

I look at the cut of Mary's/my mother's shoulders as I say, "She asked me not to mention it."

"I know." He puts his hands in his pocket shorts. "She told me, though. And whatever you said or did seems to have worked."

"Yeah?"

"She's going to check into that clinic. Get herself back on track. Deal with the depression and all."

"That's great." I nod. "Really great."

We're silent for a while and I don't know what he's doing, but I'm studying the lines of my newest figure, realizing I'm done and that it's time to move on.

"Why didn't you tell me?" He steps up to the wall. "And the one in the café."

I'm nervous now and I just shrug. What if he thinks I'm an idiot for spending all summer learning how to cut paper? What if he thinks I stepped over a line by putting his parents in the beach party scene? What if I don't care? What if this is bigger than him?

"They're amazing," he says. "Totally amazing."

"Really?"

Relief sweeps over me and then I'm wondering what James is doing here, and what that means for us, but at the same time I'm just staring at the wall and thinking about what has to happen there next and how it's *huge*.

"Really," he says. Then after a pause: "Hey, so I have something in the car for you. Do you want to maybe go for a ride?"

But I'm too distracted by the task ahead of me. His words barely sound like English, barely make sense. Then he says something about going back down to the wall, but he's like a riptide pulling me away from what I need to do and I don't like it. I say, "I'm kind of in the middle of something," and all I can think is that the moment is upon me . . .

"Okay." He moves toward the stairs. "I guess I'll see you at work."

. . . and it's thrilling and terrifying and I'm desperate to keep my footing.

"Yeah." The basement wall is a siren, calling me. "Definitely."

Then he's gone and there's a roar in my head because it's *time*. I somehow never anticipated this but it's as inevitable, as obvious, as exhilarating as nightfall.

It's time to cut a self-portrait.

chapter 25

the morning is crisp and cool and I'm eager to slip into my warm colonial clothes. September is in the air and I'm thinking of clean new notebooks and plaid and tree leaves the color of fire. At work, I'm getting water out of the well by the pond, watching the ducks glide lazily and thinking about how they'll be heading South soon, the lucky things that they are. I wish I could know the precise moment when they'll leave, so I could be here and watch them lift off and turn from lazy ducks into birds that flap and fly. I'm wondering if maybe my next project should involve ducks somehow. I'm trying to dream up a cool water scene—maybe a slice of pond life that shows life on the water and life below, maybe even a sunken pirate ship—when James startles me with a "Hey."

I look at him and his face is red. He's holding something wrapped in some kind of cloth. "I made this for you so you might as well have it." He holds it out to me but looks away.

I freeze for a second but then keep pumping the well. "I ·

don't want it if that's how you're going to give it to me."

"I don't know what you want from me." He pulls his arms back in, still holding the parcel.

"And I don't know what you want from me. I said I was sorry. It was stupid. He's an asshole. I can't spend the rest of my life apologizing."

"I'm not asking you to."

"Then what are we talking about?"

"Last night. I asked you to, you know—" He keeps looking away, running his hand through his hair, vulnerable, tortured. "To go down—"

"I was in the middle of something."

"—to the wall."

I finally understand his hurt, sort of remember hearing him say those words. "You asked me to go to the wall?"

He nods.

"I honestly don't remember hearing you say that." I wish I could explain to him how it feels, to have found this part of myself I never knew existed, to have found something I love doing, something that lights up my mind with ideas, something that's all mine.

"You don't remember?" He looks confused, like everything he knows is wrong.

"No. I don't." I put down the bucket, finally full. "That's weird. I don't know if I can explain it."

He half smiles. "And if you did remember. What would you think of that? Of me asking you that?"

Loretta comes down and silently takes the bucket away from me. I say to James, "I think that would be a fine idea," and hear Loretta mutter, "We don't have all day."

"Oh," James says, realizing he's gotten himself all worked up over nothing. He looks around, then takes my hand, and says, "Come with me."

He starts walking toward Buckman House. I want to ask him what he's doing, where he's taking me and why, but I don't because on another level I already know. In the garden maze, the air around us seems liquid, our footfalls like those of ghosts. I think of Julia Buckman and wonder whether she and her husband, John, ever stole kisses in their garden maze back in England, whether she's looking down on us, or peeking through a shrub. Whether she's happy. Whether she's jealous that I'm alive and in love and she's not.

The maze feels different with James leading me through it. It's because he knows the way. Because there will be no wrong turns this time. No dead ends. The place that used to give me the creeps has turned, with my hand in his, into a beautiful hiding place. We turn and turn—left and right and right again—and then I lose track and then we're in the center of the maze where there's a marble fountain, and we stop and he turns to me and he leans down and then we're kissing.

I hear giggling and pull away from James and see a little kid poking his head around a corner and looking at us. His mother rounds the bend and joins us in the center of the garden and says, "Oh, I'm sorry."

"'Tis a beautiful day, madam. Wouldn't you say?" James says, recovering faster than I can.

"Yes, it is," she says. "Come on, Leo. Let's find our way back."

She takes his hand and starts to lead him out of the center of the maze and there's something about the light and the white top and shorts she's wearing; I see her now like a silhouette in reverse.

White light against dark green shrubbery walls. Right then James says, "I wanted to give you this last night but I don't know. I got freaked out when you didn't want to go for a ride with me."

He hands me the bundle. It's about six inches by six inches, and when I open it I see it's a Ferris wheel cut out of wood.

"Ohmigod," I say, noting that it's practically a duplicate of the one I cut out of paper. "I have an idea," I say, as two thoughts come together in my mind. "And I need your help."

When I explain to James what I have in mind—and how I'll get the go-ahead from Rudolph—he still doesn't get it. He says, "I still don't understand what you need me for."

"Paper can't get wet," I say. "So I need something stronger. Something that can stand on its own, too. I need wood."

"Aha." It's like a lightbulb has gone on in his head. "We'll have to go to one of my father's favorite places."

"Which is?"

"You'll see."

"We don't have much time."

"We'll go after work."

"I can't tonight." There's chicken cacciatore in the Crock-Pot for the first time in months. I'm going to debut my family-of-four piece to my father and Ben. "But tomorrow?"

"Okay," he says. "Tomorrow."

Before meeting my dad in the parking lot, I stop in to Mrs. Rudolph's office and explain what I want to do.

"Hmm," she says. "Sounds cute."

It'll be more than cute, but she doesn't have to know that yet. "So I can do it?"

"Sure," she says. "I don't see why not."

"Thanks."

"No, thank *you*, Betsy." She shuffles some papers on her desk. "I had my doubts about you at the beginning, I have to say. But I'm happy to say that, well, if you'd like to come back next summer, there's a job here for you at Morrisville. And there are some part-time opportunities during the school year. We have a lot of events around the holidays."

"Thanks," I say and before I think the words just tumble out. "I'd love to come back."

She seems as surprised as I am.

"I mean," I say, "I might need to renegotiate my pay and stuff."

She smiles and says, "But of course. All right. Off you go."

At home, there's excitement in the air for the first time in a long time. Our house has sort of reeked of sadness for so long that I'd all but forgotten that it was ever any different.

"Should we eat first?" my father says. "Or view the exhibit first?"

"I think view the exhibit, right?" I've never had an art opening in my basement so I'm not sure how it's supposed to work.

"Well, let's do it right then," my dad says. He opens the freezer and takes a box of frozen hors d'oeuvres out. "Microwaveable art opening right here." He reads the box. "And wait!" He reaches way back into the fridge where there's a bottle of sparkling cider. "Get the champagne flutes from the china cabinet," he says.

"Cool," Ben says.

"It's nonalcoholic," I say.

"Oh," Ben says. "Whatever."

Downstairs I've changed the overhead lightbulbs so the room has a softer, yellowish glow. I lead the way, carrying my own glass and Ben's as he's got a platter of pizza rolls and pigs in a blanket in his hands.

"I'm taller than that!" Ben says. He puts the plate down and goes over to the wall and stands up against his silhouette. He puts a hand atop his head and then runs it straight over to the wall and it's just about perfect.

"Well, this is just great," my father says. "Really great."

"Do you really like it?"

He puts an arm around me and squeezes and says, "What's not to like?"

At dinner, my dad tells us a story about how my mother once lost her bikini top in the ocean and "oh, what a scene!" Ben pipes up with a story about how she came to an international food lunch that he was having in social studies one day and how when another mother asked why Benjamin Franklin Irving saw fit to bring in tacos, my mother lied and said that we were part Mexican. I think about telling them about the wedding dress but decide that's just for me and my mom—and I guess James. Maybe I'll tell them someday but I feel like I'm not old enough to make that decision now. Like I might regret it if they don't react the way I want them to. Instead, I tell them about the time she was driving me to the surprise party, the couple with the table. "Your mother was full of surprises," my father says with a sigh. A lump forms at the back of my throat; I figure that's the other thing worse than losing a parent. Losing a spouse. The person you dreamed with, the person you were supposed to grow old with.

He takes off his glasses and says, "I just miss her so much," and it's like a weight on me goes poof. We no doubt have a long way to go, but at least we're all—finally—in it together.

After dinner, I slip back downstairs and start working on a cutout for my next project. The Morrisville Maze project, as it's becoming called in my head. I roll out paper and cut two figures before pausing to look up at the family of four on the wall.

The sight of us there makes me sad we'll never be that way again in real life. But it seems fitting somehow—the four of us on the wall of our basement, the four of us as our foundation. I initially had Ben on the left, shooting hoops away from the other three images. And my father was looking away from him, reading from his book. My mother and I were in the middle, her facing out toward my dad, me facing out toward Ben's back. But then I changed it all around. Now Ben's basketball is just over my father's head. He's too busy with his book to notice but my mother is next to him, looking up at the ball, holding a hand to her mouth as if to cover a gasp. It's like she's saying, "Oops! That's gonna hurt."

I study my self-silhouette then, and admit that I'm pleased with how it turned out. I'm not quite sure it's exactly like me in profile but it has a certain air about it that I'd like to strive for. She seems a bit more at ease than I usually feel—probably a little touch of Liza—and maybe a little sexier, somehow, around the hip area—probably because of James. She also looks a lot like my mother around the mouth and chin and that suits me fine. She's standing behind my mother, arm outstretched, mouth open, about to say something, like maybe, "I love you." Or, "Look what I can do." Or, "There's this boy, I think you'd like him."

chapter 27

James and I stand staring at sheets of plywood. He's got a T-shirt on that says Flaming Lips—which is that band he's been playing for me, apparently—but he's still wearing his pants from work and his suspenders are hanging down his thighs. "Want to see my impression of a Home Depot shopper?" he says.

I look at him and say, "Sure," and then he turns right back to staring up at the wood. I watch him for a second, waiting, thinking how weird it is to be here with him. I somehow can't believe we're here together, that he exists at all, that I haven't always known him. That I barely know him.

"That's it?" I say, when it's clear he's doing his impersonation already.

"What do you mean, that's it? It's brilliant!" He looks up and down the aisle but there's no one else there. "Come 'ere." He takes my hand and we walk to the end of the aisle and look up the next one. There are two sets of people, staring up at ceramic tile flooring. "Ohmigod," I laugh. "You're totally right."

He drags me to the end of the next aisle and there are two people staring up at yet more tiling. James and I start cracking up.

Back at the aisle with plywood, we resume our own gawking. "Well, this is *your* baby," he says. "You need to tell me what you need."

"I think a few of these." The boards are four feet by eight feet. Farther down the aisle I see smaller pieces, in different shapes. I move toward them. "But maybe something from here, too."

James says, "That's a scraps pile so it's cheaper."

I take a small piece of plywood out of the scraps pile and rest it on the floor. An image appears to me just then.

"That one's kind of small," James says. "Isn't it? I thought we were talking life-size."

I shake my head and put the piece on our wheeling cart. "I'm the creative genius here," I say. "Let's not forget."

He smiles and, together, we get down to business. He lifts pieces of wood out—some square, the rest rectangles of different proportions—and I pick and choose the ones I want based on the images in my head. Then I realize I haven't entirely thought things through. We borrowed Will's truck—he swapped cars with James for the night, happy, I suppose, to see his apprentice engaged in a project involving wood—but beyond that . . .

"This stuff," I say. "Where are we going to take it? My father'll never let me take it in the basement. There's not really room."

"That, my dear," he says, "is where I come in. Or, more importantly, where my garage comes in."

He takes two two-by-fours down off a lumber shelf as we head to the spray paint and I say, "What are those for?"

He smiles smugly, and says, "You'll see."

White spray paint secured, we get on line and James says, "It's been too long."

"Since what?"

"Well." He leans in and kisses me and it takes my breath away. I never knew what that expression meant exactly, and now I do. My body takes a minute to reset itself, to get used to taking in oxygen again. "Too long since a lot of things," he adds. "But what I meant was, too long since you've told me a story."

"I don't feel like it," I say, even though stories have started to pile up on top of each other, like the time my mother lost her contact lenses in our friend's pool and couldn't drive us home until my father came over with her glasses, or the time she came home, having had her hair colored, and my father called her "Red" and she turned around and went right back to the salon to get it put back to blonde. Now that my family has broken the silence and started talking about her, it's less urgent that I do so with James.

"Not in any bad way," I say. "I just, well . . . how about you tell me a story about you?"

"Well." He pushes our cart forward. "I was born on a stormy Tuesday, of humble means . . ."

"No, I'm serious." I lean into him. "I've loved hearing stories about your father but I want to know more about you."

"You already know me."

This strikes me as true even though I know it's not. Maybe I just know the big things, the important things, the things that are knowable in a look or a kiss or a touch. "I know," I say. "But I want details."

James's house is dark when we pull in—it's the first time I've been here—but a light in front of the garage comes on when he pulls the truck in. "Where's your mom?" I say as he turns off the engine.

"She's out of town." The second he says it he realizes maybe it sounds weird. "Should I have told you that?" He smacks himself on the head. "I'm so stupid. I wasn't thinking. I should've told you that."

"No, no," I say. "It's okay."

"You're sure."

"Yeah, it's fine." I don't admit that I actually prefer it. That other people's mothers have started to freak me out. To make me sad.

"We'll stay in the garage." James gets out of the car. "I'll keep one foot on the ground."

I want to tell him that I don't want to stay in the garage, that I don't want him to keep one foot on the ground, but I'm not sure what I want. Mostly, I want to get to work, to see if this idea has wings. It's like a new compulsion with me, this silhouetting thing. I want to think of a new word for it, though. Something more modern and cool sounding.

"Okay." He slides a piece of plywood out of the back of the truck and together we carry it into the garage and then lean it against a wall. It's a piece about four feet wide and six feet tall. "Where do we start?"

I go back to the truck and grab the poster holder I've been toting around all day. I snap the lid off and slide out some rolled-up cutouts. I unroll them, then lift the first figure off the pile. "I think we tape this to the wood and then you get the saw out."

"Me?" James asks.

"Uh, yeah. What did you think? That *I* was gonna do it?"

It's our second-to-last week of work and Liza and I break some serious rules; she gives me a driving lesson on our lunch break. In costume. Driver's ed has ended without additional incident or fanfare and my road test is scheduled for the day before my birthday. My father is still hinting that he might not let me get an actual license but now that I've started pulling my weight around the house, he seems to have forgotten about the night I went to the party with Danny Mose. Thankfully, I've started to forget, too.

"Thank God I wasn't born in the eighteenth century," Liza says. She has her feet stuck out the passenger side window and her bonnet straps are dangling in the wind. "Do you realize how long it takes to get anywhere by horse and carriage? I'd never survive. Plus, the way your butt must hurt. Man."

I realize, too late, that I need to change lanes in order to turn right and head back to Morrisville. Our lunch hour's almost up. "Shit," I say. "I'm screwed."

Liza pulls her feet in and sticks her head out the window. "Pardon me, kind sir," she says to the guy in the right lane whose window is also open. "Might you have the kindness of heart to let two damsels in distress into your riding lane?"

I start laughing and hear the guy say, "Gahead."

"Thank you kindly," Liza says, so when the light changes I pull ahead of him and turn right. "You're getting better at this," Liza says. "No more fear."

"Well, I have you to thank." I make another turn, a left one, and feel confident, free.

"I feel like I'm always asking you for favors but I have another one," I say once we pull back into the village parking lot. "A big one."

"What, mayhap, could it be?"

I'm driving so I can't really look to judge her reaction when I say, "Mary needs help with cheerleading."

"You've got to be shitting me."

"Please."

"She's never had a nice word or thought about me, I can tell you that much."

"She doesn't know you. It'll be different. Really."

Liza's just shaking her head.

"Unless maybe you're just not up to the job."

"Fuck that," she says. "Who better than me?"

"You'll do it?" I ask, as I park in the parking lot.

"Yeah," she says. "I'll do it."

I toss her the keys when we get out of the car, and she says, "I think you should schedule your road test."

I think she's right.

As we walk back to the farmhouse, Liza starts cheering. "Give me a one!"

So I say, "One."

"Give me a seven," she says.

So I say, "Seven."

"And another seven!"

"Seven!"

"And a six!"

"Six!"

"What does it spell?"

"They're numbers. They don't spell anything."

"Seventeen seventy-six!" she screams. When I roll my eyes, she shakes her head and says, "And you call yourself a patriot."

That night, in the garage, James hands me a saw and I look at him like he's crazy.

"I can't do this," I say, but it's already in my hands somehow. "That's your job."

"Nuh-uh," he says. "Just think of this as a pair of electric scissors. And think of this as really thick paper."

Loretta sends Liza to deliver butter to Buckman House one morning and, not long after, comes into the front hallway, frantic. "Girls," she says. "Incoming. Very important tour group."

She looks around. "Where's Liza? She's not back yet?"

"No." I get up and fix my skirt and apron. "I can handle it."

"Are you sure?"

"Sure, I'm sure." I go to the front door and look over the bottom half. "Who is it? George Washington?"

"No," Loretta says. "But it might as well be. If this guy doesn't keep writing checks we're all out of jobs."

"I got it," I say. "No problem." I smile at Loretta, who looks like she might throw up an entire summer's worth of cornbread and chicken soup. I say, "T'won't take but a minute."

"Do *you* want to?" I ask James. We're on the couch in his den one night. His mother is away all week.

"Of course." James buries his nose in my hair and says,

"Mmmn." He perches up on his elbow, so he's lying beside me. His finger traces a pattern on my belly. "I mean, obviously. But at the same time, no."

"I know what you mean." I close my eyes and try not to laugh. His finger-tracing is just shy of a tickle.

"Let's wait." He flattens his palm on my stomach and bends his neck forward to kiss me. "This is fun, too."

After we kiss some more, I look at my watch, hooking my arm around his neck. "Break's up." I tap his back. "We've got work to do."

"Do it again," Liza says to Mary. I invited them both over and they're going into their second hour of cheerleading tryout preparations.

"Man." Mary picks up a bottle of water and takes a swig, then returns to the center of the deck. "How many freakin' times am I gonna have to do it?"

Liza, in a lounge chair, takes a sip of her iced tea. "Until you get it right."

I watch them—I'm actually reading *1776*—and laugh a little inside. Mary. And Liza Henske. I just never thought the day would come.

James is spreading plastic tarps around in the garage so I'll be able to spray-paint with relative abandon. I'm shaking the can and the rattle of it conjures some long-ago memory. Some project I did with my mother, just beyond recall. I shake and shake and shake the can and think maybe it was Christmas. Pinecones. The spray paint silver and gold. I find that I miss things now, before they're even gone. Like the ducks, who will lift off and flap away for the winter soon. Like the taste of Loretta's chicken soup, with way too much pepper. Like summer evenings spent with James in this garage.

I watch him as he works and say, "I keep thinking I have to say good-bye to you because you're going away to college."

He's crouched down, spreading a tarp into a crevice between two of my pieces. "Ah, but that's the genius of it. I get to go away without going away."

I haven't told him how relieved I am. How I couldn't handle it. Another leaving.

"Okay." He stands up and comes to my side. "You ready?"

I'm still shaking the can and it sounds like my heart. It's alert, it's jumping, it's ready for action. "Ready," I say, then we kiss quick and then I spray and each figure seems born again.

My father's standing at the stove reading *1776* while sautéing vegetables. Confused, I look in my bag, where James's copy of *1776* is. "Did you buy that book?" I ask him.

"Huh? What?" He looks up. "Yeah. Great stuff."

He puts the book down and turns the burner down, stirs some veggies with a wooden spoon. "I wrote my first chapter this morning."

"Hey," I say. "That's great. Congratulations."

"Might not be a *New York Times* bestseller like this one, but you never know, right?"

I think how true that is. Even when you think you do, you just never know.

"I'm applying for a grant so I can take some time off from teaching." He slides the vegetables onto a platter on the counter. "Really get this thing going."

"That's great, Dad." I go and kiss him on the cheek. "And dinner smells amazing."

"I think we're done." I step back to admire my work, though in the garage it's hard to tell if it's going to work once we take it out of the garage. The figures are all lined up—and freestanding, thanks to those two two-by-fours, out of which James fashioned bases. They look like a parade, maybe celebrating an Independence Day long ago.

He's rolling up the last of the tarps, and he says, "You mean, *you're* done."

"I couldn't have done it without you, though." I think of Nora then, and wonder whether she'll be home in time to see the exhibit. She's been e-mailing James from the common room at the clinic—she brought the gull and Frog Bog photo with her—and says she's doing a lot better and seems to be on the right medication. She's deferred college a year but is thinking about applying to art schools instead. I wonder if maybe I should think about art schools, too.

"What I mean"—I go to kiss James—"is that I wouldn't have *wanted* to do it without you."

chapter 28

Liza puts on an especially good show on our last day of work. She and I are gasping and swooning over the second general store robbery of the day—rather unconvincingly, it's true, but at least I'm not blamed this time—when she shouts, "Ask the new apprentice in Mr. Williams's shop where he's been. And get 'im to empty his pockets! There's been nothing but trouble since he rolled into town." Liza nudges me and whispers, "Check this out. It's going to be good."

"Miss Elliot, please. Calm down." The sheriff nods at her somberly before approaching James. "Sir, might I satisfy the lady's curiosity, and my own, as well, and see what you've got in those pockets."

James's hands are already in his pockets. The crowd has silenced itself in anticipation. Like me, they wait. It looks like he's going to empty his pockets, but instead, in a split second, James takes off running.

"Catch the bastard," Liza shouts.

What can the sheriff do but start to run after him?

"Liza, really," Loretta says, all knee-jerk colonial mom. "Your language!"

The sheriff says, "Don't worry, folks. We'll get 'im." He's been backed into a corner by the scene and he doesn't look happy about it. The sheriff's about forty-five and probably hasn't had to run in a while. To his credit, he takes off after James anyway. "Loretta!" he shouts, already out of breath. "Send one of the girls to the jailhouse and tell them to send my deputy out on horseback!"

"Yes, sir, Sheriff!" Loretta says. "Well, go on, Liza. What are you waiting for?" she says to Liza.

"Yeah, *Liza*," I say. "What are you waiting for?"

She smiles and starts up Main Street toward the jailhouse, whistling an Elvis tune, "Jailhouse Rock." It's so offkey, I don't think anyone else notices. The crowd has mostly dispersed, wandering off to the tavern, where, if I were a betting woman, I'd bet good money there's about to be a brawl.

"James is pissed!" Liza declares when she comes back to the house. Loretta and I are cleaning up the kitchen and Loretta just tsks. "I don't know what he's so worked up about. Somebody different gets blamed every time. It's nothing personal." It's the last day the three of us are working together and I'm all sorts of melancholy.

Loretta clears her throat. "We're all very excited about your seemingly newfound improvisational skills," she says. "I think it might be a good idea, however, to give people at least an inkling of what you're up to."

Liza splays herself out over a wooden chair, like a rag doll. "But that takes all the fun out of it," she moans.

"Yeah, well," Loretta says. "Maybe we're not all here for your amusement."

"Gosh, darn," Liza says. "You learn something every day."

"I will say this, though." Loretta pulls a pan of corn bread out of the oven. "Things are definitely going to feel a bit dull without you two around."

"Well, shucks, ma," Liza says.

At day's end we all shift gears to help set up for dinner. All week Liza and I have been helping Loretta make fruit pies for dessert: rhubarb, blueberry, cherry, every kind of fruit available. We've churned more butter between us than any twenty-first-century girls ever should, and have been assigned spots on a buffet line as serving wenches.

Buckman House has never looked lovelier. The main space is filled with long picnic-style tables, covered with white tablecloths and set with pottery plates and tumblers. Each table has a vase of wildflowers and gas lanterns to light after dark. Near a back "exit" to the ruins—a hole in the wall that opens up onto the lawn—men in colonial garb have already started up a fire and hung large pieces of meat over it. There's an actual pig on a rotisserie and a part of me wants to be grossed out but I'm not. Mostly, I'm hungry.

Liza and I load up wagon after wagon, shuttling pies down to the mansion, while the catering staff busies themselves with large platters of roasted vegetables and bread.

"Can you believe the summer's over?" Liza says as we take the last wagon up the hill.

"I'm firmly in denial."

"I'm actually gonna miss hanging out with you, Irving."

"Don't get all soft on me now, after all this time."

"I'm not!"

"Anyway." I adjust one of the pies; it looks like it might topple over. "We don't have to stop hanging out."

"That bonnet must've done something to your brain." Liza guides the wagon over an especially jagged patch of cobblestone.

"What?! I'm serious."

"I don't know. I just don't see you hanging out with a cheerleader."

I just look at her as if to say, huh?

"Mary talked me into trying out next week."

My mouth drops open. "You can't possibly be serious."

Liza looks around—sees that the coast is clear—puts her wagon handles down to rest the cart, and says, all cheerleaderlike, "Readyyyyyyyy! Go!" She slaps her hands and arms around in a sequence of claps and smacks and says, "Gooooooo team!"

"Ohmigod, that's hilarious."

She picks up the wagon handles again, back to normal Liza, and we continue on our way. I picture all of her plaques and ribbons and trophies and just know she'll make the squad. I say, "Meadow Montgomery is gonna flip. Out."

Liza and I have been tasked with circulating among the guests as they arrive and helping them with the puzzles left on the tables. I've become a master at the iron key puzzle and actually get a kick now from taking it out of someone's hands—"May I?"—and unlocking the puzzle with ease, then putting it back together and handing it back to them as their brains work so hard I can practically see it.

Mrs. Rudolph sees me do it one time and slides over to me. "Not bad," she says. "And the garden maze, well, it's just great. We love it. Everyone loves it."

"Can I go see?" I say. I set up the exhibit but haven't seen anyone looking at it yet, discovering it. I want to be a spy.

"Of course. But quickly, okay?"

I walk off toward the garden maze with my heart thumping wildly. When I enter the maze I slow my pace. Even still, I catch up to a young mother and two boys as they round a corner. One of the boys shrieks and the other boy and the mom laugh. They've encountered the first of my life-size silhouettes made of wood. It's a man in a top hat and cane, one foot crossed over the other, just standing there looking at you head on when you round the bend. One of the boys knocks on the wood and the mother says, "Don't touch, Peter."

I backtrack and head down a different pathway, where I know what I'll find. I'm alone when I come across my favorite structure. An old, crouched woman in a bonnet making a shushing gesture with her one hand and holding a candle lamp in her other. I make a shushing sign back to her, then backtrack again to take another path. This one will lead me by a young woman being trailed by a small girl, and then onto a small dog, tongue stuck out panting and tail alert, high in the air. I wind my way to the center of the maze—I know it like the back of my hand now, can't imagine having ever gotten lost here and panicking about it—to my second-favorite piece. A couple lightly kissing and holding hands. She's holding a parasol over her head—that wasn't easy; it required another trip to Home Depot—and he has a bunch of flowers behind his back.

"Oh, would you look at that." A middle-age woman in a

garden dress is holding a clear cocktail and pointing. "Isn't that lovely, Camille?"

Her friend turns and joins her. "Very cute," she says. "They look so happy."

"And so young."

"I think I need another drink."

On my way out I pass the same woman and her two boys. Now one boy is pretending to pet the dog while she takes his picture. She sees me and says to him, "Peter, step out of the way."

I say, "Don't mind me."

She says, "Say cheese."

I pass when they're done and wind my way through green walls of shrubbery. I know the exit is around the next bend and when I turn the corner, I see James standing at the opening. I say, "Hey," before I notice the woman standing next to him. She has his same hair color, the same curve of the top lip. She looks soft, inviting, despite her thin frame. They're a family of two and for a second that makes me sad for him, for her.

"Hey." He walks toward me. "I want you to meet my mom."

I hold these truths to be self-evident. That it's a good thing Liza and James and I were born when we were, that the quest for freedom from tyranny wasn't left in our hands. That no one gains anything—not a boyfriend, or a friend, or even a driver's license—without losing something else. That loss—great and small—is as unavoidable as the change of seasons. That liberty is a privilege and a curse.

I hold that we are endowed by our creator with certain unalienable rights, that among these are fuckups, and hissy fits, and the pursuit of boys. That no one—no teacher or parent or ghost or bottle or asshole from school—is the ruler of my spirit. And that the best surprises aren't the ones that require you to hide behind a door or chair or couch while someone peeks out a window and shushes you. There are ways to scream "surprise!" at life around every corner, at every stoplight, every day.

She smiles and holds out her hand for me to shake and I do, and it feels open, strong. She has tiny wrinkles around her eyes and they crunch up and I can picture her laughing at a red toilet stuffed with roses, at a husband tumbling overboard as she watches a whale fly into the sky, otherworldly and majestic. I hope she and James tell each other stories the way he and I do.

"Mom," James says. "This is Betsy." He looks at me and smiles and adds, "My girlfriend."

I somehow can't believe there was ever a time when I didn't know him, somehow know that my mother would have adored him, if only because of who he's helped me to become, what he's helped me to discover inside myself. He nods at the man in the top hat, takes my hand, and says, "This is Betsy's art."

"It's wonderful," his mother says, and I feel something old and familiar course through my blood. It fills all four chambers of my heart, and I think maybe, just maybe, it's happiness.

Your attitude. Your style.
MTV Books:
Totally your type.

Cruel Summer
Kylie Adams

First in the *Fast Girls, Hot Boys* series!

Life is a popularity contest...and someone is about to lose. In sexy Miami Beach, five friends are wrapping up high school—but one of them won't make it to graduation alive. . . .

Bad Girls
Alex McAulay

The name of the game is survival...and good girls finish last. Welcome to Camp Archstone, a bootcamp for troubled teen girls. But the girls' true troubles begin once they arrive....

Life as a Poser
Beth Killian

First in the *310* series!

Sometimes you have to fake it to make it....Eva spends an intoxicating summer in glamorous Hollywood with her famous talent agent aunt in this witty, pop culture-savvy novel, first in a new series.

Plan B
Jenny O'Connell

Plan A didn't know about him....When her movie-star half brother—a total teen heartthrob—comes to town, one very practical girl's plans for graduation and beyond are blown out of the water.

Available wherever books are sold.

MTV | BOOKS

Published by Pocket Books
A Division of Simon & Schuster
A Viacom Company

www.simonsays.com/mtvbooks

13647

As many as 1 in 3 Americans
have HIV and don't know it.

TAKE CONTROL.
KNOW YOUR STATUS.
GET TESTED.

To learn more about HIV testing,
or get a free guide to HIV and
other sexually transmitted diseases.

www.knowhivaids.org
1-866-344-KNOW

09764